Mary E. Pearce was born in London but moved out of the city as soon as she could, working for a number of years as a librarian in Cornwall before settling in the beautiful hill country of the Malverns, where she lived in a delightful three-hundred-year-old cottage in the village of Kempsey, before moving into a bigger property – with a solitary apple tree in its garden – on the outskirts of Tewkesbury. She tackled various jobs before settling down to write seriously in the 1960s. Her career began with the appearance of short stories in magazines and has led, with the publication of six novels, to her present success.

By the same author

Apple Tree Saga

Apple Tree Lean Down
The Sorrowing Wind
Jack Mercybright

Cast a Long Shadow
The Land Endures
Seedtime and Harvest

MARY E. PEARCE

Polsinney Harbour

PANTHER
Granada Publishing

Panther Books
Granada Publishing Ltd
8 Grafton Street, London W1X 3LA

Published by Panther Books 1984

First published in Great Britain by
Macdonald & Co (Publishers) Ltd 1983

Copyright © Mary E. Pearce 1983

ISBN 0-586-06157-6

Printed and bound in Great Britain by
Collins, Glasgow

Set in Bembo

For
Carole, Roger, and Caryn
and
in memory of Delyth

Chapter 1

1869

Strangers were rare in Polsinney and the girl attracted attention at once, from the moment she was first seen, a tall figure, slim but well-made, carrying a bundle slung over her shoulder, coming down the rough track that wound its way over Wheep Moor to join the road leading into the village.

It was an evening in July and up on the moor, close beside the track, three men were cutting turfs. They stopped work and leant on their spades, watching as the girl came over the brow, past the old ruined engine-house of Bal Kerensa, and across the footbridge over the stream. A little way along the stream she paused and got down on her knees on the bank, letting her bundle slip to the ground while she cupped her hands into the water. The men watched her drink and bathe her face.

'What maid is that?'

'She's a stranger to me.'

'Ess, and to me,' the third man said.

The girl rose, shouldering her bundle, and came on down the track, one hand shielding her eyes from the sun as she gazed upon the roofs of the village, huddled together, below the moor, with the glittering blue sea beyond. When she drew level with the men she stopped again and spoke to them.

'What is the name of this place?'

'Why, this is Polsinney,' one man said.

'Is there work to be got there?'

'What sort of work?'

'Anything.'

The turf-cutters stared in astonishment. A stranger was rare enough but when that stranger was a young girl, tramping the roads and asking for work, it was a thing that passed belief. They eyed her with stern disapproval, noting that her skirts were grey with dust from the frayed hem, drooping about her ankles, right up to the very waist. Noting, too, that she wore no hat – not even a kerchief over her head – and that consequently her face and neck were burnt brown by the sun. And she, seeing that they were struck dumb, put another question to them.

'Is there seining in Polsinney?'

'Ess, there's three seines in Polsinney, but seining haven't started yet.'

'Perhaps I could get work on the farms?'

'I dunnaw. Maybe you could.' The man who spoke was scratching his chin. 'You could try Boskillyer, I suppose. Mrs Tallack has girls to help her sometimes. But they don't generally stop there long cos Mrs Tallack is hard to please.'

'Where's Boskillyer?'

'That's it down there.'

The girl looked down at the tiny farms, lying strung out, half a mile below, between the road that skirted the moor and the cliff-edge with its wind-bent trees. The man was pointing to the farm that lay farthest from the village. It had three small fields, enclosed by stone hedges, and the house, which stood with its back to the road, looked down over these fields and out over the curve of the bay.

'Mrs Tallack, did you say? I'll try my luck with her, then.'

The girl began walking away and one of the men called out to her.

'Where are you from, maid? What's your name?'

'My name's Maggie Care,' the girl called back. 'I've come from the other side of Mew Head.'

The man called out another question, but the girl was

already well on her way, walking with a long, almost boyish stride that carried her quickly down the track, so that the question went unheard. The men stood watching her for a while and then returned to their turf-cutting.

'She've walked a good many miles,' one said, 'if she've come from the other side of Mew Head.'

'Ess, you, but what's she about, trudging the roads, looking for work, a young well-spoken girl like her? I never heard such a thing in my life.'

'Maybe, there edn no work to be had, downalong, where she've come from, you.'

'And where *have* she come from, I'd like to know? "Other side of Mew Head," she said, but that dunt tell us nothing at all.'

'Maybe she didn want us to know, but Rachel Tallack, down there at Boskillyer, *she'll* get it out of her, you mark my words.'

The turf-cutting was warm work and every so often the men paused, looking down at Boskillyer, wondering how the girl had fared. But although the house was visible to them, its door and yards were completely hidden because of the clustering outbuildings, and so far, whenever they looked, there was nothing to be seen of Rachel Tallack or of the stranger, Maggie Care.

Rachel Tallack had finished milking and was turning the cows into the field. They lumbered past her, taking their time, and when the fourth and last cow began loitering in the gateway, she closed the gate hard on its heels, giving a little snort of impatience.

On her way back across the yard she stopped and looked out over the bay where the fishing fleet, some thirty-odd boats, was putting out on the first of the ebb, brown sails beginning to draw as they moved from the shelter of the harbour into the freshening offshore wind. Although she was in her early fifties, Rachel still had good sight, and she could distinguish her son's boat, the *Emmet*, among the leading clutch of five which, already picking up speed, were standing out on the tack that would carry them past Struan Point. The pilchard season had been good so far. The weather on the whole had been fair and the shoals were moving in the Channel. 'God grant it continue so,' Rachel murmured as she turned away

She was about to enter the house when she heard footsteps on the road and a girl with a bundle over her shoulder turned into the open yard.

'Mrs Tallack?'

'Yes, that's right.'

'I was told you might want help on the farm.'

'And who was so good as to tell you that?'

'I met some men cutting turf on the moor. I told them I was looking for work and they sent me to you.'

'I'm much obliged to them, I'm sure!'

The girl let her bundle slip to the ground and Rachel looked at it with distaste. She noted the dust on the girl's skirts and saw that her boot-soles were well worn down.

'Wherever have you come from, girl, to get yourself in such a state?'

'Today I've walked up from Mindren. Before that I was at Tardrew. I've been moving about these parts three weeks, working on different farms, helping with the haymaking.'

'That's no life for a young girl, living like a vagrant,' Rachel said. 'What are your family thinking of to let you roam about like that?'

'I've got no family. They're all dead.'

'Surely you must have a home of some sort?'

'I did have, once, but not any more.' For a moment the girl seemed to hesitate. Then, with a wave westwards, she said: 'I've lived all my life in one place, further down the coast from here, and three weeks ago I made up my mind to leave it and try somewhere new.'

'What's your name?'

'Maggie Care.'

'How old are you?'

'Nineteen.'

'Are you used to farm work, besides what you've done these past three weeks?'

'Yes, I've done it all my life. I worked on a farm near my home. I was dairymaid there for six years.'

'And left it to go tramping the roads!'

Rachel frowned suspiciously. The girl's story was in complete. That much at least was obvious. 'And if I had any sense at all, I'd send her packing straight away.' But Rachel had to admit to herself that help *was* needed on the farm. Only that afternoon, Brice had talked of going to Penolver to ask if one of the Pentecosts could come and help with the haymaking, but Rachel was always reluctant to ask any favour of her neighbours, and she had rejected her son's suggestion. Now this stranger stood before her: a girl she knew nothing about; but a stranger might perhaps, after all, be preferable to a gossiping neighbour.

'I've had girls working here before but they never stay long. As soon as seining starts they're off, to earn more money in the fish-cellars. I've never had a *dependable* girl, nor one who really knew how to work.'

Rachel paused. She hoped that her keen scrutiny would break down the girl's reserve but in this she was disappointed. The clear grey eyes remained steady and although the girl had come asking for work, and looked little better than a beggar, there was no trace of humility in her manner or in her glance. Rachel resumed her questioning.

'Have you got a written character?'

'No.'

'And yet you expect me to give you work!'

11

'Did your other girls have written characters?'

'They were from local families, known to me by repute.'

'Yet none of them was dependable.'

Rachel's eyebrows rose sharply. A dry smile touched her lips.

'You make your point, girl, I grant you that. And you're not afraid to speak well of yourself, promising to do better than they.'

'At least I'm not afraid of work. Certainly I can promise that. And all I ask in return is my keep.'

'Yes, very well, we shall see!' Rachel said. 'I'll take you on for a month's trial and then if I find we deal well together I'll think about keeping you on for good. Now you'd better come indoors and have a bite of something to eat. You look as though you're in need of it.'

She went into the house and the girl followed. Inside the porch, on a bench at one side, lay a coil of rope and a few cork floats and an old kedge anchor, coated in rust, with one of its flukes broken off.

'Is your husband a fisherman?'

'My husband's been dead six years. My son, Brice, is a fisherman. He's off for the night, pilchard driving, and won't be back till tomorrow morning.' Rachel spread a cloth on the kitchen table. 'Were your own family fisher-folk?'

For a moment it seemed the girl had not heard. She was stroking the big tabby cat who sat in a corner of the settle. Rachel, with a frown, repeated the question, and the answer was given reluctantly.

'Yes, they were all fisher-folk.'

While Rachel was busy in the kitchen, the girl went out to the yard again, to beat some of the dust from her skirts and to wash herself under the pump. Rachel then called her in and the two of them sat down to eat.

* * *

'You still haven't told me where you're from.'

'The other side of Mew Head, a few miles further on from St Lar.'

'It must have a name of its own,' Rachel said, 'and I am waiting to hear what it is.'

The girl remained stubbornly silent, spreading her bread with soft cream cheese, and Rachel spoke impatiently.

'Perhaps they've got the cholera there and that's why you don't want to say where it is?'

'No, there's no cholera there. The name of the place is Porthgaran.'

'Well, well, so it's out at last! And why should you make such a mystery of it? Is it such a terrible place?'

'No,' the girl said quietly. 'It's a place pretty much the same as Polsinney. A harbour town, built into the cliff, with most of the folk getting their living from fishing.'

'You don't seem to have gained much, then, by coming in search of somewhere new.'

'No. Perhaps not.'

'You say your family are fisher-folk but you don't sound like a fisherman's daughter. You speak decent English, as good as my own.'

'My mother was a schoolmistress before she married my father and she was strict about such things. But it all depends on the people I'm with. I *can* speak broad when I've a mind to.'

'You needn't bother on my account! I hear more than enough of it from my neighbours in Polsinney.'

Rachel herself had been born and raised in an inland village, two miles from Truro, where her father had been the curate-in-charge, and her tone betrayed the contempt she felt, even now, after twenty-five years, for the place she had come to on her marriage. Even when she spoke the words 'fisher-folk' it was with a faint touch of scorn. True, her own son was a fisherman, but that was because her

13

foolish husband had muddled away what money he had and as the little rented farm brought only a meagre profit, her son sought his living from the sea, going as skipper in a boat owned by his uncle, Gus Tallack.

Perhaps it was this matter of speech that had prompted Rachel, in spite of her doubts, to receive Maggie Care into her home. And now, as they sat at tea together, she noticed other things as well. The girl's table manners were good; she ate with a certain fastidiousness; and although her hands were roughened by work, they were shapely and well cared for, the finger-nails clean and neatly trimmed. All these things won Rachel's approval, and yet at the same time her doubts remained, because of the girl's stubborn reticence.

'Your mother did well by you but I wonder she didn't see to it that you were trained to something better than hiring yourself out as a servant-girl. You're intelligent enough, I would have thought, to have followed in your mother's footsteps.'

'No, I wouldn't have wanted that. I prefer to work out of doors.'

'You mean you prefer to go tramping the roads.'

'Only until I've found a place I like well enough to settle in.'

'And you think Polsinney will suit you? You are easily pleased!' Rachel said.

For a while the two of them ate in silence, but Rachel's thoughts still dwelt on what the girl had told her so far, and something was stirring in her mind.

'Porthgaran, did you say you came from? Wasn't there a fishing boat lost from there, not long ago, a month or so?'

'Yes, the *Luscinia*, lost with all hands. She capsized in a sudden thunderstorm, only a mile off Garan Head. There were six men in the crew and their bodies were washed ashore at St Lar.'

14

'No doubt the men were known to you?'

'Yes, they were all known to me.'

The girl by now had finished eating and sat, straight-backed, with her hands in her lap. For a while she stared at her empty plate but at last she looked up and met Rachel's gaze.

'The skipper was my father, John Care, and my brother David was one of the crew.' She spoke in a quiet, toneless voice, without any hint of tears in it, but her clear grey eyes had in their depths the coldness and greyness of the sea at dawn 'They were all the family I had. When they were gone, and I was alone, Porthgaran became a hateful place, especially as – '

'Yes? What?'

'My father was held to blame for what happened. The *Luscinia* was an old boat and he had been warned many times that she was not safe in bad weather. The other four men who were drowned . . . they were all young like my brother David . . . and three of them left widows and children. Their families were very bitter, because of the risks my father took.'

'He paid for it with his own life. Wasn't that enough for them?'

'No, and why should it be?' the girl demanded, and this time she spoke with vehemence; with a sudden angry catch in her voice. 'He paid for it with *David's* life and the lives of four other men besides! I can never forgive him, myself, for throwing away those good young lives!'

'They didn't have to go to sea. They knew the risks and they made their own choice.'

'I can't forgive him all the same.'

'Your father must answer to God, not to you.'

Rachel was not without sympathy, but because she believed in self-restraint, it would not easily find expression. Maggie Care's story, now it was told, was a story only too familiar all along these Cornish coasts. The churchyards were full of fishermen who had forfeited their lives at sea, but still there were many hundreds more prepared to follow the same calling because, as Brice had said once, the sea was there and the fish were in it and that was inducement enough for any man who had his living to win. The girl had suffered a grievous loss, but she was young and had her life before her. She would get over it, given time.

'So you left Porthgaran and took to the roads? I don't know that you were wise, leaving the one place where you were known, to come away among strangers'.

'The place was too full of memories. I made up my mind to start a new life and put the past behind me.'

'Didn't your home mean anything to you?'

'Our cottage was needed for someone else. The land-lord was anxious for me to leave and he offered to buy the furniture.'

'At least you have some money, then?'

'No, I put it into the fund, to help the dead men's families.'

'And got small thanks for it, I'll be bound.'

'I didn't wait for thanks. I came away that very day.'

'With nothing but the clothes you are wearing and what you've got in that bundle there! It strikes me that's not very much to start you on this new life of yours.'

Rachel strongly disapproved. She had never met with such foolishness. But the girl appeared healthy and strong and her help would be welcome on the farm. She had not asked for wages; she had asked only for her keep; and so long as she kept her promise to work, Rachel would be well satisfied.

She rose and began clearing the table and the girl followed suit. Together they washed up the tea things and then Rachel led the way out to the hayfield. There was still time to turn a few swaths before it grew properly dark.

The light was just beginning to fade when one of the turf-cutters, on his way home along the road, stopped and looked over the hedge and spoke to Rachel in the field.

'Evening, Mis' Tallack,' he said. 'Weather's holding, edn it, you?'

'So far, so good,' Rachel said.

'I see you've taken her in, then.' The man jerked his head towards the girl who worked, a dim figure in the dusk, some little way across the field. 'Think it was wise of you, midear, taking a stranger into your house, and you all alone when Brice is at sea?'

'Only time will show that, Mr Wearne, but seeing that you sent her to me, if it turns out badly I'll know who to blame.'

'Aw, twadn me, twas Alf Tremearne. I never spoke to her, not one word.' The man leant closer over the hedge. 'Where have she come from? Did she say?'

'She comes from Porthgaran,' Rachel said. 'Her name's Maggie Care and she's nineteen.'

'She's a fine-looking maid, I will say that, but supposing she should turn out a thief? Have you thought of that, Mis' Tallack, midear?'

'Yes, I've thought of it,' Rachel said, 'and I've hidden my jewels in a safe place.'

'Aw, you must have your joke, I suppose, but if anyone was to ask me – '

'Goodnight, Mr Wearne,' Rachel said, dismissing him impatiently, and the man, after a moment's pause, answered with a muttered 'Goodnight, Mis' Tallack' and went on his way along the road.

Rachel, barely able to see, tossed a forkful of hay in the air. By morning, she told herself, all Polsinney would know that Rachel Tallack, up at Boskillyer, had taken a girl in off the road. But that was something that couldn't be helped and if Maggie Care thought to escape attention here in Polsinney, where she was a stranger, she would find that she had made a mistake.

Soon Rachel was obliged to stop work. She called to the girl and they went indoors, and when the two candles had been lit, she moved about the kitchen methodically, filling the kettle ready for the morning, raking the ashes from the stove, and turning the cat out into the yard.

She then led the way upstairs, took a blanket, a pillow, and two sheets from the blanket-box on the landing, and showed the girl into her room: a tiny room with a bunk bed, a cane-seated chair, a chest of drawers, and a row of pegs in a little alcove hidden by a curtain of worn brown plush.

'The last girl who had this room kept her candle burning all night. I hope you won't do the same. Candles cost money and they're dangerous.'

'I shan't keep it burning, I promise you.'

'Then I'll say good night.'

Rachel withdrew, closing the door, and the girl set about making her bed. She then unwrapped her bundle of clothes, laid her nightdress on the chair, and hung the rest away in the alcove. Her room was at the end of the house, over the stable, and while she was getting undressed she could hear the pony shifting about in his stall below. She blew out the candle and got into bed and lay on her back in the pitch-black darkness. The pony was still fidgeting and the sounds he made were companionable. She turned on her side and went to sleep.

In the morning a mist hung over the sea, and the fishing boats, returning to harbour, came in with it swirling whitely behind them, clinging in shreds about their sails.

Rachel, as she went about her tasks in the farmyard, kept a sharp watch on the boats and when the *Emmet* came in, with the white gulls flying and crying behind her, she gave a nod of satisfaction, knowing that Brice had had a good catch.

Maggie helped her to milk the cows and afterwards herded them out of the yard, across the road and onto the moor, where they would graze throughout the day. Rachel then sent her to fetch the pony and together they harnessed him to the milk-float. Two churns of milk were put aboard and Rachel got in and took the reins. Maggie stepped in behind her and they drove slowly out of the yard, along the road skirting the moor, and down one of the turnings leading into Polsinney village.

Their first stop was in front of the church and Rachel's customers, on the alert, emerged from their houses with their jugs and came hurrying down the street, knowing that if they kept her waiting she would whip up the pony and move on.

'Good morning, Mis' Tallack. You're some early this morning. Dunt ee never sleep late at all?'

The women, gathering about the float, stared with frank curiosity at the girl, Maggie Care, as she dipped her measure into the churn and filled the first jug handed up to her.

'I see you've got a new dairymaid. Now where've she come from all of a suddent? I've never clapped eyes on her, dunt believe.'

'She comes from Porthgaran,' Rachel said, 'and her name's Maggie Care.'

'Porthgaran? My dear life! That's a pure long way from here.' The first customer, receiving her jug, put a coin into Maggie's hand and looked hard into her face. 'And what've brought you to Polsinney, if I may be so bold as to ask?'

'I came looking for work and Mrs Tallack has taken me on.'

'You got relations hereabouts? Or a chap you're sweet on, perhaps?'

'No, there's nobody,' Maggie said.

The woman was about to question her further but Rachel now spoke sharply.

'Make room, Mrs Prideaux, please. Mrs Tambling is waiting her turn. And be so good as to tell your boy not to keep jogging the float.'

Each of the twenty-one customers was at last served with her milk; the coins jingled in Maggie's satchel; and Rachel, with a flip of the reins, drove past the church and into Tubb's Lane. The milk-float made ten stops altogether and at each of them Maggie was questioned. She was asked about her age and her prospects of marriage, about her past life in Porthgaran, and whether she was church or chapel; and all these she answered with polite brevity; but whenever her questioners probed too close, Rachel took it upon herself to answer brusquely on her behalf.

'She's got no family. They're all dead. Her father and brother were drowned last month. Now move aside, Mrs Roberts, please. I haven't got all day to linger here.'

Their last stop was down at the harbour, outside *The Brittany Inn*, and from there they drove to the fish-quay. This was the busiest part of Polsinney, now that the drifters had all come in, and there was a loud babble of voices as the fish-merchants from Porthcoe and the local jowsters, jostling together, called out to the fishermen the prices they were willing to pay for the pilchards glistening in the holds. At the edge of the crowd stood a number of fishermen's wives and daughters, each with a basket on her arm, and as the milk-float came slowly by, they turned to nod to Rachel Tallack and to stare at the stranger accompanying her.

The *Emmet* occupied a berth halfway along the jetty and

Brice, together with his crew, stood on a plank across the hold, picking the last few fish from the nets as he bargained with the noisy buyers standing in their carts above. When the milk-float drew up at the back of the crowd, he threw down his section of the net and picked up a basket of pilchards, hoisting it high onto his shoulder. He stepped out onto the jetty, made his way through the crowd, and came to where his mother waited. His sea-boots and short blue smock were covered with glistening fish-scales and his hands were stained with blood and oil. His cap was pushed back from his forehead and his face was smeared with sweat and dirt.

'Who's this you've got riding with you?'

'Her name's Maggie Care,' Rachel said. 'I've taken her on to help on the farm. But never mind about that now. Let's have that basket aboard, quick sharp, so that we can get out of this crowd.'

Brice and the girl exchanged a glance and Brice put a hand to the peak of his cap. He went round to the back of the float and, with a little twist of his body, swung the basket down onto the floor, beside the two empty milk-churns. The girl moved to make room for it, pressing herself against the float's side, and Rachel turned to look down at the fish.

'Better than yesterday, anyway.'

'Yes, they're all prime fish,' Brice said, 'and the biggest catch of the season so far.'

'See that you get the price they deserve.'

The float moved away along the jetty, to a place where there was room to turn, and Brice went back to the boat. The crew had finished clearing the nets and were counting the pilchards into the baskets. Brice stepped into the fish-hold and Ralph Ellis spoke to him.

'I didn't know your mother had got a new dairymaid.'

'I didn't know myself till now.'

21

Above him the merchants and jowsters were clamouring for his attention. He paused in his counting to look up at them and his blue eyes were suddenly keen.

'Well, gentlemen, and what's the best bid?'

Rachel and Maggie, leaving the quayside, drove along the harbour road, past the shops and the warehouses, the fish-cellars with their dwellings above, the coopers' huts and the customs house and the tiny stonebuilt fishermen's chapel dedicated to St Peter.

At the other end of the harbour, where it completed its horseshoe curve, there was a second quay with a slipway, now fallen into disrepair and used only by smaller craft, punts and dinghies and lobster-boats. Above this old quay stood a small cottage, built on the edge of the sea-wall itself, backing onto the foreshore, but facing inwards across the harbour. Beside it there was a big cobbled yard and on the inner side of the yard stood a sail-loft and some stonebuilt sheds. Outside the cottage, an elderly man in a wheelchair sat with a spyglass to his eye, looking across the curve of the harbour to the fish-quay on the opposite side. As the milk-float drove past the yard the old man swung his spyglass round and watched it until it passed from sight. Rachel was well aware of this but kept her eyes on the road.

'That's my brother-in-law, Gus Tallack. He's an invalid, as you see, and got nothing better to do all day than spy on people with that spyglass of his, minding everyone's business but his own.' Then, in the same acid tone, she said: 'He owns my son's boat, the *Emmet*, and he'll be on tenterhooks till he knows how much money Brice got for his catch.'

She whipped the pony to a trot and turned up the steep winding road that followed the curve of the cliff.

* * *

As soon as they had washed out the churns and sluiced the spilt milk from the floor of the float, they set to work on the basket of pilchards, splitting them open and cleaning them, cutting off the heads and tails, and laying the fish down in salt in two big earthenware bussas. Maggie worked with extreme quickness and Rachel noted approvingly that when she topped and tailed the fish she did it precisely, without waste, and that when she laid them in the bussa, each layer was perfectly even, with the salt pressed well down round each fish.

The bussas were put away in the cellar, the offal was given to the pigs, and the empty basket and chopping-board, already attracting flies, were scrubbed clean under the pump. By now the sun was scorching hot, the dew had dried from the hayfield, and Rachel and Maggie, with their big wooden rakes, began drawing the hay into rows, ready for putting up into pooks.

At nine o'clock Brice came home and Rachel went in to prepare breakfast. On his way up from the harbour, he had been stopped by a great many people, enquiring about the girl, Maggie Care; but, as he said to his mother in the kitchen, *they* had told him a lot more than *he* had been able to tell them.

'I hear you took her in off the road and somebody said she'd tramped all the way from Porthgaran. But what brings her here to Polsinney?'

'Her father and brother were both drowned when their boat was lost off Garan Head. It was in the papers a month or so back. Do you remember reading about it?'

'Yes, I remember,' Brice said. 'The boat was unsafe. I remember that.'

'She's got no family left now, she says, and after she'd buried her father and brother she decided to leave Porthgaran for good. It strikes me as very strange that she should leave her own home town to come away among

23

strangers, but it seems that people in Porthgaran had some hard things to say about her father, so she upped one fine day and came away. She's been roaming about these past three weeks, doing casual work on the farms, and last evening she turned up here saying she'd heard I needed help.'

'Well, that's true enough,' Brice said, 'though yesterday, when I mentioned it, you told me you could manage alone.'

'You mentioned asking the Pentecosts. I can certainly manage without *them*.'

'You prefer this Maggie Care?'

'I said I'd give her a month's trial. After that – well, we shall see.'

Rachel now had a good fire going. She pulled the frying-pan onto the hob and dropped six rashers of bacon into it. She then began laying the table. Brice, standing at the kitchen window, could see the girl out in the hayfield: a tall, slim, rather boyish figure, dark hair bare to the sun, strong arms moving rhythmically as she raked the loosely scattered hay and drew it into windrows.

'Judging by what I see, she's no stranger to work,' he said.

'So far, so good,' Rachel agreed. 'But that's often the way with these young girls. They begin well enough but then they get slack. They take advantage. You've seen it yourself.'

'She doesn't look that sort of girl.'

'You can't judge people by their looks.'

'What did *you* judge her by when you decided to take her on?'

'Whatever it was,' Rachel said, 'I could still turn out to be mistaken.'

'Don't you trust her?'

'I don't know. She seems anxious enough to please and

she says she's looking for a place where she can settle down for good. She wants to start a new life, she says, and put the past behind her. But I don't begin to understand her. Not yet at least. It seems to me she's a hard nut to crack and she has a way of looking at you sometimes as though she cares not a penny piece for anything you say to her.'

'Not very surprising, perhaps, considering what's happened to her.'

Brice was young. He was twenty-three. And although he favoured his mother in looks, having the same stubborn jaw and the same keen blue eyes, deeply set, his nature, taken as a whole, was more like that of his dead father. The story of the girl's double bereavement therefore touched his sympathy and he was young enough to be stirred by the thought of her courage and resolution in setting out all alone to start a new life for herself. He began to say something of this to his mother but she cut him short.

'You may call it courage if you like but I have a different word for it! What would have become of that girl if I hadn't taken pity on her and given her shelter in my home?'

'I suppose she would have gone elsewhere and you would have lost a good worker.'

Rachel snatched a fork from the table and went to turn the bacon sputtering in the frying-pan.

'Are you going to get yourself washed? Then hurry up or your breakfast will spoil.'

Brice, sitting opposite Maggie at breakfast, was able to study her at his leisure. His first meeting with her on the quay had shown him a girl of striking good looks, but if he had never met her again, all he could have said in describing her was that her eyes were a pure, clear grey. Now, however, as he studied her closely, he saw how shapely her features were and was struck by the way fineness and strength were blended in the structure of her face.

Her cheekbones, perhaps, were almost too strong, but were softened and rendered beautiful by the delicate hollows underneath and by the perfect curve of her chin. Her mouth had forgotten how to smile and in those clear grey eyes lay a shadow that robbed them of expression; but surely, not so long ago, that mouth had expressed tenderness and those eyes had been full of humour and warmth; and one day, in God's good time, Brice thought, those things would surely be restored.

He wanted to know more about her but was shy of asking direct questions. Instead he talked of the night's fishing and described how he had shot his nets three miles west of the Oracle Rocks.

'The night was perfect, dark as dark, and the sea was as docile as a lamb. We got three hours sleep while the nets were out and when it came time for hauling them in everything went like clockwork. But then we decided to shoot again and that wadn smart, as Billy said, for it meant we had our work cut out making harbour in time to get a good berth.'

'How much did you get for your catch?' Rachel asked.

'Ninepence the long hundred.'

'Less than yesterday, then, although they were better quality.'

'There were big catches all round, that's why. The *Speedwell* did better than us and the *Ellereen* ran us close.'

'I know that. I saw for myself. I knew it would bring the prices down.'

'I banked a cheque for twenty-four pounds. That's not bad for one night's work. Uncle Gus won't grumble at that.'

'Tommy Bray must have made twice as much, judging by what I saw of his catch.'

'You don't grudge Tommy his bit of luck? He hasn't had much this season so far.' Brice looked at Maggie Care.

'Do you know my mother's prayer when I go out for a night's fishing? – "Send them in with your blessing, Lord, but only into my son's nets"!'

A glimmer came into the girl's eyes and she gave a faint smile. She had not quite forgotten how, after all, and Brice felt pleased with himself at having won this response from her.

'And what,' Rachel asked, 'is your own prayer, my son?'

'That all the dogfish in the sea should turn and devour one another, and that when only one is left it should sink to the bottom, never to rise.'

One of his nets had been badly holed by dogfish that night. He had brought it home with him and had hung it over the farmyard wall, and as soon as breakfast had been cleared away, Rachel and Maggie went out and began repairing the torn mesh. Brice, on his way to the hayfield, paused and stood watching the girl's quick hands skilfully plying bodkin and twine.

'I can see you've mended nets before.'

'Yes, I've done it all my life.'

'And does the last mesh come out square at the end?'

'Oh, yes. Usually.'

Rachel turned and frowned at her son.

'You are standing in our light,' she said.

The day's heat had become intense. There was thunder in the air. Brice worked in his shirtsleeves, forking the hay from the windrows and building it up into pooks, each as high as his shoulder. At noon his mother and Maggie Care, having finished repairing the net, joined him in the hayfield, and they toiled together in the sun. Such was the heavy heat of the day that they worked in silence, the three of them, but once, when thunder crackled overhead, Rachel paused and looked up at the sky and said in a voice of great vexation:

27

'Yes, you *would* break now, I suppose, just in time to spoil the hay!'

The storm, however, was passing them by. The clouds were moving away to the west and at half past one, when Rachel went in to prepare dinner, Brice and Maggie, still in the field, could see the dark thunder-shower spending itself out at sea. The storm-clouds hung like a tattered curtain and were lit by flashes of lightning.

'Crockett Lighthouse is getting that. They say if there's any lightning about, Crockett will always bring it down.'

'Can you see the lighthouse from here?'

'Yes, but you have to stand on this hedge.'

Brice climbed onto the stonebuilt hedge and, stooping to give the girl his hand, pulled her up to stand beside him. They could now see as far as Burra Head and its reef of rocks running out into the sea, but Crockett Lighthouse was hidden from them behind the dark curtain of rain. In a moment, however, as they watched, the rain fell further away and the lighthouse suddenly stood revealed, a dazzling white in the glare of the sun, rising, tall and graceful, from its rock at the outermost end of the reef.

'I used to stand here sometimes when I was a boy, watching it being built,' Brice said, 'and later, when it was finished, I was allowed to stay up late to see it lit for the first time.'

'We could see the light from Porthgaran, on clear nights in winter, sometimes,' Maggie said. '"That's Crockett," my father would say, and it always seemed like another world.'

Brice turned his head and looked at her.

'I'm sorry about your father and brother. My mother told me what happened to them and I know something about it from reading the news in *The Cornishman*. The lifeboat couldn't get out, I believe.'

'The crew were not willing to try. They said it was too dangerous.'

'Do you feel bitter about that?'

'I don't think so. Perhaps. I don't know. There was so much bad feeling afterwards. . .Everyone blaming everyone else. . . My father'd been warned not to go out, so of course he was blamed more than anyone. The whole town was full of bitterness and there was a lot of ugly talk.'

'That's why you came away.'

'Yes.'

Brice got down from the hedge and turned to give Maggie his hand, but she leapt lightly down without his help. She took her rake and went back to work, drawing the last strands of hay from the grass and spreading them over the top of the pook. Brice also took his rake but only to stand leaning on it, watching her as she worked.

'Didn't you have any friends in Porthgaran? And didn't they try to stop you?'

'Nobody could have stopped me. I'd made up my mind. I felt I had to get right away . . . I didn't know where, I left that to chance . . . And as it was haymaking time I knew I was bound to get work.'

'Chance brought you here to us. Do you think you will stay for good?'

'That depends on Mrs Tallack and whether she chooses to keep me on.'

'I hope she will,' Brice said. 'There's always a lot to do on the farm, small though it is, and the nights are very lonely for her, especially in wintertime. It would ease my mind a lot if only she had company at such times.'

The girl was looking at him with a frown. Something seemed to be troubling her and he tried to guess what it was.

'Am I looking too far ahead?'

'Perhaps.'

'But you must have *some* plans for your future. You surely don't want to spend your life wandering from place to place?'

'No, I should want to be settled,' she said, 'but I'm only here on a month's trial and – a lot can happen in a month.'

'Perhaps you have already heard that my mother is a difficult person to please?'

'Yes. She told me so herself.'

'Well, it's perfectly true, I suppose, but she could be a good friend to anyone who won her respect.'

'And to those who don't?'

'Then,' Brice said, 'she is quite the reverse.'

The girl turned away from him and he watched her removing the strands of hay that had wound themselves round the teeth of her rake. He was about to speak again; there were many things he wanted to know; but at that moment Rachel appeared, calling to them that dinner was ready, and they put up their rakes and went indoors.

By half past four that afternoon all the hay had been safely pooked and Brice was well pleased with the day's work. Now the thunderstorms could do their worst, but if by good luck they still kept off, that hay could be carted next day, he thought.

At six o'clock he was in the yard, dressed in sea-boots and short canvas smock, getting ready to go down to the boat. He went to collect the pilchard net that was hanging spread out over the wall and began gathering it together, folding it carefully into festoons. While he was doing this Maggie came out of the cowshed and he called her over to give him a hand. He could quite well have managed alone but it was easier with two and it made an excuse for talking to her. She was on her way out to the moor to fetch the cows in for milking but she leant her stick against the wall and began helping to fold the net.

30

'There are other cows up there besides ours,' Brice said. 'How will you know which to bring?'

'I helped to milk them this morning. I think I know which ones are which.'

'Well, watch out for yourself or they'll lead you a dance. They're often frisky in the evening after grazing out there all day.'

In a few moments more the net was folded and hung from the wall in a neat double truss. He got his shoulder under it, and the girl eased it away from the wall, freeing the mesh where it caught on the stones. He stood upright, taking the weight, and hunched his shoulder two or three times until the net lay comfortably, an equal burden before and behind. His mother came out of the house with the linen bag containing his crowst: pasties, raw onions, apples, cheese, and half a loaf of crusty bread: enough, he said, to last the whole week.

'You say that every night, my son, but the bag's always empty when you bring it home.'

With the heavy net over one shoulder and his bag of crowst over the other, Brice went swinging out of the yard and along the road that led to the village. Before turning down the hill he paused and looked back and saw the girl, Maggie Care, steadily climbing the narrow path up over the edge of the moor. Clumsily, because of his burden, he put up a hand and waved to her, but she was intent on her task, searching the slopes of the moor for the cows, and apparently did not see him. Disappointed, he turned away.

Chapter 2

On her second morning at the farm, and every morning afterwards, Maggie went out on the milk-round alone. It was a chore Rachel detested and she was only too glad to have it taken off her hands. And unlike all her previous girls, who had taken the whole morning over it, Maggie always completed the round as quickly as Rachel did herself.

'I will say this for you, my girl. – You don't waste time gossiping.'

Every morning, at the end of the round, Maggie drove onto the fish-quay and if the night's catch had been a good one, Brice would have a basket of pilchards ready to put into the float. As his luck was well in at this time, Rachel was soon telling him that no more pilchards were needed at home. She had salted down some twelve hundred fish and that should certainly be enough to see them through the winter months.

'Will it be enough now that Maggie is with us?'

'Winter is a long way off. Maggie may not be here by then. But yes, twelve hundred will be plenty, even for three of us.'

Brice and his mother were alone in the house. Maggie was out feeding the hens.

'You haven't made up your mind, then, whether you will be keeping her on?'

'The girl is here on a month's trial. I shall make up my mind when that month is up.'

Rachel would not commit herself. The habit of caution was too strong. She wanted to know a good deal more about this stranger, Maggie Care, before she finally made up her mind, and this was proving a difficult thing. Most young girls of nineteen revealed themselves in no time at all; their thoughts, their ambitions, their vanities, came out, whether they wished it or not, in their lively prattle as they worked; but Maggie Care never prattled, never gave away her thoughts, and Rachel, at the end of a week, knew no more about her than she had done at the very beginning.

Brice, when his mother said this to him, was inclined to be impatient,

'You always complained that the other girls wasted too much time with their talk. If Maggie doesn't talk so much it's because she's getting on with her work.'

'Something goes on in that head of hers and I should like to know what it is.'

'Only five or six weeks ago her father and brother were drowned at sea. I would have thought it was plain enough that her mind is still full of that.'

'Yes. Well. Perhaps you're right.'

Certainly the girl was willing to work and whatever task she undertook she proved herself very capable. Rachel was a stickler for cleanliness and everything had to be done just so, but even she could find no fault with the way Maggie scrubbed a floor or blackleaded the Cornish slab or beat the mats on the garden wall. Rachel was an excellent cook but Maggie had a hand equally light when making pastry or bread and she had a way with under-roast that Rachel found better than her own. Altogether it seemed, sometimes, as though the girl was too good to be true.

It was the same out in the fields. Whatever she did was done well. The hay had been carted and ricked now and Brice had begun singling the mangolds in the half-acre strip behind the barn. Sometimes Maggie helped him there and he saw with what clean, confident strokes she hoed the weeds out of the rows and how, if she came on a deep-rooted dock, she would stoop and pull it out by hand. Nothing was too much trouble to her. She took more pains than he did himself.

Once when he turned to look at her he saw that she had put down her hoe and was searching for something on the ground; making her way back down the field, bent double, arms outstretched, hands turning over the weeds that she had left scattered between the rows. She had lost the small silver locket that had hung on a ribbon round her neck and there was distress in her face as she searched through the weeds.

Brice went to help her look for it and saw it almost immediately, glinting two or three rows away, half covered in dry-crumbled earth. He picked it up and gave it to her and her hand closed over it gratefully, and such was the look in her eyes that he felt quite ridiculously pleased because, although it was only luck, *he* had been the one to find this thing which plainly was very precious to her. She tied a new knot in the ribbon and hung it round her neck again, tucking the locket inside her dress.

'It used to belong to my mother,' she said. 'I've worn it ever since she died.'

'She was very dear to you?'

'Yes, she was dear to all of us. If only she had been alive when my father was told the boat was unsafe, *she* would have made him give it up. But he wouldn't listen to anyone else. He sailed that boat for another two years and in the end six lives were lost.'

'You find it hard to forgive him for that.'

'Yes, I do.'

'And yet you grieve for him all the same.'

'I grieve for him because he's dead but I can't pretend I was fond of him.'

They turned and walked back along the field. Brice

34

picked up her hoe and gave it to her and she stood for a moment looking at him. For once she seemed inclined to talk.

'My father was rather a hard man and my brother tried to be like him. They had no friends in Porthgaran and nobody ever came to the house . . . except the rest of the crew, of course, and even with them there were arguments. My father was always quarrelsome and after my mother died it got worse. He thought the whole world had a down on him and in a way I suppose he was right.'

Brice was impressed by her honesty. Nothing was as simple as it seemed. At first he had been rather shocked, hearing her deny having loved her father, but he quickly began to understand that this lack of love in her father's lifetime only added another burden to the grief she felt for him now he was dead.

She was only nineteen. There had been little happiness in her life and she faced the future all alone with a terrible tragedy fresh in her mind. He could see by her eyes how it haunted her and he found himself filled with a fervent hope that the future would bring enough happiness to make up to her for the past. He tried, not very lucidly, to say something of this to her, and she took him up on it straight away.

'I don't know about happiness but the future is there, certainly, and something has got to be made of it.' She spoke with a touch of youthful defiance and a certain light came into her eyes which, just for a fleeting instant, drove the shadow right away. 'I intend to make a new life for myself . . . Start again, from the very beginning . . . And whatever the future brings me, be sure I shall make the most of it.'

She and Brice were standing quite close, grey eyes looking straight into blue. Then, abruptly, she turned away and, finding her place in the row, resumed her work of singling the mangolds. Brice went back to his own place and they worked in silence, three rows apart, moving steadily down the field. But secretly, every now and then, he would turn and glance at her, wondering about this new life of hers which, in spite of everything, she looked to with such faith and confidence. God willing, he told himself, he would play some part in that future of hers, though exactly what that part might be he was not yet willing to consider, even in his innermost mind.

The affairs of the *Emmet*, in common with those of most other fishing boats in Polsinney, were organized on a system of shares. Every day, when Brice had sold his catch on the quay, he would bank the cheque with Thomas Kemp, landlord of *The Brittany Inn*, and Thomas would then send the cash to Brice's uncle, Gus Tallack, who, as owner of the boat, kept a rough and ready 'log' of its profits and losses. On Saturday Gus divided the week's takings into eight equal shares: two for the boat, two for the nets, and four to be split between skipper and crew; and at intervals, during the afternoon, each man would call to collect his share.

There was no fishing on Saturday night because in Polsinney, as elsewhere throughout Cornwall, the sabbath was very strictly observed. On Saturday evening, therefore, after working in the fields, Brice would wash and put on clean clothes and would stroll down to his uncle's cottage, to collect his share of the week's takings and stay for an hour or two gossiping with the old man.

'I'm going down to see uncle Gus,' he said, seeking his mother in the dairy. 'I thought perhaps I could take him some eggs, unless you intend calling on him after church tomorrow morning, in which case you could take them yourself.'

'No, indeed I do not!' Rachel said. 'I called on him last

Monday, on my way back from market, and only got shouted at for my pains. He gets more cantankerous every day and the state he's let that cottage get into is too disgraceful for words.'

'He *is* a sick man,' Brice said.

'All the more reason, I would have thought, for him to take heed of good advice.'

'What advice?'

'Oh, never mind! I should have known better than waste my breath on him. But I'm certainly not going again to be shouted at and abused.'

'In that case I'll take the eggs myself.'

Brice stood waiting obstinately and after a moment Rachel gave in. She put a few eggs into a basket and handed it over with an ill grace.

'I hope for your sake that he's in a better temper today than he was last Monday afternoon.'

Gus Tallack was fifty-two: a tall man and solidly built: almost as tall as Brice himself when he stood upright and straightened his back; but this he was rarely able to do because of the obscure wasting disease which, two and a half years before, had struck him down out of the blue, leaving him partially paralysed.

His condition varied mysteriously: on good days, with the aid of two sticks, he could walk about the house and yard and could even climb the steps to the sail-loft; but on bad days, and they were more frequent now, he had barely enough strength to crawl out of bed and put on his clothes and get himself into the chair on wheels that the Polzeale blacksmith had made for him.

Gus had been a powerful man and indeed his great shoulders and chest gave an impression of strength even now, so that, sitting hunched in his wheelchair, he looked not unlike a latterday Samson held and constrained by invisible bonds. He had a round head of unruly grey curls and a grey curly beard, trimmed short, that encroached high on his thick-fleshed cheeks. But whereas Samson had been blind, Gus had a pair of dark brown eyes that looked out hungrily on the world, missing nothing, and often burnt with the rage he felt at his own weakness and helplessness.

As always in fine weather he sat outside in the yard. From there he could look out to sea and, with the aid of his spyglass, could watch whatever vessels passed. To the right he could watch the big ships that sometimes put in at Polzeale, hidden beyond Struan Point; to the left he could see across the harbour to the sands of Porthvole and Pellow's Reach, completing the eastern curve of the bay, and, above Volley Head, the four little grey-and-white villages of St Inna, St Idric, St Jean and St Owe, with the green slopes of Goonwelter behind.

'My mother sent you some eggs,' Brice said, 'and asked me to say she hoped you were well.'

Gus cocked a bushy eyebrow at him.

'Either you are a damned liar or your mother's a damned hypocrite!'

'Here are the eggs, anyway. At least *they* are honest enough.'

'Be damned to the eggs!' his uncle said. 'And to the rest of the things she sends! She only keeps on the right side of me cos of getting my property when I'm gone. She wishes me dead, the old catfish, and the sooner the better, that's what she thinks.'

'That's not true.'

'Oh yes it is. I know that mother of yours, by God! She was in here a few days ago and had the cheek to tell me that since I am failing in health and can't run my business properly I ought to hand it over to you and let you run it for me!'

'She had no right to say that. She certainly wasn't speaking for me and I have absolutely no wish – '

'Tes all the same if you have or not! The sail-loft and the barking-house are nothing whatever to do with you, at least not while I'm still alive, and I pretty damn quickly told her so!'

'Then I hope that will be the end of it.'

Brice drew up a wooden box and sat down beside his uncle. The old man took a pinch of snuff.

'So Rachel's got a new dairymaid? Some poor wretch of a girl that she can bully and put through the hoop! She've come from Porthgaran, I hear, and been tramping the roads looking for work. According to the rumours flying about, her father and brother were fishermen and were lost at sea a month or two back.'

'Rumour has told the truth for once.'

'She's all alone in the world, then? Well, that'll soon be changed, I daresay. She looks a fine docy maid from the little I've seen of her, driving past, and if she've come in search of a husband, she'll soon pin one down for herself, no doubt.'

'Why should you think that of her?'

'I never saw a maid yet that wasn't anxious to get married.'

'Maggie is different from most other girls.'

'Then maybe you've got ideas yourself?'

'She's only been with us four or five days.'

'Long enough for you to find out that she's different from other girls.'

Brice smiled but was not to be drawn and after a while his uncle Gus, although plainly curious, began talking of other things: chiefly of the affairs of the boat and the prospects for the rest of the pilchard season, based on the catches so far.

'You've had a good week this week. Shares worked out

thirty shillings a man. Your crew have already been for theirs. You'll find your own on the table indoors. Go in and help yourself and while you're there put these damned eggs away and bring out the rum and glasses.'

Brice went into the kitchen and picked up the pile of coins his uncle had put ready for him. Among the clutter of odds and ends that covered the bare boards of the table lay the remains of his uncle's supper: half a loaf, already stale, and a piece of dark, greasy cheese; and when he put the eggs into the larder he saw that the shelves were almost bare. The kitchen was dirty and comfortless and looked as though it had not been touched since his visit the previous Saturday. The stove was stuffed full of rubbish and the hearth underneath was so choked with ash that it fell out over the fender onto the stone flags of the floor. He found the rum and two glasses and returned to his uncle in the yard.

'Has Mrs Kiddy been in today?'

'No, she've got a bone in her leg.'

'She promised to cook you a meal every day but that slab can't have been lit for days.'

'Seems you've been having a good look round.'

'She's supposed to come in and keep the place clean – '

'I know what she's *supposed* to do!' the old man exclaimed, flying into a rage. 'The place is a pigsty! I know that! D'you think I don't *know* what the place is like?'

With an effort he tried to control himself but his temper, once roused, was hard to put down.

'Tes just the same in the sail–loft! Dirt and rubbish everywhere and Isaac Kiddy so bone idle he never comes in till half past eight, sometimes nearer nine o' clock. They take advantage, all of them, but what am I supposed to do? I can't *make* the beggars work when I'm stuck in this chair like a sack of beans!'

Brice poured out two glasses of rum and put one into his uncle's hand.

'Would it be a good idea if I had a word with Isaac Kiddy?'

'No, damme, it would not!' This suggestion made matters worse. 'You may be skipper of the boat but you're not skipper here yet, by God! You'll have to wait till I'm dead for that!'

The old man glared at Brice. His lips were parted in a little snarl. He took a deep breath, trembling, and swallowed his rum at a single draught. Gradually he calmed down and after a while, when he spoke again, his voice was quiet and matter-of-fact, although it still had an edge to it.

'You won't have to wait much longer,' he said. 'This damned disease, whatever it is, is beginning to get a hold on me and two or three years should see me out. Dr Sam has made that plain. I asked him and he told me straight.'

Brice knew that this was true. He had spoken to Dr Sam himself. The wasting disease, which began in the spine, attacked the muscles and the nerves, causing progressive atrophy. Almost nothing was known of its cause and there was no hope of a cure. All Dr Sam could say was that the wasting would spread throughout the system and that when in time it reached the lungs it would inevitably bring death.

'Dr Sam could be wrong,' Brice said.

'Don't talk widdle. It makes me tired. At least your mother spares me that. She never makes any bones but that I'm a dying man and Isaac Kiddy is the same. They're all as bad, the whole boiling of'm, and take as much account of me as if I was dead already!'

The old man refilled his glass and sat staring into it. Then he looked out to sea.

'I *try* to be a good loser,' he said. 'Tes all in the luck of the draw, after all, and if God've singled me out like this,

41

well, he's in the position to have the last word. But I wish he'd chosen something quick. There've been plenty of times in my life when I've had to ride out a gale in the *Emmet*, with great seas coming over her, higher than the top of her mast, when God could've finished me off like that!'

Gus gave a snap of his hard, horny, misshapen fingers.

'But instead he cuts me down from behind . . . Takes all my strength, inch by inch, and leaves me so helpless as a worm . . .' He turned his head and looked at Brice and there was a kind of childlike puzzlement in his eyes as he said: 'Now why should God do a thing like that? I can't make it out at all. He must have some reason for cutting me down and maybe if I knew what it was . . . I'd be better able to say "Amen."'

There was a pause. Gus sat slumped in his chair, the evening sun full in his face and a faint breeze stirring his hair where it curled from under his seaman's cap. On the old quay below the cottage some boys were fishing with a handline and there was a sudden commotion among them as they landed a handsome mackerel. A few gulls gathered, screaming; trod the air for a moment or two; then wheeled away overhead; over the cottage and sail-loft and sheds and down onto the foreshore beyond.

'I don't know,' Brice said. He could not think of anything to say to this stricken man who was trying to wrest some meaning from the cumbered life that was left to him. 'I just don't know.'

'Of course you don't! Nobody does!' Gus, coming out of his mood of abstraction, dismissed the subject with a wave of his hand. 'Take no heed of my ramblings. Let's talk about something else. Did you know that Martin Laycock is building a new boat for George Newpin? He came to see me to order the sails . . .'

★ ★ ★

42

When Brice got home to the farm, his mother was busy in the yard, filling her pails and churns at the pump to cool them ready for the evening milking. Brice took over working the pump and when he had finished he said to her:

'I hear you've been telling uncle Gus how to run his own business. That's why you had words when you saw him last.'

'I tried to give him some good advice and he threw it in my face,' Rachel said. 'That business is going to rack and ruin. The barking-house has been closed for months – goodness knows how much money is lost by that – and the sail-loft will soon go the same way if half the tales I hear are true. Your uncle has lost his grip on things and if he had an ounce of sense he'd hand the business over to you. With your good schooling and your brain you're wasted as a fisherman and I've said so from the very first.'

'I don't want to take over the business. I'm quite happy as I am.'

'You'll *have* to take over when your uncle dies, unless you decide to sell it up, and the way things are going at present there soon won't be anything left to sell. The cottage and sheds will tumble down if something isn't done soon – '

Rachel broke off and became silent, for Maggie had come out of the byre and was crossing the yard to the gate, on her way to the moor to bring in the cows, and Rachel did not want her to hear this private discussion of family affairs. Brice also remained silent, giving the girl a little salute, but when she had gone out of the gate he turned again to his mother and said:

'We have no right, either of us, to interfere in my uncle's affairs. He's always been very good to me and whatever *your* feelings may be *I* have nothing but respect for him. The sail-loft and the barking-sheds are his property – his alone – and what he chooses to do with them is no concern of ours while he lives.'

'I don't agree,' Rachel said. 'You're his only living relation and the property's bound to come to you and although you may take a high moral tone you can't pretend you don't care what is happening to your inheritance.'

'That's as maybe,' Brice said, 'but if you try to interfere you'll only antagonize uncle Gus and no good will come of that.'

The good practical sense of this was plainly indisputable and Brice saw from his mother's face that he had succeeded in silencing her. He turned away feeling satisfied. The discussion had been disagreeable to him and he was glad it was at an end. He could now turn his mind to other things.

'I think I'll go after Maggie and give her a hand with the cows.'

'There's no need for that. She can manage alone.'

'I think I'll go up all the same.'

He strode away out of the yard and Rachel stood frowning after him. The other girls who had worked on the farm had never attracted his interest at all and she had always been thankful for it. But this girl, Maggie Care, had only to walk past him and he could not wait to follow her. Rachel gave an angry sigh. It was a problem she had not foreseen.

During the first week in August Brice cut the three acres of dredge-corn in the field furthest from the house. His mother and Maggie bound up the sheaves and set them up into shocks and the wheat and barley, ripening together, whispered in the warm dry wind. Everywhere, on the neighbouring farms, harvest was well under way and the bustle of it filled the air. Reaping-machines churred all day long and the voices of the reapers could be heard calling from one field to the next.

Down in Polsinney itself there was bustle of another kind, for it was now the time of year when the pilchard shoals, making their way down the Channel, were expected to come close inshore, and this was when the seine-fishers expected to reap their own harvest. The seine-crews had been put into pay and the boats lay out in the bay day and night, each to its own allotted stem, while the huers up on the cliff at Porthvole took it in turns to watch for the shoals which, when they came close enough, would betray their presence to a keen eye by the darkening and thickening of the waters and a turbulence on the sea's surface.

The seine owners, in smart frock coats and stovepipe hats, were up on the cliff day after day, but so far the shoals had proved shy. Brice strolled up one afternoon and lingered for a while with the crowd of people who, in a state of high expectation, kept the huer company, all staring out to sea. John Lanyon, who owned the New Venture Seine, offered Brice a large cigar and spoke to him in a jocular way that only half hid his fretted nerves.

'You drifter chaps are no friends of ours. You break up the shoals and drive them away. I shall be on the rocks myself if the season's as bad as it was last year.'

Brice refused the proffered cigar and stood staring out at the bay.

'The shoals will come in. They always do. And so long as they come in on your stem all you need worry about is your warps.'

This was a sly joke on his part for twice during the previous season a shoal, enclosed by the New Venture Seine, had been lost because the rope had parted while the beachmen were hauling it up the shore.

'It won't happen this time. I've made sure of that.'

Lanyon now began to ask how things were on the farm.

45

He was Brice's landlord and liked to show a friendly concern.

'I hear you've got a new dairymaid. A mystery girl from down the coast that your mother took in off the road. That was a Christian act on her part.'

'It has been amply repaid,' Brice said, 'for Maggie is a good worker.'

'Your mother is pleased, then?'

'Yes, indeed.'

'And what is your own opinion of her? Is she as comely as they say?'

'No doubt you'll meet her one of these days,' Brice said, 'then you'll be able to judge for yourself.'

He turned and walked home along the cliff.

The hot dry weather continued and soon the dredge-corn was carted and ricked. The seine-boats still lay out in the bay and the huers still kept watch on the cliff but so far no shoals had come inshore. Once a shoal was seen in the distance but it veered away off Burra Head and the groan that arose from the disappointed watchers could be heard in the fields at Boskillyer.

But although the seiners were so far unlucky, the drifters were enjoying a good season. Because of the calm, easy weather Brice was able to fish every night and catches were consistently good. His uncle, paying his share one Saturday evening, did so with a teasing remark.

'If you *are* thinking of getting married, at least you needn't plead poverty.'

'You are in a great hurry, suddenly, to get me married off,' Brice said, 'yet you've been a bachelor all your life.'

'Rumour tells me you're keen on the girl.'

'Does it indeed!'

'Why, isn't it true?'

'I think myself,' Brice said, 'that people should mind their own business.'

'The day they begin doing that,' Gus said, 'it will be the end of the world.' He looked thoughtfully at Brice and said: 'Of course, I can quite understand that you've got to mind your p's and q's, courting right under your mother's nose. She won't exactly be over the moon to see you marry her servant-girl.'

'Maggie's no ordinary servant-girl and I'm sure my mother would say so herself.'

'You think she'll give it her blessing, then?'

'I hope she will.'

'And what if she won't?'

Brice considered carefully.

'I shall be very sorry,' he said, 'but my mother doesn't rule my life.'

'I'm glad to hear it!' his uncle said. 'But it's not for want of trying, eh?'

Brice, as he walked home that evening, was full of a young man's irritation at knowing that he and Maggie Care were the subject of gossip in the village. His feeling for her was still new to him, a secret thing, shut away in his heart, and it was an unpleasant shock to find that onlookers with busy tongues had already been at work bringing out into the open something he had thought safe and secure.

And now, in talking to his uncle Gus, he had been led into making an admission before he was properly ready for it, and this caused him some disquiet. Still, however, it couldn't be helped, and he could only hope that his uncle Gus would at least respect his confidence. As for the rest, his uncle was right: such talk was inevitable and he would just have to accept it; but it irritated him all the same and he knew he would have to be on his guard.

* * *

Every morning, coming up from the boat, as soon as he reached the top of Cliff Hill and turned onto the level road, he would look for Maggie in the fields. He would call to her over the hedge and she would glance up and give him a wave. Once he brought home an enormous hake and held it up for her to see. 'Did you ever see such a monster?' he said. 'Its father must have been a shark!' And once he brought home a string of whiting because she had said it was her favourite fish.

One day Brice went up to the moor and brought home a cartload of turfs which he had cut early in June. Maggie helped to unload them and stack them up in the back yard, and while they were working thus together, he spoke about the St Glozey sports, to be held the following Saturday.

'St Glozey sports are a great affair. Wrestling, running, sheaf-pitching, and tea afterwards in the marquee. I hear there's to be a German band and the hand-bell ringers are coming from Steeple Lumbtown to compete with the ringers from Polzeale.' Brice took a pile of turfs from the cart and put them into Maggie's hands. 'I wondered if you'd come with me,' he said. 'It's time you had an outing away from the farm.'

She stood quite still, looking at him, and her eyes were full of deep-questing thought. What she was thinking he could not divine but it seemed to cause her uneasiness and after a moment she turned away to place the turfs on the growing rick.

'No, I don't think I should,' she said.

'Why ever not?' Brice asked. He was somewhat taken aback. 'Is it because you think it's too soon after losing your father and brother?'

'I don't know. Yes. Perhaps.'

But her glance had now become evasive and he saw that she had been too quick to grasp the excuse he had offered her.

'No one in Polsinney would expect you to keep such strict mourning.'

'Wouldn't they?'

'No, they would not.'

'I'd sooner not come all the same. It's kind of you to ask me but – I don't really like watching sports.'

'In that case, of course, there's no more to be said.'

Brice was disappointed and piqued but, brooding afterwards on her refusal, he wondered if his mother might have something to do with it. He decided to find out and spoke to her that very evening. They were alone in the kitchen together. Brice was getting ready to go down to the boat and Rachel was preparing his food for the night.

'St Glozey sports?' she said blankly. 'It's nothing to do with me, my son, if the girl has refused to go with you. I've heard nothing about it till now.'

'I realize that,' Brice said, 'but I've seen the way you look sometimes when Maggie and I are talking together and I thought perhaps you had said something to make her feel you disapproved.'

Rachel took a deep breath. His challenge had taken her by surprise. She had been conscious from the beginning of the interest he took in Maggie Care and the problem of it had vexed her sorely. She had decided to bide her time but now that Brice had broached the matter she knew she would have to speak her mind.

'I've said nothing to Maggie Care but I *have* got plenty to say to *you*. I would have thought you'd have had more sense than to fix your attentions on a girl employed as servant in this house. You can do better for yourself than marry the daughter of a fisherman who hasn't a penny piece to her name and I hope you'll take heed of what I say before it's gone too far.'

'As I am a fisherman myself I can see nothing wrong – '

'You needn't be a fisherman all your days and well you

49

know it!' Rachel said. 'When your uncle's property comes to you : means you'll be able to give up the sea, and once you've built up that business again and got it properly on its feet, you'll be able to live the life you are best fitted for.'

'You don't seem to understand that none of that means anything to me. The sea is my life. It's all I want. But whatever I may do in the future – ' Here Brice paused for thought because once again he was being led into making a premature admission. And yet – was it really premature? No, it was not. He knew his mind. 'Whatever I do in the future,' he said, 'I should still want Maggie as my wife.'

'A girl you know nothing about, that I took in off the road?' Rachel said.

'Don't you like her?'

'That's not the point! What I know I like well enough. It's what I *don't* know that worries me. There is something about that girl that's not quite right and I can't quite bring myself to trust her.'

'Maybe you haven't tried hard enough,' Brice said, quietly, 'but now that you know what my feelings are, I hope you will try for my sake.'

This was the nearest he had ever come to a serious quarrel with his mother and he hoped, by appealing to her in this way, to ease the friction between them before he left to go down to the boat. He could see he had made her very angry but anger came so readily to her that he was almost inured to it and he had enough faith in her to know that, given a little time, she would take his words to heart and do what she knew was best for him. Watching her as she packed up his food, he could see her struggling with herself, and when, in a while, she turned to him, he could see that she had reached some resolve.

'You haven't mentioned marriage yet?'

'No. Not yet. It's much too soon. Maggie – ' He searched for the right words. 'Maggie is like a wandering bird, looking for a place to rest,' he said. 'She needs time to find herself.'

He took the bag containing his food and slung it over his shoulder.

'You won't say anything to her, will you, about St Glozey or anything? I think it's better to leave it alone.'

'Don't worry, my son,' Rachel said dryly. 'I don't intend to do your courting for you. You're a grown man and you know your own mind – even if you *are* a born fool!'

Brice left the house feeling relieved. The quarrel, he thought, had cleared the air. Things would be easier from now on and all that remained for him to do was to woo and win the girl of his choice.

Rachel, during the next few days, was much exercised in her mind. She still felt bitterly angry over her son's foolishness and wished with all her heart and soul that she had turned the girl away instead of receiving her into her home. But it was too late to wish that now. She would just have to make the best of things. The trial period of one month was now drawing to an end and as far as her work was concerned the girl had given complete satisfaction.

Her one and only fault was that she had engaged Brice's affections and this she had done unconsciously. Unlike the previous servant-girls, who had flaunted themselves in front of him, Maggie had gone about her business and had never for a single instant deliberately put herself in his way. And Brice, who had treated the other girls with good-humoured indifference, had been ensnared by Maggie's reserve. Perhaps after all she knew this. Perhaps she had been more subtle than they. But Rachel had to admit to herself that, shrewdly though she watched the girl, she could detect no guile in her.

Maggie was so wrapped up in herself that she seemed

51

unaware of Brice's interest, and that was a curious thing in itself, singular in a girl of nineteen. But it was only a question of time before awareness dawned on her and once that happened she was sure to respond for no girl, Rachel thought, could resist a personable young man with prospects once she knew she had his love.

Rachel, at the kitchen window, stood watching Maggie out in the yard, taking the washing off the line and dropping it into a basket. The girl had good points, there was no doubt of that, and if Brice had set his heart on her, was it such a bad thing after all? 'I wish I knew!' Rachel exclaimed to herself. 'I wish I could see into that girl's mind!'

Maggie now came into the kitchen and tipped the washing onto the table. She filled a bowl with warm water and began damping down the clothes, dipping her fingers into the bowl, flicking water over them, and rolling them up into tight rolls.

'If only you'd picked them in earlier, you'd have been spared that job!' Rachel said.

Try as she would, she could not always entirely suppress the irritation that rose in her, for what did they know about this girl beyond a few bald facts that told them little or nothing of her character? Rachel respected her for her competence and Brice thought he was in love with her but she was as much a stranger to them now as on the day she had first arrived.

'Tomorrow is Tuesday and you will have been here a month,' Rachel said. 'Do you wish to stay on?'

The girl looked up from damping the clothes.

'If you are willing to keep me, yes, I would like to stay,' she said.

'Very well, it's settled, then.' Rachel gave a little sigh.

'You're a good worker, I will say that, but mind and see that you keep it up.'

For a moment it seemed as though the girl was about to say something more and Rachel waited expectantly. But the moment passed in silence, the girl went on with her task, and whatever she had intended to say remained unsaid.

The following morning, when Maggie went out on the milk-round, she was gone longer than usual and when she returned at half past eight Rachel was looking out for her.

'What kept you, miss?'

'I don't know. Everything seemed to take a long time.'

'Are you all right?'

'Yes. Oh, yes.'

But the girl, Rachel thought, was looking wisht. There was a cloudiness in her eyes; her forehead and upper lip were moist; and although the two milk-churns were empty, the effort of lifting them from the float left her palpably breathless.

'Are you ill?' Rachel asked.

'No. I'm just feeling the heat.'

This was a piece of arrant nonsense, for the weather had turned cooler now, and the girl's excuse only served to deepen the suspicion quickening in Rachel's mind.

For the moment, however, she said no more; she pretended to be fully occupied with the business of sluicing out the float; but all the time she was keeping watch and when Maggie went to unyoke the pony, reaching up on tiptoe to lift the collar from his neck, she noted what a strain it was to her and saw how, when the task was accomplished, the girl was overcome by giddiness and had to put one hand on the float to steady herself until it had passed.

Rachel went to her, took the collar and harness from her, and carried them into the stable. She then let the pony into the pasture and when that was done she returned to

Maggie, who still stood beside the float, pale-faced but recovering.

'Come with me,' she said crisply. 'It's time we had a little talk.'

In the kitchen she motioned the girl to a chair, fetched a cup of water for her, and stood over her while she drank.

'I felt all along there was something left out of the tale you told when you first came and now I know what it is. You are going to have a child?'

'Yes.'

'Don't you think it was deceitful, wheedling your way into my house without telling me the truth?'

'Would you have taken me in if you'd known?'

'No, I would not. But where was the point in deceiving me? You couldn't keep your secret for ever.'

'I thought perhaps, by the time you knew, you would be willing to let me stay. I thought if I worked hard enough – '

'Then you were a fool,' Rachel said. 'How many people, do you think, would be willing to give house-room to a girl with an illegitimate child? Very few, let me tell you, and I am not one of them.'

'Even though I am willing to work without any wages except my keep?'

'No, it's out of the question, and you should know better than to ask.' There was a pause and then Rachel said: 'Who is the father of your child?'

'His name was Jim Kenna,' Maggie said. 'He was one of my father's crew and he was drowned along with the rest. We were to have been married in September.'

'It's a pity you didn't wait. You'd have saved yourself a packet of trouble.'

'No, that's not how I feel,' Maggie said. 'I'm glad I'm having Jim's baby. It's all I have to remember him by.'

'Have you no sense of shame, girl, at bringing a love-child into the world?'

'No, Mrs Tallack, I don't think I have.' Maggie was quite composed now and although her face was still deathly pale, her eyes were steady and clear again and her chin had a certain lift to it. 'It's a bad start for a child, I know, but . . . I shall try to make up for that in every possible way I can.'

'And how are you to do that when you are all alone in the world?'

'I don't know. But I shall, somehow.'

'What about your lover's family? Couldn't they have helped you?'

'Jim had no family,' Maggie said. 'He was brought up in an orphanage.'

'Well,' Rachel said, and drew a deep breath. 'This is a pretty problem indeed but you've only yourself to blame for it. If you've got any sense at all you'll go back to Porthgaran where you belong and let your own parish look after you.'

'No. I shall never go back there.'

'If it's the gossip that worries you, you'll find it the same wherever you go, as soon as people know the truth.'

'Gossip doesn't worry me. I know I shall have to face that. But Porthgaran is an unhappy place, full of bitter memories, and I shall never go back to it now. If I can't stay here – '

'And you certainly can't.'

'Then I must move on somewhere else.'

'If you go tramping the roads again, you'll soon be arrested as a vagrant, my girl, and then you'll be packed off back to Porthgaran whether you like it or not.'

'I shan't be arrested. I'll make sure of that.' The girl rose and went to the stairs. 'I'd better go up and pack my things.'

Rachel, exasperated, clicked her tongue.

'You don't need to be so hasty as that. I'm quite willing

to let you stay until you've had time to think yourself out. I'll give you until the end of the week.'

Briefly the girl seemed undecided but in a moment she shook her head.

'There's nothing to be gained by putting it off. I think I'd as soon go straight away.'

'And where do you mean to go, may I ask?'

'I don't know. I haven't thought. I shall think about it on the way.'

'Such a mess you've got yourself into! I can't think what's to become of you! You don't seem to have the slightest idea of the dangers you're running tramping the roads!'

Rachel was angry and upset. True, her discovery of the girl's condition had lit a flame of triumph in her, and never once had she doubted her wisdom in sending the girl away from the farm. But Maggie's predicament worried her and the haste with which the girl was departing made her feel uncomfortable.

Still, perhaps it was all for the best. In two or three hours, when Brice came home, she would have to break the news to him, and that would cause him pain enough. But at least if the girl was already gone he would be spared the added pain, not to mention embarrassment, that meeting her was bound to cause once he knew the sorry truth. Yes, indeed, it was all for the best, and this reflection did much to ease the disquiet in Rachel's mind.

Upstairs, in her little bedroom, Maggie collected her few belongings and put them into the old worsted shawl. It was a task soon done and she wasted no time over it. She tied the shawl's corners into knots and, thrusting her arm through the loop, pushed the bundle up high so that it hung, satchel-wise, comfortably over her shoulder. She took a last look round the room, making sure she had left nothing, and went downstairs.

Rachel, seeing her off at the door, tried to press money into her hand, but she pushed it away.

'I don't want charity, Mrs Tallack.'

'Hah! That's all very fine!' Rachel said. 'But what were you looking for when you came here, if it was not charity, pray?'

'I was looking for friendship,' Maggie said.

She turned and walked out of the yard and Rachel, after a brief delay, followed her as far as the gate to see which way she had gone. The girl had turned left along the road but was already crossing it to take the steep winding track that led up over the moor. For a while Rachel remained at the gate, watching the girl's lonely figure making its way up the lonely moor, under a sky that threatened rain. That was the last of Maggie Care, she said to herself as she turned away, but although her chief feeling was satisfaction, it was not entirely unmixed with regret.

The girl was made of good strong stuff; her help would be sorely missed on the farm; and if circumstances had been different she might even, Rachel admitted, have made a suitable wife for Brice. But circumstances could not be changed and Rachel would not allow herself to waste time in vain regrets. She still had to face Brice with the news and that prospect was enough to drive all other thoughts from her mind.

Maggie's objective, as she climbed the steep moorland track, was the old ruined engine-house of Bal Kerensa, standing close beside the stream on the level ground at the top of the slope. The morning's events had tired her; she needed time to rest and reflect; so when she came to the engine-house she left the track and went inside. Against the far wall, as she already knew, there was a heap of dead bracken, cut by some farmer the winter before and stored there for future use, and on it she made herself comfortable, leaning back against the wall and folding her hands over her stomach.

This morning, for the first time, her baby had moved inside her womb. The lurching of it had caused her pain; it had made her feel giddy and sick, bringing a darkness that clouded her senses; but the pain had been welcome to her and her heart had leapt in response to it, because of the life thus asserting itself, making demands upon her body, giving her own life meaning and purpose.

For this child was fruit of the love and the tender overwhelming passion that she and gentle Jim Kenna had known in those few happy weeks before he had been taken from her. She hoped and prayed it would be a boy, who would grow up to be the sort of man Jim had been: strong and gentle, quiet-voiced, full of good humour and kindliness; but whether it should be boy or girl, she would love it and cherish it just the same, for Jim's sake, because it was his. Indeed she loved it fiercely already and was eager for the feel of it moving underneath her hands. But the baby was quite still now and she pictured it curled at rest in her womb; and in her mind she spoke to it, saying: 'Yes, you are there. You've let me know. I don't mind if you bring me pain so long as I know you are there and alive.'

Jim had known about the baby and he had wanted to bring their wedding forward because of those people in Porthgaran who, as he said, could always be relied on to count up to nine and would take delight in doing so. Maggie had merely laughed at that. 'They will still count, whatever we do, but I don't care what they say so long as we're together, you and me.' But with Jim dead it was a different matter. Her father had been disliked all his life and after his death he had been reviled, and because she could not bear the thought that her child would be born and would grow up among people filled with such bitterness, she had turned her back on the place and had set out into the unknown. Had she been foolish? Yes, perhaps. For here she was, friendless and homeless, glad to seek temporary shelter in this old ruined building, without any roof overhead and without even a door to close against marauding cattle and sheep.

Still feeling sick and faint, and knowing a moment of hopelessness, she instinctively sought comfort by drawing out the silver locket she wore on a ribbon round her neck. She took it off and opened it and looked at the two pictures inside. One was of her mother, sad but serene, looking at her with tired eyes. The other was of Jim Kemma and although the picture was small and dim it was enough to bring to her mind his good, plain, honest face with its kindly look and crooked smile. The picture made her ache for him and after she had closed the locket she sat with it clenched tight in her hand, yielding herself to her memories, of his voice and his touch and his tenderness, and allowing herself to be overcome by the hopelessness of her longing for him.

The longing and the hopelessness passed. She hung the locket round her neck and tucked it away inside her dress. The sickness and faintness also passed; she was feeling herself again; and as her youthful strength and courage began to reassert themselves she sat up straight, hugging her knees, and began to think about the future.

Rachel Tallack's warning, that if she was arrested for vagrancy she would be taken back to Porthgaran, weighed heavily on her mind and she recognized the dangers of taking to the road again in search of work on other farms. Farm-work was what she did best; it was what she was used to; but there were other kinds of work available to girls like herself and she didn't mind what she did so long as she earned enough money to rent a lodging and buy food. In her pocket she had two shillings; enough to live on for at least a few days; but after that, if she failed to find work, she would either have to beg or go hungry.

She rose and went to the open doorway and stood looking down at Polsinney, built hugger-mugger, the houses close-packed, tucked into the cliffside and running steeply down to the sea. The harbour itself was hidden from her but she could see where, out in the bay, the seine-boats still lay-to, their patient crews waiting and watching for the pilchard shoals to come inshore. She could also see that part of the cliff where the huer had his look-out place and she could see that a large crowd still kept the huer company. The shoals were late coming in this year but when they did at last come there would be work for scores of people down in the fish-cellars on the wharf.

Maggie now reached a decision. She went to where she had left her bundle, took a square cotton scarf from it, and hid the bundle among the bracken. A light rain was beginning to fall and she tied the scarf over her head. She then left the old engine-house and set out over the brow of the moor to that part, well away from Boskillyer, where a second track ran down to the road. From there she took one of the alleys that led, by many a twist and turn, down to the harbour and the wharf.

Here, too, as on the cliff, scores of people were gathered, all looking eagerly out to sea. Many of these were the women and girls who, when the great moment came, would be rushed off their feet in the cellars, receiving the hundreds of thousands of pilchards brought ashore from the seine: tipping them out on the cellar floor, arranging them neatly, row by row, one layer upon another, each layer spread with salt, until they rose shoulder-high and formed a solid wall of fish. The women would work by shifts, day and night, till every last silver pilchard was safely in cure in the bulk, and for this work they would earn good wages, sometimes as much as fourpence an hour.

As Maggie mingled with the crowd, people turned to look at her, and one old woman, meeting her eye, tut-tut-tutted with toothless gums, pointing her long, bony chin in the direction of the bay.

'They old pilchers!' she exclaimed. 'They dunt seem to realize that we've been waiting a week or more. But they will come in pretty soon, I believe, for the stones've been rumblen these three nights past and there's no surer sign than that.'

'I hope you're right,' Maggie said.

She stood in the rain looking out to sea and the old woman eyed her up and down.

Brice, on getting home to Boskillyer, missed Maggie immediately and asked where she was.

'The girl has gone,' Rachel said.

'Gone? Where? On an errand, d'you mean?'

'No, she's gone for good, my son, and please do not fly out at me until you've heard what I have to say.'

'Do you mean you've sent her away?' Brice asked in a tight voice. 'Because if you have I must warn you – '

'That precious girl of yours,' Rachel said, 'is three or four months gone with child, and I counsel you to think on that before you begin speaking to me in a way you may well regret.'

She made no attempt to mince her words for she fully intended to shock him, and even when she saw from the look on his face that she had succeeded all too well, she gave no sign of the pity she felt, for he had a hard lesson to learn and the sooner he learnt it the better, she thought.

'I knew from the start there was something not quite right about her. I felt it in my very bones. For one thing it isn't natural for a young girl to have so little to say for herself and if you remember I said so to you – '

'How did you find out?' Brice asked.

'I used my eyes,' Rachel said.

'Did she admit it?'

'Of course she did. She could hardly do anything else.'

'I don't understand it,' Brice said. His face was still stiff and numb with shock but he had great powers of self-control and was beginning to use them. 'Who was the man responsible?'

'He was one of her father's crew. He was drowned with the rest. She was to have married him next month, it seems.'

There was a silence in the room. Brice took a deep and difficult breath.

'Poor girl,' he said at last. 'To lose not only her father and brother but the man she was going to marry as well . . .'

'Yes, poor girl indeed,' Rachel said, 'but what I can't quite forget is her slyness in coming here to me, persuading me to take her in, and all the time practising such deceit.'

'You lost no time in turning her out.'

'I gave her until the end of the week. It was she who chose to leave straight away.'

'Where has she gone?'

'I don't know.'

'Didn't she say what she meant to do?'

'No, she did not,' Rachel said. 'All I can tell you is that she went the same way as she came – up the track and over the moor.'

'How long ago?'

'About two hours.'

'Then I'd better go after her.'

'Oh, for pity's sake!' Rachel said. 'Are you such a poor witless fool that you hanker after her even now?'

Brice, with a gesture, turned away, impatiently scorning his mother's suggestion. His feelings were still too tender, too raw, for him to discuss them openly, but no, Maggie was nothing to him now that he knew the truth about her, for he saw with terrible clarity that the girl he had come so close to loving had never really existed at all.

The real Maggie Care was someone quite different; a girl with a past life of her own that he knew nothing about; a girl who, when he had looked at her with a young man's innocent desire, had carried this secret thing in her, this seed of knowledge in her womb, implanted there by another man. He felt no anger against her, – at least he told himself he did not – for never by a single word or glance had she ever encouraged his interest in her, so how could she be held to blame? There was no question of that. Only he himself was to blame, for his blind, simple-minded trustfulness.

Yet even while he assured himself that no blame could attach to her, he could not prevent some bitterness from creeping into his thoughts of her. Her secret, now it was out, had altered his feelings utterly. He thought of her clear grey eyes, looking at him so steadily, and he thought of how, unsuspected by him, this knowledge had lain hidden in her; this thing that set her completely apart and made her just a stranger to him; and gradually, as he dwelt on it, his heart began to close against her.

But he could not help pitying her, for she was all alone in the world, victim of a terrible tragedy, and, turning back to his mother, he said:

'The girl is in trouble. She needs help. Something must be done for her.'

'You'll never catch up with her now,' Rachel said. 'There are three roads out at Nawmenvennor. She could have taken any one of them. And what if you did catch up with her? What would you do then?'

'Bring her back here, I suppose.'

'You are talking like a fool. Can't you see what will

63

happen if you bring that girl back here? As soon as people find out about her condition they will say the child is yours.'

'That's ridiculous,' Brice said. 'Maggie has only been here a month and if as you say she's three months with child – '

'People will forget the facts,' Rachel said, 'if the fable has more spice to it.'

Brice stood irresolute. He knew what his mother said was true. And because he was rather a puritan, at least where his own conduct was concerned, the thought that people would point at him, linking him with the girl's trouble, was more than enough to give him pause. And Rachel, seeing she had scored a hit, made haste to drive it home.

'If she's never seen here again, nothing will be known about the child, and no harm will be done,' she said. 'People here will soon forget her and that will be better for all of us.'

'What on earth will become of her?'

'I don't know. I told her she should go back to Porthgaran and let her own parish take care of her. She said she wouldn't but who knows? – Perhaps after all she changed her mind. Anyway, whatever happens, she will no doubt fall on her feet. That sort of girl always does.'

'That sort of girl? What sort is that?'

'You know what I mean.'

'Whatever you may think of her, Maggie is certainly no slut.'

'No, well, I grant you that. But she was a ship that passed in the night and if you take my advice, my son, you will put her out of your mind. She has no claim on either of us.'

'Not even the claim of humanity?'

But his mother was right after all. Maggie had already

gone on her way and the matter was best left as it was. And although he was still troubled by guilt when he thought of her tramping the roads he could not help feeling some relief that he would not have to see her again.

Rachel, reading all this in his face, remained silent, giving him time, and after a while, when he spoke again, she saw by his altered expression that she had nothing more to fear.

'When people ask why Maggie has left us,' he said, 'what do you think we ought to say?'

Rachel shrugged.

'Other girls have come and gone and this one has done the same. There's nothing strange about that.'

'You won't tell them about her trouble?'

'No, now that she's left the district, there's no need for anyone here to know.'

The following morning, however, when Rachel went on her milk-round, she soon heard that Maggie Care was still in Polsinney, for the girl had been seen the previous day, loitering down on the wharf, apparently hoping for work in the cellars. Rachel was furiously angry at this and when her customers, all agog, asked why Maggie had left Boskillyer, she answered at once with the bald truth.

'Maggie Care is with child. She's three or four months gone with it. A girl of that sort can only spell trouble and I was obliged to dismiss her.'

She felt no compunction in spreading this news, since the girl, by lingering in Polsinney, had only brought it on herself. The truth would emerge soon enough, anyway, and Rachel quickly made up her mind that *her* account of it should be heard first.

Brice, when he berthed at the quay that morning, heard the gossip immediately from the quayside loafer, Dicky Limpet, who came aboard cadging for fish.

65

'So that girl you had up at the farm have got herself into trouble, then, and your mother have turned her out of the house?'

'Who told you that?' Brice asked sharply.

'Why, tedn no secret, surely, cos Alice Cox told me she had it from Mrs Tallack herself, and Gladdy Jacka told me she'd seen the girl and asked her straight out and the girl said yes, it was true, sure nuff.'

'Seen her?' Brice said. 'You mean she's still here?'

'Ess, for sure. Didn't you know?'

'No, I thought she'd gone away.'

'My dear life, no, she'm here bold as brass. Any number of people have seen her walking about the place, and Gladdy Jacka spoke to her only half-hour ago, I believe.'

Brice gave Dicky a string of fish and bundled him out of the boat but the crew had already overheard. Most of them kept a discreet silence but Ralph Ellis came to Brice and clapped a hand on his shoulder.

'Twadn you, by any chance, that got the girl into trouble, was it?'

'No. It was not.'

'I was only asking, that's all.'

'Well, now that you've had your answer,' Brice said, 'perhaps you'll get on with clearing these nets.'

He was not surprised, on going home, to find his mother full of the news and in a thoroughly bad temper about it.

'I thought we'd seen the last of that girl but oh, no, not a bit of it! – She's chosen to stay on in the district to be the bane of both our lives. The whole place is buzzing with gossip from Churchtown down to the quay.'

'And you have been adding to it, I hear.'

'I only added the truth, my son. Surely you don't blame me for that?'

'No, I don't blame you,' Brice said. 'You've spread the

truth about Maggie's child to protect me and I'm grateful for it. What you said yesterday, about people twisting things round, has already come to pass. I had my first taste of it from Ralph Ellis this morning and no doubt there will be more before I'm many days older. But at least, thanks to you, people know the truth, and until the gossip has died down we shall just have to bear it as best we can.'

Having thus spoken Brice went to wash and Rachel, brooding over his words, was able to find some comfort in them. It seemed that twenty-four hours of reflection had done Brice a great deal of good. His tone, when speaking of Maggie Care, had had a coldness and hardness in it and although he now knew where she was, he no longer talked of helping her. It seemed he had cut her out of his heart and that at least, Rachel thought, was something to be thankful for.

Chapter 3

The huers had been keeping watch for ten days; so had the crews of the seine-boats lying-to out in the bay; and now at last, on the afternoon of the tenth day, a shoal was sighted off Volley Head: a red-brown shadow darkening the sea, coming on and on and on, over the sandbar and into the bay, closer and closer inshore until the movement of the water could be plainly and unmistakably seen, breaking the surface of the water and chopping it up into sharp-pointed waves.

The huer's great cry rang out, shouted through his long tin trumpet, 'Hevva! Hevva! Hevva! Hevva!', and was at once echoed by the crowd gathered beside him on the cliff. People now appeared from everywhere and came running down the streets of Polsinney, swarming onto the jetties and wharves, climbing onto the coopers' sheds, and spreading over the beach at Porthvole. And the cry went up on all sides, 'Hevva! Hevva!', again and again, until the whole harbour rang with it.

The shoal came into that part of the bay allotted to the Nonesuch Seine and the Nonesuch owners, Mark Hall and his son, stood on the cliff beside the huer who, with a furze bush in either hand, was signalling to the boat in the bay, directing it into position. The seine-crew bent to their oars; the boat went cutting through the water and came up close beside the shoal; and the huer gave the signal to stand. Now there was a hush on the watching crowds. A stillness lay over all the bay. Then the huer, using his trumpet, gave the order:

'*Shoot the seine!*'

Again the boat began to move, its steersman watching the huer's signals, and as it moved the net was paid out, splashing down into the sea. Round and round came the seine-boat and when the shoal was almost enclosed the follower moved into position ready to shoot the stop-net that would close up the opening of the seine. While this was being done the lurker-boat stood by and there was a great deal of splashing and noise as the lurker crew, with their long oars, beat at the water again and again to prevent the writhing silver fish from escaping through the opening. At last the shoal was fully enclosed and the team of hauliers on the beach began hauling in the warps, drawing the seine, with its millions of fish alive in it, into the shallower waters inshore. Soon the warps had been secured. The hauliers raised their caps and cheered and the cheer was echoed by the crowd. Mark Hall shook hands with his son and the two of them hurried down to the beach. The seiners were working the tuck-net now and as the fish were raised to the surface the ravening gulls gathered there in a desperate frenzy of movement and noise.

The sky was darkly overcast and there was more rain in the offing. Maggie, with her scarf over her head, moved among the crowd on the wharf, watching the dipper-boats putting out to bring the pilchards in from the seine. Behind her, Mark Hall's cellar was already alive with people bustling about with buckets of salt, making ready to receive the fish as soon as they should be brought ashore. Many of the cellar-girls stood outside, sleeves rolled up, ready for work, laughing and chatting in small groups, excited at the taking of the season's first shoal, and as Maggie moved among them they watched her with inquisitive eyes. It was three days since she had left Boskillyer and by now, as she well knew, her story was common property.

Three of these girls, watching her, were whispering and laughing together, and suddenly one of them, nudged by the others, spoke out in a loud voice.

'Some folk should go back where they belong and have their babies where they were got. Porthgaran, wadn it, or someplace like that?'

Maggie stood still and looked at them and with one accord they turned their backs. But another girl, standing nearby, met her gaze and spoke to her.

'You needn't pay heed to Biddy Grose. Her chap've gone off with Nolly Geach and chance'll be a fine thing if she ever find herself another.'

The girl, who was short and stoutly built, stood with her bare arms folded, picking at the skin on her elbows. She had a broad freckled face and hair as thick and red as a fox's and she wore a man's cloth cap. One of her front teeth was missing and she kept sucking the gap with her tongue.

'You're Maggie Care, aren't you? You were dairymaid up at Boskillyer and Mrs Tallack turned you out. I saw you down here yesterday and the day before, I believe.'

'Yes, I'm hoping to get work.'

'Have you worked in the cellars before?'

'Yes, in Porthgaran,' Maggie said, 'but only two or three times, that's all.'

'Mr Hall will take you on. I'll tell him you're a friend of mine.' The girl took hold of Maggie's arm. 'My name is Martha Cledra but everyone d'call me Bussa,' she said.

The dipper-boats had begun to come back and already the first gurries, wooden handbarrows filled with fish, were being carried up to the cellars. There was a lot of laughter and noise. Children ran about everywhere, trying to flip fish from the gurries, and the carriers bawled abuse at them. Up on the cliff there was more excitement. Another shoal had come into the bay. The huer was shouting through his trumpet.

'Seems they're coming in fitty now. That one's on the Regina stem.' The girl turned again to Maggie. 'Got a place to live, have you, since being turned out at the farm?'

'No, I've been sleeping up at the bal.'

'Aw, my dear life, that'll never do! Not in your condition it won't. You'd better come home with me tonight. There are nine of us but we'll squeeze you in somehow.'

'What about your mother? Won't she mind?'

'My sister Kate's in the same boat as you so none of *us'll* cast any stones.' Martha suddenly squeezed Maggie's arm. 'There's old Mark Hall now,' she said. 'Come with me and I'll get you signed on.'

Gus Tallack sat alone in his cottage looking out at the heavy rain which had kept him indoors for almost a week. The cottage kitchen was very dark for the windows, on the outside, were so thickly encrusted with salt that even today's downpour did nothing to wash it away. In his lap, as he sat by the window, he held his big brown bible, open at Ecclesiastes. He had been reading for some time and the words of one verse still ran in his mind, and now, as he stared at the white rain sluicing down the window-panes, he spoke them aloud to the empty room:

'Whatsoever thy hand findeth to do, do it with thy might; for there is no work, nor device, nor knowledge, nor wisdom, in the grave, whither thou goest.'

Gus was not a pious man. He rarely attended church service. But he had been a fisherman and he had a fisherman's simple faith, and in the two and a half years since his illness had first struck him down, he had turned more and more to the Scriptures, hoping to find guidance there. Often in the evenings, especially in winter, the bible was his only companion. He would read some favourite passage aloud and argue it over with himself. It did not always bring comfort, however, and once he had been so

71

enraged by the sheer inscrutability of the Word of God that he had flung the bible across the room. But Ecclesiastes contained good cheer. It was full of simple truths. There was charity in it and plain good sense.

'For to him that is joined to all the living there is hope, for the living dog is better than a dead lion. For the living know that they shall die, but the dead know not anything, neither have they any more a reward, for the memory of them is forgotten. Go thy way, eat thy bread with joy and drink thy wine with a merry heart, for God now accepteth thy works.'

Gus leant forward in his chair and laid the bible on the window-sill. He took his watch from his waistcoat pocket and compared it with the clock on the wall. It was nearly half past twelve and he gave a little fretful sigh, for his nephew should have been here by now. For some days Brice had kept away; he had not even paid his Saturday visit and his share of the previous week's takings still awaited collection; but this morning Gus had sent a message asking Brice to call at the cottage on his way home from the quay.

At a quarter to one Brice came, shedding his oilskin and sou'wester and hanging them up in the porch. He was still wearing his sea-boots and as he came into the kitchen he left a wet trail across the flags.

'Isaac said you wanted to see me.'

'I've been waiting to see you for twelve days! What happened to you last Saturday?'

'I went to St Glozey for the sports.'

'Surely you can't have stayed there all day?' Gus looked up at him irritably. 'Aren't you going to sit down?'

'Well,' Brice said. He glanced at the clock. 'I wasn't really intending to stay. I'm already late as it is.'

But he pulled a chair close to the window and sat down opposite Gus. He was not in the best of moods this morning, for the night's work had been arduous, due to the rain and the squally winds. Neither he nor his crew had got any rest and by morning tempers had become badly strained and then, when the catch had been sold and unloaded, he had quarrelled with Ralph Ellis over cleaning out the fish-hold. Brice was particular about this: not a single fish-scale must be left to taint the next night's catch; but Ralph had no time for such womanish ways and it was not the first time that he had refused to do his share. 'I'm going home to sleep!' he had said, and because the other four men had been inclined to take his part, Brice had sent them all home and had cleaned out the fish-hold himself.

Now, tired and out of sorts, he had to face his uncle Gus, and he could quite easily guess why the old man had sent for him.

'So that girl of yours is expecting a child and your mother has turned her out of the house!' Gus's upper lip curled in contempt, showing his strong, white, irregular teeth. 'How exactly like Rachel, by God, to make no allowance for nature!' he said. 'And she a woman who goes to church, calling herself a Christian.'

'You can't expect me,' Brice said, 'to join you in abusing my mother.'

'I don't see why not if tes what she deserves!'

'I hear Maggie's got work in Hall's cellar so no harm has come to her.'

'Have you also heard where she's living?'

'Yes, with the Cledras in White Hope Lane.'

'And you say no harm has come to her! From what I know about that girl, the Cledras' is no place for her, and you know it as well as I do myself. Nick Cledra's a drunkard and a thief and his slut of a wife is almost as bad.'

'Nobody made her go to them. She should have done as my mother said and gone back to Porthgaran where she belongs.'

'Is that all you've got to say about her? A girl you had working on your farm? A girl you as good as told me you loved – '

'No! I never told you that!'

'What *did* you tell me, then?'

'Whatever it was – ' Brice began.

'Yes? Well? Spit it out!'

'Whatever it was, I made a mistake,' Brice said, coldly. 'I feel sorry for her, of course, as I would for any unfortunate, but – she is nothing to me in *that* way.'

'Not any more, I can see that! You're just about chokeful with it all. Now that you know the girl had a lover and is going to bear his child it's turned you against her properly and you can't even bear to think of her. You'd like to be able to clap your hands and hey presto! – She doesn't exist!'

There was so much truth in this that Brice, for a while, could find nothing to say and sat in silence, feeling ashamed. But he was tired, both in body and mind, and his uncle's contemptuous attack had roused some stubborn resentment in him so that, for the moment at least, whatever pity he felt for Maggie was deadened by the pity he felt for himself.

'And what,' he asked, eventually, 'would you expect me to do for her?'

'Go and find her, of course, and take her back home with you.'

'That is out of the question. Whatever you may say about my mother, she is mistress in her own house, and I am bound to consider her.'

'You told me not so long ago that your mother didn't rule your life.'

'No, she doesn't, but then neither does Maggie Care.'

'If you had an ounce of spunk in you, you'd marry the girl, baby or no. Your mother would have to accept her then. She would just have to make the best of things.'

'You are joking, of course.'

'Am I? Yes, perhaps I am. You're too much of a stick, my boy, to do what's plainly the bestmost thing. Too much tied up in your dignity. Too much afraid of what folk will say!'

'I certainly don't want a second-hand wife, if that's what you mean by my dignity.'

'You loved her once. You could love her again. And she could come to love you in time, if only you were to give her the chance.'

Brice felt he had had enough. He rose and pushed back his chair.

'Maggie has already loved one man – '

'And that man is dead, so I've been told.'

'Yes, he was one of her father's crew, and they were all drowned together.'

'Father, brother, lover!' Gus said. 'All lost to her in a single night.' He looked up at Brice with dark-gleaming eyes. 'And the only thing *you* can think about is that *you* have suffered some hurt to your pride!'

'I would help her if I could but marriage is out of the question,' Brice said. 'And now, if that's all you wanted with me, I'd just as soon be getting home.'

'Oh, get home by all means, back to your mother!' Gus exclaimed. And then, over his shoulder, he said: 'Don't forget to pick up your share. You'll find it on the mantel-shelf.'

Brice collected the heap of coins and went to put on his oilskins. As he let himself out he called, 'I'll see you again on Saturday,' but his uncle did not answer him.

Gus, left alone in the cottage kitchen, had taken up the bible again and it lay in his lap, between his hands. But he was not reading it; he was staring into space; and between his bushy, grizzled brows there was a frown of intense

75

concentration, for something was working in his mind. His bearded lips were pressed close together and his breath came heavily through his nose.

He was used to sitting long hours in his chair but whereas, most days, he shifted about restlessly, easing his body this way and that, now he sat perfectly still, so deeply absorbed in his thoughts that the old ornamental clock on the wall chimed away the quartered hours without once drawing his fretful glance.

When at last he bestirred himself, it was with a sudden alertness and quickness, humping himself round in his chair and gazing, sharp-eyed, about the room as though to catch it unawares in all its squalor and shabbiness. His upper lip curled in disgust. A little growl moved in his throat. And his hands, taking hold of the heavy bible, slammed it shut and held it aloft.

'Whatsoever thy hand findeth to do, do it with thy might,' he declaimed, 'for there is no work, nor device, nor knowledge, nor wisdom, in the grave, whither thou goest.'

He laid the bible down again and wheeled himself towards the door. At the onset of his illness, he had had a double wooden ramp laid down at the threshold, so that he could wheel his chair up and over the doorstep; and outside the porch door he had had an old ship's bell hung up so that he could summon help when needed. He now wheeled himself outside and rang the bell and its clangour echoed round the yard, and when he looked up at the sail-loft windows, he could see two startled faces looking palely down at him. Rain was still falling heavily, so he wheeled himself back indoors and sat waiting impatiently, and after a while Isaac Kiddy came in, half in eager anticipation that perhaps some calamity had occurred, half in reluctance in case it had not.

'I want you to go to Mark Hall's cellar and find that girl,

Maggie Care. Tell her, when she's finished her shift, I want her to come and see me here.'

Isaac stared.

'What do ee want with the likes of she?'

'Never mind what I want her for. Just go and give her the message.'

'This is the second time today I've had to go out on messages,' Isaac said, grumbling. 'First I had to go down to the quay and take a message to Brice and now I've got to go to the cellars and find this maid, Maggie Care, though whether tes right to call her a maid – '

'Are you going, then?' Gus roared.

'Ess, surely, I'm just on my way. I've only got to finish the bit crowst I was eating when you rang that bell and then I'll be off with this message of yours, though just what tes you've got in mind, wanting to see a maid of that sort, is just about past my comprehension . . .'

The old sail-maker went at last and his errand took him almost an hour. He returned smelling strongly of drink, having broken his journey at *The Brittany* for a nip of something to keep out the wet.

'I gave the maid your message, you, and she said she'd come at eight o'clock. She was besting to know what you wanted her for but of course I couldn't tell her that – '

'She'll know soon enough when she gets here,' Gus said. '*You* can get yourself back to your work.'

It was dark by the time Maggie arrived, for the rain, which was still falling steadily, had brought the day to an early close. Gus had already lit the lamp and it stood on the hob of the fireless stove and in its half circle of light he and the girl, sitting one at either side of the hearth, looked at each other appraisingly.

'We've never met, you and me, but we know as much about each other as the folk in Polsinney have to tell, and

77

that's plenty to be going on with, I seem. Have you been told I'm a dying man? Yes, you're sure to have heard that, having been at Boskillyer a month, and what you didn't hear there you'll have heard in the fish-cellars, no doubt.'

'Well,' Maggie said. She was at a loss.

'You don't have to worry about my feelings, cos what they say is only the truth, and the only difference between them and me is that *I* know when it's going to happen, though not to a navvy-gravvy, of course. There are compensations in that. It gives a man the chance to think and see about putting his house in order.'

Gus gave a sardonic laugh and his glance flickered round the room.

'As you can see, it needs it,' he said.

Maggie also glanced round the room. There was a patch of damp on one wall and the wallpaper was black with mould. Neglect was manifest everywhere and after the recent heavy rain a cold clamminess hung on the air so that, as she looked around, her skin came out in gooseflesh and a shiver ran over her. Her shoes were full of water from the puddles she had walked through and her wet skirts clung coldly over her knees. She turned to look at Gus again and found him watching her intently. So far she had scarcely spoken. She had left it all to him. But now, in a quiet voice, she said:

'Why have you sent for me, Mr Tallack? What do you want to say to me?'

'I wanted to see for myself what sort of girl this Maggie Care was that I've been hearing so much about.'

'And now that you've seen, are you satisfied? Am I what you were led to expect?'

'I suppose, after the treatment you got from my sister-in-law, you're a bit suspicious of us Tallacks, but I mean you no harm, I promise you.'

'Mrs Tallack only did what many another would have done.'

'She put you out in the road,' Gus said. 'Don't you bear her a grudge for that?'

'No, I don't think so,' Maggie said.

'And what about my nephew Brice?'

'I don't quite understand what you mean.'

'He fancied himself in love with you. Surely you must have realized that.'

'I think he'll have changed his mind by now.'

'Maybe you could change it back.'

'I wouldn't want to,' Maggie said. 'There was only ever one man for me and he is dead. I shall never love anyone else.'

'What was the young man's name?'

'Jim Kenna.'

'He brought you a packet of trouble before he went and got himself drowned.'

'No more than I brought on myself.'

'Life, in this Christian country of ours, can be very hard for a young girl with an illegitimate child to bring up. At present you're lodged with the Cledras, I hear, but that's no suitable place for you, or for your child when it comes.'

'No, I know,' Maggie said. 'The Cledras have been good to me but we sleep three in a bed and I certainly can't stay there long.'

'Well, I'll come to the point,' Gus said. 'I'm not a rich man – far from it – but I *have* got a bit of property. This cottage is mine, such as it is, and so are the sail-loft and barking-house. The barking-house is not in use – I sacked the man who worked it for me and I haven't bothered to find another – but the sail-loft brings in a bit of money, and of course there's the boat but you know about that.'

'Yes,' Maggie said, 'I know about that.'

But she could not follow the trend of his thoughts and waited, still puzzled, for him to go on.

'Well, I've got a proposition in mind and I'll put it to you fair and square, without beating about the bush.' For a moment Gus sat looking at her and his dark brown eyes, in their crinkled lids, reflected the glow from the little lamp. 'If you would consent to marry me, it would give you and your baby a home and some security for the future, cos when the time came for me to snuff out, my bit of property would come to you.'

Maggie sat perfectly still. Whatever she might have expected, it was certainly not this, and she was struck dumb. But Gus was in no hurry for her to answer. There were still a number of things he wanted to make clear to her and he was glad to have the chance of doing it in his own way.

'Don't make any mistake about it. This is a business proposition and nothing else. I'm a sick man and I'm soon for the grave. All I want from you is that you should keep house for me and bring some comfort into the place. I shouldn't want to come to your bed – much good it'd do me if I did! – and you and me would have separate rooms. I thought I'd better make that plain so as not to give the wrong idea and frighten you off before I've begun.'

Gus paused and took a deep breath. Talking always taxed his strength.

'Of course, I *could* just ask you to come as my paid housekeeper and still leave my property to you,' he said. 'But it would be better if we married cos that'd make everything right and tight. Oh, I know folk'll talk just the same! They'll wink and nod among themselves and say they know what's behind it all . . . But marriage, even of this sort, is legal and binding in every way and people have great respect for it. You'd have my name and so would your child and when you came into the property there'd be no room for argument about the rights and wrongs of it. No one could interfere with you. No one could ever take it away.'

Once again there was a pause. The clock on the wall could be heard ticking and rain could be heard on the window-panes. Maggie sat, straight-backed, her hands folded in her lap. Her grey eyes were full of thought and Gus could see uncertainty in them.

'I don't expect you to answer at once. You'll need time to brood on it. And if I read your face aright, you've got a few questions you want to ask.'

'Yes,' Maggie said. 'One question at least. Why should you want to do this for me?'

'It's not just for you. It's for both of us. I've got two or three years at the most and Dr Sam Carveth has said that my end will not be an easy one. At present I can still use my legs but it costs me something, I can tell you, to get myself across this room. In a year or so I shall be worse. Helpless. Dependent on *you*. That won't make me an easy man to live with day in, day out, and I reckon by the time you've seen me through, you'll have earnt what you're getting in return. You need to consider that side of it. You'll have your child to think about and you may decide it's too much to take on.'

'Can't the doctor do anything for you?'

'No. Nothing. He've said so straight. Any more questions you want to ask?'

'Yes. I'm wondering about your nephew, Brice, and your sister-in-law, Mrs Tallack. Won't they, being family, expect you to leave your property to them?'

Gus gave a cynical laugh.

'You're right about my sister-in-law. What she expects would fill a book. But don't worry your head about that. My brother Henry, years ago, sold his share of the business to me and put his money into a copper mine over

81

to Goonwelter. It was Rachel who made him do that. She thought it'd make him a rich man. But instead he lost every penny he had. So whatever hopes Rachel has about getting her hands on my property, she've got no rights in the matter at all, and if you accept my proposition, one of the things that'll please me most is giving *her* a smack in the eye.'

Gus broke off and took a rest. He was breathing heavily.

'Well?' he demanded, after a while. 'Does that shock you, Maggie Care?'

'No. Not in the least.'

'Rachel's had me dead and buried a dozen times in the past two years so what do I owe her? – Not a groat! As for boy Brice, well, a few disappointments here and there won't do him a ha'porth of harm. He's a young man, fit and strong, and he can make his own way in the world. But you're a girl and you're all alone, so surely you won't refuse my help just because of some foolish qualm over putting my nephew's nose out of joint?'

'No,' Maggie said. She shook her head. 'I have my baby to think of and that's more important to me than anything else in the world. But – '

'What?'

'It still seems strange that you should want to do this for me, someone you've never met before, a stranger you know nothing about.'

'Damme, why should it seem so strange? It seems simple enough to me.'

Gus sought to brush the matter aside, but Maggie looked at him in such a way that his gaze faltered before hers and he sat for some time in complete silence, frowning at the oil-lamp on the stove.

'There *is* another reason of sorts and I may as well make a clean breast of it. It's an old story, out of the past, and I've kept it to myself till now.'

Gus shifted in his chair. Somehow the lamp was bothering him and he leant forward to turn down the flame. Then he slumped back again.

'I started life as a fisherman. That was when I was twelve years old. When I was twenty my father died and left me the money to buy my own boat. In winter I used to go up to Bigbury Bay for the herring fishing and one winter there I met a girl. We became lovers, her and me, and we planned to get married just as soon as we could get her father's consent. He was one of the Plymouth Brethren. Too sanctimonious by half for me. Anyway, at the end of the season, I came home to Polsinney for the long-lining, and I didn't go back again till June. By then Ellen had gone. I'd got her into trouble, you see, and her father had turned her out of the house.'

Gus stared at the lamp on the hob. His story was bringing old wounds to life and he still felt some of the rage he had felt as a young man of twenty-two.

'Nobody knew where she'd gone. She'd slipped away without a word. But I'd only missed her by four days and I thought I should find her in no time at all. I spent three weeks tramping the roads, asking at turnpikes, villages, towns . . . But by the time I got news of her it was too late and she was dead. It seems she'd set out to walk down into Cornwall to find me here in Polsinney but on the way she'd caught a chill and been taken into the workhouse infirmary at Dunsett. It turned to pneumonia and she died. She was buried as a pauper in the churchyard at Bayle.'

Gus looked up and met Maggie's gaze.

'I was too late to help Ellen and do what I ought to have done for her but I *can* help you and your child instead. It's the one last useful job I can do before I have to hand over the helm and when I meet up with Ellen again, to give an account of myself to her, I know she'll say I've done the right thing.'

'How old was she?'

'She was eighteen. It happened thirty years ago. But no one in Polsinney knows the tale and I would prefer to keep it that way.'

'I shan't tell anyone,' Maggie said.

Gus gave a nod. He was satisfied.

'There's something about you, somehow, that makes me feel I can trust you,' he said. 'Do you think you can trust me the same?'

Before Maggie could answer, however, he stopped her with a brusque command.

'Don't answer that! I'm asking too soon. You need time to go besting about to find out something of what I'm like. You'll be told some rare tales, I daresay, and when you've heard them you can make up your mind.'

'I don't need to go besting about. I've been in Polsinney long enough to know what people say about you.'

'Hah! Is that so? And what *do* they say?'

'For one thing, they say you're fond of the rum bottle.'

'Damme! And what if I am? Would they grudge a dying man the one bit of comfort left to him? What else do the beggars say about me?'

'They say you don't suffer fools gladly.'

'Nobody does, except he be a fool himself, and even then he's a lot more shrewd with other folk's foolishness than he is with his own. What else do they say?'

'They say you've got a quick temper and that once you've got an idea in your head you can be peggy as a mule.'

'Is that the whole reckoning?' Gus asked.

'Yes,' Maggie said, 'I think it is, and it seems to me, if that's the worst, I haven't got a lot to worry about.'

'Does that mean you're willing to consider my proposition?'

'Yes.'

Maggie now rose to her feet and took her wet cape from the back of the chair. She drew it round her and tied the cord.

'I'll come in the morning, before work, and let you have my answer,' she said. 'That'll be just before eight.'

'That's not very long to be thinking all round a step that will settle the whole of your future life.'

'It's as long as I shall need,' Maggie said.

At the back of her mind she already felt sure that she would accept his proposal of marriage and the conditions that went with it. Astonishing though the proposal was, her mind had quickly adapted to it, and she had soon begun to feel that everything that had happened to her since her arrival in Polsinney had been bringing her slowly to this point. She had been in Gus Tallack's company for less than an hour but somehow, during that time, because of what had passed between them, a conviction had grown and taken root that their lives were already linked by fate.

But certainly she needed to think; to look coolly and critically at all the possible implications; to weigh the problems against the advantages, especially with regard to her child, and to try, with what honesty she could command, to sort out the rights and wrongs involved in accepting a dying man's proposal.

On reaching the door she paused and looked back, and what she saw was an old man, aged prematurely by disease, his big body, once powerful, now misshapen and made slack by the slow wasting of his muscles and nerves. But there was a look of strength even now in the set of the head on the powerful neck and as he turned his bearded face towards her, she saw how fiercely the flame of life still burnt in him, glowing in the broad, thick-fleshed cheeks and lighting up the dark brown eyes with a kind of angry energy.

'Well, does it give you pause,' he said, 'to see what a wreck of a man I am?'

'I was thinking, if we do marry, I shall want to speak to that doctor of yours, to see what can be done for you.'

'I've already told you, there's nothing to be done. That's how I come to be sitting here, offering to make you wife and widow all in the space of two or three years.'

'Yes, well, we shall see,' Maggie said.

When she had gone, Gus sat for a while without moving, staring fixedly into space. The clock on the wall struck nine. He looked at it and gave a scowl.

'Get a move on, will you?' he said.

During the night the rain stopped and by seven o'clock the next morning Polsinney was steaming dry in a sun that shone, burning hot, from a cloudless sky. Gus had wheeled himself out to the yard and sat watching the drifters unloading their catches onto the quay on the opposite side of the harbour. He had brought his breakfast out with him: two thick slices of bread and a hunk of cold fat bacon; but after two or three bites it lay untouched on the plate in his lap.

Just before eight Maggie came. Gus had set a stool for her, and she sat down on it, facing him. She came to the point without delay.

'I've thought it over and the answer is yes.'

'Are you sure?'

'Yes. Quite sure.'

'You won't change your mind later on and leave me looking a damned fool?'

'No. I promise you faithfully.'

Gus took a long, deep, quivering breath. His face was flushed with satisfaction. He looked as though he would burst with it. But there were lingering doubts.

'I'm not a saint. You know that. And sickness doesn't

bring out the best in a man who's only flesh and blood. Have you thought what it'll mean, seeing me through to my end? Have you any idea what you're taking on?'

Maggie tried to answer honestly.

'I can't see into the future, Mr Tallack, but I promise I shall do my best to fulfil my side of the bargain and so long as you're good to me and my child – '

'You will be my wife,' Gus said, 'and your child will be like my own child, and the day we are married I shall make my will leaving my property to you, so that it's all watertight as anything on this earth can be.' After further thought he said: 'In some ways we know a lot about each other. In other ways we know nothing at all. It may be I'm doing a bad thing, persuading a young girl like you to marry a sick old man like me, but I mean only good to you and your child, and this much I swear by Almighty God.'

Maggie nodded but made no reply. She trusted him absolutely.

'Are you church or chapel?'

'Church,' she said.

'Then as soon as Isaac Kiddy comes, I'll send him up to fetch the parson, to see about calling the banns. There's no sense in wasting time. Are you agreeable to that?'

'Yes.'

'So be it. I'll see to it.'

'I must go now. I'll be late for work.'

'There are things we shall need to discuss. You'd better come and see me again tonight.'

'Yes. All right. I'll be here at eight.'

When she had gone out of the yard Gus, in a sudden surge of feeling, took his breakfast from the plate in his lap and hurled it piece by piece to the gulls who swooped instantly, screaming and flapping, to snatch it up in mid air.

At half-past-eight Isaac Kiddy arrived and immediately Gus sent him out again.

'I want you to go to the parsonage and ask the parson to step down here. I want to see him straight away.'

'What do ee want with the parson, you?'

'You can tell him I've got a job for him.'

Even before the first banns had been read in church, news had spread throughout Polsinney that Gus was to marry Maggie Care. Hall's cellar was agog with it. The women and girls could not leave it alone. And just as their hands were ceaselessly busy laying out the pilchards and spreading the salt, so their tongues were equally busy with this latest piece of news.

'You must've known a thing or two when you came to Polsinney, Maggie Care. You'll be sitting some pretty when the old man dies and leaves you his bit of property even if tes all tumblen down.'

'If I'd known old Gus was looking out for a wife, I should have made up to him myself. But tedn no good talken like that. I should have had to get into trouble before I stood a chance, I suppose.'

'Aw, just listen to Deborah Larch! If *she* haven't got herself in trouble it can't be for want of running the risk!'

'Maybe Kate Cledra can give her some hints.'

'If at first you don't conceive – '

'The church'll be full on Sunday, you. Even the chapel folk'll be there to hear Gus Tallack's banns shouted out.'

'Any just cause or 'pediment, en?'

'Only a little one, that's all.'

'Dear of'n, too, tedn hardly his fault.'

'Maggie'll have to make the most of this cheeld. She won't get another from old Gus.'

The noisy gossip went on and on and Maggie let it flow over her. The women and girls, for the most part, were friendly and sympathetic to her, now that her story was fully known, for their own menfolk were fishermen and the tragedy that had befallen her was one that touched them very close. Rough their jokes might be, but they were meant in good fellowship, and Maggie knew it. As for the rest, the spiteful few, she was completely indifferent to them. Their barbed remarks left her untouched. She found she was able to shut them out.

The only thing that mattered to her was the child she carried in her womb and she thought about it constantly. All her life's hopes were wrapped up in this child and to safeguard its future she had agreed to marry a man almost three times her age. An ailing man, close to death. A man she knew almost nothing about. Yet none of this seemed strange to her. Instead it seemed like providence. Gus Tallack might be a stranger to her, but he had appeared in her hour of need, and he had her trust and her gratitude. People would say, and it would be true, that she was marrying him for his money; but a bargain had been struck between them and so long as she kept her side of it there need not be any feelings of guilt; and when his property came to her she would keep it and hold it, for her child's sake, whatever the world might think of her.

All these things so filled her mind that the babble of gossip in the fish-cellar made no impression on her at all. She felt perfectly safe and secure, now that her baby's future was settled, and she followed her own trend of thoughts.

'One thing I should dearly love to see,' said Martha Cledra, at her side, 'and that's Rachel Tallack's face when she hears you're going to marry old Gus.'

Chapter 4

Rachel's anger was bitter indeed and Brice had to bear the brunt of it.

'It was a bad day for us when that girl came to the district!' she said. 'She's brought nothing but trouble, right from the start, and to think I took her into my house! If only I had had the sense to send her packing as she deserved! But no, I took Christian pity on her, and this is how I've been repaid!'

'It surely wasn't Christian pity that made you turn her out of the house, and perhaps if you hadn't done that, none of this would ever have happened.'

'So that's the way it's to be, is it? *I* am to take the blame for it all?'

'It's too late now to talk about blame. All we can do is face the facts. The girl was in trouble and uncle Gus felt sorry for her. This is his way of helping her.'

'Don't you believe it!' Rachel scoffed. 'He's doing it to spite you and me!'

'Why should he want to do that?'

'Because it's the kind of man he is! He's always disliked me, merely because I speak my mind, and now it seems he's spiteful enough to take his feelings out on you!'

'You needn't worry on my account. The property is nothing to me. And my uncle has a perfect right to do whatever he likes with it.'

'Don't speak to me about his rights! You are his brother's only son and what he is doing is cheating you. That business of his may be run down but if only you had the running of it, and got good men to work for you, who knows what would have come of it? Why, you could have been as big a man as John Lanyon or Mark Hall, if only you'd got your proper rights!'

'I have no wish to be like them. I'm just a plain fisherman and quite content to stay that way.'

'Even after your uncle is dead and that girl becomes owner of the boat? Yes, you can stare, you poor innocent fool! You hadn't thought of that, I suppose?'

No. It was true. He had not thought of that. And the realization came as a shock.

'How will you like it then, my son, when you have to go cap in hand to *her*, to answer for the boat's affairs?'

Brice looked at his mother with a cold blue gaze. Just for a moment he hated her. Then abruptly he turned away.

'If the worst came to the worst, I could always go as skipper on some other boat, but I'll cross that bridge when I come to it. And, after all, there's always the farm.'

'The farm! The farm! What good is that? Fifteen paltry rented acres and more than one third of it covered in stones! What profit this farm brings in could just about be put in my eye! Your uncle knows that, devil as he is, and yet you're still foolish enough to stand up for him!'

'Fool I may be but at least I can accept the facts. Whether my uncle is right or wrong, there's nothing we can do about it, so where's the sense in wrangling like this? For my part I've had more than enough so please let there be an end to it.'

'There will *never* be any end to it!' Rachel said, in a passion of anger. 'We shall have to live with it all our days, seeing that girl, when your uncle dies, coming into property that should be yours and passing it on to her bastard child. Oh, how she must smile to herself, having wormed her way into such a good berth! And oh, how the folk in Polsinney are looking on and enjoying it all!'

'It will all die down in time. We'll just have to bear it as best we can.'

But for Brice the gossip was in fact the hardest thing of all to bear. At first, when he had heard the news, he had not believed it; he had thought it was one of Dicky Limpet's jokes; and by the time he knew it was true, he had already betrayed the fact that his uncle Gus had not seen fit to take him into his confidence. Four of the five men in his crew had kept a considerate silence, for they were men of fine feeling and were very well disposed towards him, but Ralph Ellis had been quick to make the most of his discomfiture.

'So the old man've done the dirty on you and pinched your girl from under your nose? I'd have thought at least he'd have told you first, instead of springing it on you like this, but maybe you've fallen out with him?'

'No, I haven't fallen out with him, nor do I intend to,' Brice said.

'You don't mean to say you aren't sore at the trick the old devil's played on you?'

'What my uncle chooses to do is no one's business but his own.'

'Will you be going to the wedding, then?'

'That depends on whether I'm asked.'

'Yes, well, of course,' Ralph said, 'you've got to keep in with him, I suppose, if only on account of the boat.'

Ralph was frankly jealous of Brice because, when Gus had first become ill, Brice had taken over as skipper, a job Ralph felt should have been his.

'Seems there edn much profit in being the old man's kin after all. I reckon I'd just as soon be as I am. At least I can call my soul my own.'

All this from Ralph was only a sample of what Brice had to endure on his way up through the village that morning and of what he would have to endure for a good many days and weeks to come. His mother was not much liked in Polsinney and many people relished the thought that she had been taken down a peg. He himself was liked and respected: among men, who knew him to be a good seaman, and among women because he was a fine upstanding young man who treated them with courtesy; and from some he received friendly words that showed he had their sympathy.

'I would never have thought of your uncle Gus doing a thing like that,' old William Nancarrow said to him, 'but you mustn't take it too much to heart, for your uncle Gus is a sick man and seemingly tes affecting his mind.'

But the gossip, whatever form it took, was all equally hard to bear and Brice was often sick at heart. The sympathy of some; the slyness of others; the jokes, the probing, the lewd remarks: all were equally hateful to him because, whichever way he answered, he was made to feel a fool. Still, he was determined to put a good face on it, if only for the sake of pride, and one of the first things he knew he must do was to call on his uncle Gus.

When he arrived at the cottage he found it the scene of unusual activity. Jimmy Jenkin, the Polsinney builder, was perched high at the top of a ladder, removing the old rusty launders and pipes which, having leaked for six months past, were the cause of the dampness in the walls. Another man was repairing the chimney and a third was repairing a hole in the roof. And down in the cobbled yard below, Gus, in his wheelchair, sat watching them.

For more than two years now the place had been falling about his ears and he had lacked all heart to order the necessary repairs. But in three weeks' time there would be a woman in the house and that would be a different matter entirely. For her sake, and for her child's, when it came, every inch of the cottage was to be made good, inside and out. New launders and drainpipes were to be put up; the stonework was to be washed with lime; and the roof was to have a coat of cement to keep the slates firmly in place when the south west gales came blowing in. No expense was to be spared, and Gus watched with critical eyes, determined that the work should be properly done.

'I suppose you've heard that I'm to be married?' he said, as Brice stood before him.

'Yes, and I've come to wish you well.'

'No hard feelings, then?'

'No. None.'

'You understand what it'll mean? That Maggie will get my property?'

'Yes, of course,' Brice said. Then, with some dryness, he said: 'I could hardly fail to know since any number of kind folk have been busy pointing it out to me. Polsinney can talk of nothing else. The gossip's enough to stop the church clock.'

'Well, it seems you're taking it pretty well, and seeing we've got three witnesses watching from up there on the roof, I think it would be a good idea if you and me were to shake hands.'

Brice had no hesitation whatever; he had always valued his uncle's friendship; and as their hands met and clasped he knew it was more than just a show for the benefit of the onlookers: he knew that the friendship was still intact. His uncle had said some hard things during the course of their previous meeting but Brice was willing to forget them now, and whatever difficulties lay in the future, so long as he had the old man's goodwill, he would do his best to face up to them.

Gus looked up at his nephew with a certain quizzical understanding. He could guess what deliberations had brought the young man here today. Brice had shown what Gus saw as weakness in his behaviour over Maggie but there was little fault to be found in his behaviour today.

'I suppose it's too much to hope that your mother shares your view of things?'

'I'm afraid it is.'

'The wedding is fixed for September the tenth. Will you come?'

'If you wish it, yes, of course.'

'Would you be willing to do more and give Maggie away?' Gus asked.

Brice stared. He was taken aback. It was more than he had bargained for. But Maggie, as he well knew, had nobody of her own.

'Yes. Very well. I'll give her away.'

'I'm thankful to see that you've got more of your father in you than your mother. Sometimes I've wondered about that.'

'My mother will get over this – in time.'

'I don't much care if she does or not. I've never got much joy from her company so tesn't a thing I'm likely to miss.' Gus looked up with a mischievous gleam. 'Still, you can tell her, if you like, that she's welcome to attend the wedding,' he said.

But Rachel, as Brice expected, only found this message provoking.

'I will *not* be present at the wedding, nor will I ever set foot inside your uncle's house again, and as for that sly, scheming slut of a girl, if we should ever chance to meet, I shall have *nothing* to say to her.'

During the next three weeks people in Polsinney said that the dust rising from Gus Tallack's cottage could be seen from the top of Teeterstone Hill. Gus had succeeded in persuading Maggie to give up her work in the fish-cellars and to turn her energies instead towards putting her future home to rights.

'I've got Mrs Kiddy in and I've told her to give the place

a good clean but she needs keeping up to the mark and you would be better employed if you were here to see to it.'

So Maggie now spent her days at the cottage and, in Mrs Kiddy's words, was turning the place inside out. The sail-maker's wife was not best pleased at receiving orders from this slip of a girl, and the high standard of cleanliness that Maggie expected her to achieve was, she considered, unreasonable.

'Why, this old house is so black as a shaft, and no amount of rubben-and-scrubben is ever going to make it come clean. And where's the sense of it, anyway, when Jimmy Jenkin and his crew are coming in presently to put new paper on the walls and paint everything spick and span? *They'll* soon cover up the dirt and no one will ever know tes there!'

But this would not do for Maggie and she said so in no uncertain terms. Every room, upstairs and down, had to be thoroughly scrubbed out before she pronounced herself satisfied, and even when this was all done there was still no rest for either of them, for the rugs and mats had to be cleaned, the curtains and bed-linen had to be washed, and constant warfare had to be waged on the mice that infested every cupboard. Mrs Kiddy was run off her feet. She had never worked so hard in her life.

'Such a skimmage there is down there!' she told her neighbours in the backlet. 'I'm sure if old Gus Tallack had known what he was letting himself in for he'd have changed his mind before twas made up!'

In fact Gus was enjoying it all. The bustle and stir pleased him no end. It was the first time in years that this old neglected cottage of his had seen such a spate of activity and he sat all day out in the yard, looking on with undisguised glee as Mrs Kiddy steamed to and fro, carrying pails of water from the pump to fill the copper in the scullery, where Maggie was washing blankets and sheets.

The only thing that troubled him was the fear that Maggie was working too hard.

'You want to take it easy, young woman, and leave Mrs Kiddy do a bit more, instead of rushing and tearing about, wearing yourself down to the cheens.'

'I'm all right. I'm as strong as a horse.'

'And what about your baby?' he said. 'Supposing you was to do him some harm?'

But Maggie knew what she could do. Her unborn baby was too precious for her to take any risks with it, and although she worked throughout the day, she was careful never to strain herself. As for Mrs Isaac Kiddy, complaining of her own aches and pains, Maggie had no scruples in keeping her hard at work, for Gus was paying her a shilling a day and if, as happened all too often, Mrs Kiddy skimped some chore, Maggie would make her do it again.

'I d'feel sorry for this poor old house, getting pulled and pummelled about,' Mrs Kiddy said to Gus. 'Tes just about been scrubbed to the bone and there edn a stick nor stitch inside'n that haven't been rummaged through and through!'

'And not a moment too soon, neither,' Gus said.

He himself was full of admiration for the way Maggie was doing things for he, as an old fisherman, respected order in all things, and always, in the old days, just as his boat had been one of the best-kept craft seen on this south Cornish coast, so had this cottage of his been object of the same pride and care. The boat, under Brice's skippership, had been kept up to the same high standard, but Gus, since the onset of his illness, had allowed his home to fall into decay. Now it was all being put to rights; he had the incentive, the will, the drive; and with Maggie firmly in charge, the place was now being restored to its former brightness and comeliness, with everything ship-shape and Bristol fashion, neat and tidy and spotlessly clean.

Of course, a great many things would be needed yet to make a comfortable home of it, fit for a woman and her child, but there would be plenty of time for Maggie to buy whatever she needed, and meantime the most important thing was to see that the dirt and dampness were banished and that Jimmy Jenkin did a good job with his repairs and renovations. And when at last, two days before the wedding, everything was done that could be done, even Mrs Kiddy had to admit that perhaps after all it had been worthwhile.

'The house d'look a picture,' she said. 'I wouldn mind living in it myself. And to think they old curtains belonged to be red when all these years I've thought they were brown! As for that old slab of yours, Maggie must've used a ton of blacklead, getting it to shine like that, and I reckon if you was minded to, you could see to comb your hair in it. This cottage is just about as fitty as any bride could wish to come into and it strikes me that Maggie Care is doing better than she deserves.'

'*I'll* be the judge of that!' Gus said.

At noon on the day before the wedding, when Maggie called on Gus to make a few last-minute arrangements, he was absent from his usual place in the yard, and when she walked into the kitchen she found him, not in his wheel-chair, but standing a short way away from it, supporting himself on two walking-sticks.

'What are you doing?' she asked, alarmed.

'I'm practising how to walk,' he said.

'Is that wise?'

'I don't know. But that's what I'm doing all the same.' Cautiously, without turning his head, he looked at her out of the sides of his eyes. 'I *can* walk just a short way, you know, so long as the groundswell is not too bad. I'm not completely done for yet and tomorrow when I get into church I intend to stand on my own two feet. Tes just a question of trying it out. Finding my sea-legs, as you might say.'

'Is there anything I can do?'

'Yes, you can look the other way!'

But she was too nervous on his behalf to obey this curt command and she stood close by, watching over him, ready to help if necessary. The effort it cost him to lift one leg and put one foot down in front of the other required all his strength and concentration and he had to lean heavily on the two sticks. With his back slightly bent and his shoulders hunched, he took a few painfully difficult steps and then came to a halt again, breathing stridently through his nose. The exertion was too much for him and the perspiration, pouring from his forehead, dripped down his cheeks and into his beard. His strong teeth were clenched together and his lips were drawn back from them in a little snarl of rage.

'Damn! I'll get as far as that wall even if it takes all day!'

'Don't you think you're being foolish?'

'Tes my two legs that're being foolish, and if they think I'm giving in to them, they can damned well think again!'

With a stubborn effort he moved forward again and Maggie watched him in distress. She hesitated to go to him, for he was still a stranger to her, and she knew not how he would react. But she feared very much that he would fall and do himself an injury and it was a great relief to her when a knock came at the half-open door and Brice walked in.

Gus, turning to look at Brice, swayed and was in danger of losing his balance. His brief burst of strength was almost spent and he was trembling from head to foot. But Brice, seeing at once how it was, went and put his arms round him and held him in a strong, close grip, and when Maggie pushed the wheelchair forward, the old man, with a scowl of defeat, suffered himself to be lowered into it and thrust the two sticks into Brice's hands.

'I'm to be married tomorrow,' he said, 'and I wanted to be married standing up, not stuck in my chair like a Guy Fawkes!'

'Better stuck in your chair,' Brice said, 'than falling down on the floor in church.'

'You mean I might fall dead, I suppose? Yes, well, you're right, I can't risk that. Not until I've made Maggie my wife.'

Exhausted but resigned, Gus sat back, closing his eyes for a little while and taking deep breaths that filled his lungs. Gradually the tremors passed. He took a handkerchief from his pocket and wiped the sweat from his forehead and cheeks. Then he looked up at Maggie and Brice and a self-mocking grin spread over his face. 'Well, I may not get married standing up, but at least I shall look some smart!' he said. 'I've had the barber in this morning, clicking and fussing over me, and he've left me smelling like a dockside moll! I've got my Sunday suit on, too, to get the smell of mothballs out of it, and if I don't look the part tomorrow it only means folk are hard to please!'

Gus was highly amused at himself and turned his head this way and that to show off his neatly trimmed hair and beard. He also pointed out his boots, for he had polished them himself and was proud of the brilliant shine on them. And over his head, as he rattled on, making boyish fun of himself, Maggie and Brice looked at each other.

It was the first time they had met since Maggie had been at Boskillyer and it meant there was some constraint between them. Although he had known he might meet her today, he was still foolishly unprepared, and he felt a sudden cowardly urge to make some excuse and depart post haste. But Maggie, perhaps understanding this, looked at him in such a way that he found his mind growing quiet and still and in a while, as his uncle's self-banter petered out, he found himself speaking quite normally, as though what lay between him and this girl had no significance whatever.

'I thought I'd better call on you and find out if everything is fixed for tomorrow.'

'I think it is. Yes, I'm sure. And thank you for your kindness in agreeing to give me away.'

'The wedding's at half past eleven,' Gus said. 'I hope you'll be back in harbour in time to get the fish-scales washed off yourself?'

'I shan't be going out tonight. I don't want to risk being late. Ralph will be skipper for tonight and Joe Tambling is going along to make up the crew.'

'Everything's settled, then?'

'Yes,' Brice said. 'I'll be here at eleven o'clock.'

'I've been thinking out how it will be when Maggie becomes my wife,' Gus said. 'She'll be your aunt-by-marriage, of course, but she won't expect you to call her that. As for her child, when he comes, he will be your cousin, I suppose,'

'He?' Brice said, with a little smile.

'Yes, she've set her heart on a son, to be called Jim after his father.'

'Well, I hope that Maggie's son and I will be more than just cousins-by-marriage,' Brice said. 'I hope, perhaps, when the time comes, I'll be asked to be one of his godparents.'

How this idea had come to him and how it had found expression so glibly he could not have explained to anyone; and afterwards, as he walked home, he wondered if he had been guilty of a piece of blatant hypocrisy. But on the whole he was pleased with himself because, by making this gesture of his, he was putting on a face that the world at large would have trouble in reading. People might

101

surmise as much as they liked, but no one would ever really know what his feelings had been for Maggie Care, nor would they know what his feelings were at seeing her marry his uncle Gus.

There was much comfort in this; he commended himself on his cleverness; and then he realized, with wry self-scorn, that these precious feelings of his were a mystery even to himself.

The wedding day was misty and warm, typical of September month, with a smell of dying leaves in the air.

Brice, as he wheeled his uncle Gus up Bryant's Hill and into the church, found him unusually subdued and perceived with a twinge of sympathy that he was nervous and unsure of himself. But he also perceived, on entering the church, that the sight of Maggie, serene, self-possessed, instantly set his uncle at ease and that in the look that passed between them there was complete understanding and trust.

There were very few people at the wedding and this was as Gus and Maggie wished. Mr and Mrs Kiddy were there, with the younger sail-maker, Percy Tremearne, and Martha Cledra was there, as Maggie's friend. And behind them were gathered those villagers, numbering two or three score, who, having nothing better to do that day, the tenth of September, 1869, had come together into the church to see Gus Tallack put his ring on Maggie Care's finger and to hear them pronounced man and wife.

The ceremony was so simple that many people thought it austere. No hymns were sung; no music was played; and when the couple left the church, there was no sound of wedding-bells. Martha Cledra threw some rice, and a small girl, waiting at the lych-gate, put a bunch of poppies into Maggie's hands, but these were the only festivities. There was not to be any wedding breakfast and Brice, pushing his uncle's wheelchair, was the only person to accompany the bride and bridegroom home. Even he did not go inside; he excused himself on the grounds that he had to go down to the quay and see that all was well with the boat; and so, within an hour of being married, Gus and Maggie were alone in their home.

'Well, here we are, then, man and wife.'

'Yes,' Maggie said. She looked at him.

'No regrets?'

'No. None.'

'I hope it will always be like that.'

'I hope so, too. On your side, I mean, as well as my own.'

'We're talking like strangers, aren't we?' he said. 'But time will cure that, I suppose. – Such time as I have left to me.'

'Don't talk like that.'

'No. Very well. But it's something we've got to face all the same.'

'Is it?' she said. 'Well, we shall see.'

That afternoon, at three o'clock, Frank Rogers the solicitor came, and Gus made his will. Maggie, as his wife, was already his heir, but he intended to make quite sure that no doubt could ever exist regarding his intentions. So the will was made and Isaac Kiddy and Percy Tremearne were called down from the sail-loft to witness Gus's signature. They each got a glass of rum for their pains and so did Mr Rogers, and the three of them drank the couple's health. None of it took very long, for the will was simplicity itself, and everything Gus possessed was left to Maggie.

Gus, with his new responsibilities, was anxious that his property should bring in the maximum profit, and soon he was talking of opening up the barking-house and putting it into business again. The problem was to find a man who would run it honestly and efficiently, and as soon as Isaac Kiddy got wind of the plan he wanted the job for his son Eugene.

'If your son is anything like you,' Gus said, 'I don't want him near the place.'

'What are you talking about?' Isaac said.

'I'm talking about that suit of sails you're making for Matt Crowle,' Gus said, 'that should've been ready two weeks ago and aren't finished even now.'

'Twadn *me* that promised those sails would be ready by October fifteenth. Twas *you* that went and promised that. I do my best. I can't do no more. And I've only got one pair of hands, you know.'

'No, you haven't, you've got two! – Your own and Percy Tremearne's!' Gus said. 'And if two grown men who call themselves sail-makers can't get a suit of sails cut and stitched inside a month there must be something wrong with them!'

Isaac began making excuses but Gus cut him short.

'I'll tell you what I'm willing to do. You get those sails finished by the end of this week and your boy Eugene can have the job of running the barking-house for me.'

This promise worked like a charm. The sails were complete within another twenty-four hours and Isaac duly reported to Gus.

'Can I tell boy Eugene he've got the job?'

'I promised you, didn't I?' Gus said. 'But just you let me tell you this. – Things've got to be different from now on. No more kiddling about, coming and going just as you please, but a full day's work every day, and sails got ready on the dot. And another thing I expect to see is that sail-loft kept tidy and clean. If it isn't – just you look out!'

Eugene Kiddy arrived the next day and quietly, without any fuss, took possession of the barking-house. Gus had already got in a load of cutch and soon the acrid smell of it as it boiled and bubbled in the vat, with the *Maid Molly's* nets steeping in it, was wafting all around the harbour and up into the terraced town, pungent evidence of the fact that Gus Tallack's barking-house was working in full swing again.

There was no lack of customers because fishermen who, in the past eighteen months, had been obliged to take their nets to be barked in St Glozey, now returned to Gus Tallack and put their names on his waiting-list. Soon the barking-house and yard were full of noise and activity, just as they had been in the old days, and Gus, sitting out in his wheelchair, with men of his own kind to talk to and plenty of business to occupy his mind, found himself closely in touch again with the stirring, bustling life of the sea.

All this he felt he owed to Maggie, because she had given him a sense of purpose, and the will to see that this business of his was working to its proper capacity. He was doing it all for her sake, so that she and her child should lack for nothing when he was dead and in the grave, but what he was doing for Maggie's sake brought rewards for himself as well. He had taken on a new lease of life and although he knew that its days were numbered, there was work and device enough in them to make them rich and meaningful.

Maggie also was content, for she and Gus got on well together, and when, early in the morning of the twelfth of January, her baby was safely delivered to her, after a labour lasting ten hours, she felt that God had been good to her and was making amends for what lay in the past. For her baby was a fine healthy boy and when she held him in her arms and smelt the soft warm smell of him she knew that he, more than anything else, would ease and allay the aching void that his father's death had left in her heart.

News that she had given birth to a son reached Brice on the quay that morning and when he was on his way home he met Annie Tambling, the midwife, coming away from his uncle's house.

'Ess, tes a boy, sure nuff, brave and handsome as any I've seen. Weighed eight pounds if he weighed an ounce and was screamen fit to burst his lungs almost before I'd turned him up.'

'Is Mrs Tallack all right?'

'Ess, for sure. No trouble at all. Did what I told her, good as gold, and never so much as yelled wunst. As for your uncle Gus, well, he's about as bucked with it all as though he'd fathered the cheeld himself.' Mrs Tambling squinted at Brice. 'Going in to see them, are you?'

'Not right now,' Brice said. 'I think I'd better wait a while.'

On getting home he found that his mother, too, had heard the news.

'So your uncle's wife has got a son? A bastard child with a borrowed name! And in time he will come into property that should by rights have been yours.'

Brice walked past her into the house.

When he did call at his uncle's cottage, one wet afternoon, on his way to the boat, Maggie was sitting in the kitchen and it happened that she had been suckling her child. Brice would have withdrawn at once but his uncle motioned him into the room.

'Maggie won't mind you stepping in. Women don't fuss about such things. They've got more sense than us men.'

It seemed that this was perfectly true, for Maggie's glance was quite composed and she showed no signs of prudishness. She sat in a low nursing-chair, close beside the kitchen table, and the light of the lamp, in its pink-frosted globe, fell on her baby's warm flushed face as he

106

lay in her arms, almost asleep. The small mouth had become slack; the shadowy eyelids were slowly closing, and one tiny hand, with fingers curled, lay in the opening of her dress, in the soft warm hollow between her breasts.

'So this is Jim?'

'Yes,' Maggie said.

'You wanted a son.'

'Yes. I did.'

Brice, though he stood in front of her, was still awkwardly keeping his distance, and his uncle Gus remarked on it.

'You needn't be afraid of going close. Neither she nor the child will bite you.'

'Well,' Brice said, and looked down at himself. His dark red oilskins were wet with rain and a puddle was forming on the floor. He had taken his sou'wester off and it hung, dripping, from his hand. 'As you see, I'm not really fit.' But he moved forward a pace or two and, leaning down from his great height, looked closely at the sleeping babe and touched it gently on the arm. 'I can't stay long. I'm due at the boat. But I felt it was time I called on you to offer my good wishes and see young Jim Tallack for myself.'

'And what do you think of him?' Gus asked.

Brice stood up straight again.

'Mrs Tambling called him a brave handsome cheeld and it seems to me she was right,' he said.

The baby stirred in Maggie's arms and she bent over him, holding him close, shifting sideways in her chair so that his face was screened from the light. For a moment she was completely absorbed and Brice saw and understood how it was that the bond between a mother and child, forged in such moments of closeness and warmth, came to be the strongest in the world. He saw that Maggie's whole life was centred on her baby son and that nothing else

107

mattered to her; he saw, too, that motherhood had made her more gently beautiful; and by the sudden twist in his heart as he turned away from her and her child he knew he was still in love with her.

'Going already?' Gus said.

'Yes. I must.'

'You've got a wet night's work ahead of you.'

'At least there's a good wind,' Brice said. 'It's been too still the past few nights and the herring haven't been coming to us but maybe tonight our luck will change.'

Outside in the wind and the rain he pulled his sou'wester onto his head and turned his collar up to his ears. The afternoon was as black as pitch and the rain fell like rods of glass, slantways on the north-west wind blowing down from Mump Head. Most of the drifters had already gone but a few were just pulling away and he saw their lights gleaming fuzzily as they made towards the harbour mouth. Only the *Emmet* remained at the quayside and the crew were waiting impatiently, bowed figures in gleaming oilskins, under sails that hung like wet rags.

'God! What a night!' Ralph Ellis said as Brice jumped down into the boat. 'Tes what you get for grumblen all week about it being too damned fine!'

Chapter 5

Gus's prediction proved correct and Maggie, from the day she married him, found herself treated with respect. Tongues still wagged, inevitably, for Maggie's history was such that it would bear telling and re-telling for many a long day to come. But whatever people said behind her back, to her face they were all civility, such was the standing endowed upon her by her marriage to Gus. She was his wife; her child bore his name; and these indisputable facts were enough to make her position secure.

Only Rachel remained hostile and this too worked in Maggie's favour, for whereas Rachel had always looked down on the ordinary people of Polsinney, Maggie was friendly with everyone.

'At least she dunt give herself airs,' the villagers said among themselves. 'And she *could* do if she had a mind that way cos tes *her* husband, edn it, you, that've got his own bit of property and she'll get it all when the old chap dies. Rachel Tallack edn nothing at all for all she d'look down her nose at we and if old Gus've put a slight on her I reckon tes only what she deserve.'

So it fell out that quite soon Maggie came to be liked for herself. The villagers accepted her and looked on her as one of themselves. And in time it also came about that even the more exalted members of the community raised their hats when meeting her, for it was seen that Gus Tallack was a man of growing consequence, and people like the Halls and the Lanyons treated his wife accordingly.

For Gus, up until this time, the sail-loft and barking-house had never been anything more than a second string to his bow; something he had been glad to fall back on when illness had forced him to give up the sea. But now all that was changed; he had acquired a taste for commerce; and in a small way, without taking risks, he was expanding his business interests.

For one thing, when he had money to spare, he bought a share in the Nonesuch Seine, and out of the handsome profits he got when the seining season proved good that year, he bought a shed at Steeple Lumbtown, installed two net-making looms in it, and engaged two women to make nets. All this was done for Maggie's sake, to make her future more secure, and right from the start he encouraged her to take an interest in his affairs because, as he said to her, 'You'll have to run things when I'm gone.'

Rachel, on hearing of Gus's new business ventures, spoke of them bitterly to Brice.

'Oh, that girl has done well for herself, marrying that uncle of yours! There's no fool like an old fool and it seems he can't do enough for her.'

'The gain is not all on Maggie's side. Uncle Gus benefits too. It's given him something to live for and he's more cheerful now than he has been for years. Maggie is a good wife to him and no one can say otherwise.'

'Wife!' Rachel said scornfully. 'And what sort of marriage is it when he is nearly three times her age and everyone knows he's a dying man?'

'Whatever sort of marriage it is, it seems to be working pretty well, and if uncle Gus is a dying man, at least his last years will be happy ones.'

Brice, calling on Gus every week to discuss the boat's business affairs, had plenty of opportunity to observe the improvement Maggie had wrought. The old man now had a comfortable home where everything was cheerful and bright and where, at every hour of the day, he was considered and waited on. He ate proper meals, at regular times, and instead of spending his evenings alone, brooding on his helplessness, he now had Maggie's company and would yarn to her by the hour. It seemed they had plenty to talk about and in spite of the difference in their ages, there was a close understanding between them, based on mutual need and trust. All these things had made their mark; the old man was in good spirits these days; and Brice felt sure that because of this his health had improved accordingly.

At first, when the boat's business was discussed, Maggie took no part in it but kept herself in the background, out of consideration for Brice. That was in the early days and Gus said nothing about it then because all Maggie's thoughts at that time were centred on her unborn child and she was everlastingly busy with some piece of knitting or needlework. But later, some few weeks after baby Jim's birth, Gus firmly insisted that Maggie should join him and Brice at the table and go through the *Emmet*'s accounts with them.

'The boat will be yours one of these days and tes only right you should know what's what. You needn't worry about Brice. He quite understands how things'll be.'

So every Saturday now, when Brice called, Maggie sat in on these discussions and heard Gus go through the weekly 'log'. She heard what each night's catch had been and what it had earnt in hard coin; she heard that so far the herring season had been slow in getting under way; and she heard that the *Emmet*'s pumps would soon need repair. Sometimes she had some comment to make and always Gus would pass her the 'log' so that she could check his figures.

'Maggie's got a better head for reckoning than I ever had in my life,' he said. 'Her mother was a schoolmistress – did you know that – so brains must run in the family.'

'Yes,' Brice said, 'I did know that.'

'Damme! What am I thinking of? I'd forgotten, just for the moment, that Maggie was up at the farm with you. You must've got to know her pretty well in that time and I doubt if I can tell you much that you haven't already found out for yourself.'

'Well, I'm not sure about that, but we're not exactly strangers, it's true.'

Brice gave his answer clumsily; he knew that the taunt was intentional; and later on that same evening the old man followed it up with a few more pointed remarks. The business discussion had been completed; Brice had received his weekly 'share'; and Maggie, as was her custom, brought out the rum and two glasses and set them down in front of Gus.

'I did the right thing when I married this girl. There's nothing suits a man so well as having a woman to wait on him. You ought to try it yourself, my boy. – Take a leaf out of my book and find yourself a decent wife. You shouldn't have to look very hard. Polsinney is full of docy maids keen to snap up a fine chap like you.'

'Is it?' Brice said, evenly. 'Then I must certainly give it some thought.'

'Don't spend too long thinking,' Gus said. 'You can miss a lot of good chances that way.'

Brice, at this point, changed the subject. His uncle's jokes were too close to the bone. And as soon as he had drunk his rum he rose to go.

'What, leaving already?' his uncle said.

'Yes. I have things to do at home. And my mother is too much alone as it is.'

'Dunt she like her own company? Well, I can't blame her!' Gus said.

These visits to his uncle Gus, now that the old man was married to Maggie, were something of a strain to Brice

112

and sometimes he thought of giving them up. But that would only create fresh problems; for one thing he had no valid excuse; and he knew he would have to resign himself to the visits and the torment they caused.

Sometimes he felt the perverse satisfaction that a man feels when he has a wound and exults in hiding it from the world, and with this went a kind of elation because he knew he had the wit to act out the part he had set himself. It was a challenge. A trial of strength. And if his uncle's barbed remarks made it more difficult, all the more triumph when he won.

The old man might suspect that his nephew was still in love with Maggie but at least he would never know for sure. Nor would Maggie herself ever know. Brice was grimly determined on this; it was important; a matter of pride. So the weekly visits continued and gradually, over the months, fell into a sort of pattern.

'Not found a wife yet?' his uncle would say. 'You're letting the grass grow, aren't you, my boy? It seems you must be hard to please!'

Mostly Brice merely laughed and shrugged but once, by way of a change, he said:

'I'm in no hurry. Why should I be? I've got plenty of time yet before I think about settling down.'

His words brought a frown to the old man's face and a shadow seemed to fall on him.

'Yes, and you're luckier than you know. You've got your life in front of you. What are you now? Twenty-four? The years go slowly for young men like you but for me they go at a rate of knots.'

Time, for Gus, was slipping away; he and Maggie had been married a year; baby Jim was growing fast and the earth was spinning relentlessly on. But there was much to be thankful for and Gus was the first to admit it.

'I'm in better shape now than I have been for years. I

have a good appetite for my meat, I get five hours' good sleep every night, and I've still got enough command of my brain to manage my bits of business affairs. Not bad for a dying man, eh?'

'Have you seen Dr Sam lately?'

'No, nor I don't intend to,' Gus said. 'He can come and see me when I'm dead and according to what he've already told me, that'll be in the next eighteen months.'

'Looking at you right now,' Brice said, 'I find that impossible to believe.'

When baby Jim began to crawl he did not go on all fours as most babies do but by sitting with his left leg under him and his right leg thrust out in front and, with little humping movements of his body, aided by movements of the right leg, propelled himself forward comfortably, remaining always in an upright position. People were highly amused at this; they had never seen such a thing before; and Gus said it showed great intelligence, for by this method of locomotion, Jim could always see exactly where he was going.

According to Gus, who doted on him, Jim was forward in every way. No other child was so sturdy, so strong, or so quick in the uptake. And certainly no other child of his age ever showed a more resolute will. Maggie said that this son of hers was in danger of being spoilt because Gus, as he sat in his wheelchair, would let the child climb all over him, doing pretty much as he liked; and what Jim liked best was to rummage through the old man's pockets where, more often than not, he would find a stick of barley-sugar or a couple of hazelnuts.

The old man's wheelchair fascinated Jim and one of the first words he learnt was 'ride'. He would scramble up into Gus's lap, turn himself round to face forwards, and, with his hands on the arms of the chair, would bounce up and

down, shouting:'Ride! Ride! Ride!' And Gus, always willing to oblige, would take the little boy for a ride round the
yard, passing so close to the barking-house door that
Eugene, if he chanced to step out, was in danger of being
run down or having his nose taken off, as he said.

As soon as Jim learnt to walk he became so adventurous
that everyone who came into the yard had to be careful to
close the gates. When the fishermen brought their nets to
be barked, they had to take extra care because while they
were wheeling their wheelbarrows in, Jim would dart out
from some hiding-place and go rushing past them into the
road. They would have to go after him and Jim thought it
a huge joke to be brought back into the yard, tucked under
some fisherman's arm or sitting astride his broad shoulders, especially if that fisherman happened to be his uncle
Brice.

'See what I've found!' Brice would say. 'Has anyone lost
a boy called Jim? A little tacker in petticoats with liquorice
all over his face? If not I shall have to keep him myself and
take him out in the *Emmet* with me – '

'Here, give him to me!' Gus would say, and Brice would
deliver the squirming child into the old man's outstretched
arms.

At this time, being so small, Jim was not allowed into
the barking-house because of the open furnace fire and the
stinging fumes of the boiling cutch, and Gus, taking him
into his lap, would keep him there under restraint until the
barking-house door had been closed. Jim would squirm
and struggle and kick and make such a hullabaloo that
Maggie would come running out of the house and Gus,
with a laugh, often said to her:

'Just see what a temper he've got in him! He's more my
son than he is yours!'

But Jim learnt better behaviour in time because Gus,
though indulgent, meant to be obeyed, and if the little boy

went too far he would receive a smart slap on his leg. So he learnt discipline early in life and because of it he and Gus were good friends. Each was amused by the other's antics and Maggie, whenever she watched them together, marvelled at the old man's patience and gave thanks for it in her heart. No child in the world, lacking a father of his own, could have had a better substitute.

Sometimes, however, she was anxious for Gus because of the demands Jim made on him.

'Don't let him climb all over you. He's so energetic, he'll tire you out. Hadn't I better take him indoors?'

'Leave him be. He's doing no harm. Just look at me! – I'm as strong as a horse!' And Gus, to demonstrate his strength, lifted Jim high in the air, holding him up at arm's length for perhaps half a minute or so, then setting him down again. 'There!' he said, breathing hard. 'I couldn't have done that two years ago. I wouldn't have dreamt of trying it. But these days I feel I could lift a whale and if only my legs were as strong as my arms – '

He gave a little wistful sigh. His legs were not much use to him. He still could not walk more than a few yards at a time.

'But if they're no better, at least they're no worse, and I must just count my blessings,' he said.

At least he could still put himself to bed, and get up in the morning and dress himself, and he valued these acts of independence, guarding them with fierce obstinacy. What he could do he *would* do and wanted no help from anyone. Maggie understood this and never tried to interfere. She would take hot water into his room; then she would come out and close the door; and only when Gus had emerged fully dressed, wheeling himself out in his chair, did she venture into the room again, to empty the basin and make the bed.

As for the hundred and one things she did for him

during the rest of the day, he accepted them without demur, even with a certain complacency. Sometimes he pretended to grumble. 'Maggie sews my buttons on even before they've come off,' he would say, and 'I have to change my clothes every week now that I'm a married man.' But in fact he enjoyed Maggie's attentions and was often touched by the trouble she took in putting his boots to warm by the fire, in bringing him hot cocoa to drink when he sat out of doors on a cold day, and in cooking those meals she knew he liked best, such as rabbit pasty with turnip and thyme and plenty of pepper in the crust.

He was always praising Maggie's cooking, especially when Brice was there, and he said that Maggie's heavy cake was the best he had tasted in his life. Sometimes when Brice came on Saturday he would stay and have supper with them and on one of these occasions Gus suddenly said to him:

'Did Maggie ever do the cooking when she was up at the farm with you?'

'Yes, she did, quite often,' Brice said.

'Then your mother must've been properly mazed when she turned Maggie out of the house. Still, there tis! Your loss was my gain. And if you and Rachel have any regrets you've only got yourselves to blame.'

Brice said nothing to this. He was inured to these jibes by now. But he noticed that Maggie, clearing the dishes, frowned at Gus reprovingly.

Gus, however, would not be reproved. He was in an ebullient mood. And when Maggie came close to his chair he suddenly caught hold of her and, pulling her roughly down to him, kissed her clumsily on the mouth.

Maggie was taken by surprise. Released, she stood staring at him, her eyes at once puzzled, vexed, amused. A flush of warm colour came into her cheeks and she turned away with a little laugh, glancing quickly towards Brice but without directly meeting his gaze.

'I don't know what's wrong with your uncle tonight. It must've been something I put in the pie.'

'Damme!' Gus said, in a boisterous voice. 'I was just showing my gratitude at having a wife worth her weight in gold.'

'Perhaps it was too much pepper and salt . . .'

'"So ought men to love their wives as their own bodies,"' Gus said, quoting the Scriptures. '"He that loveth his own wife loveth himself."'

'Indeed,' Maggie said, 'no wife can ask more than that.'

She busied herself, washing the crocks, and the two men went to sit by the fire, Gus now talking soberly of his new business venture at Steeple Lumbtown, and of how many lengths of herring-net the looms were producing every week. After a while Maggie joined them, bringing a pile of mending to do, and the evening passed as usual. But as soon as Brice had left the house she put her needlework into her lap and looked at Gus with challenging eyes.

'Why did you kiss me like that?' she asked.

'My dear soul and body!' Gus exclaimed. 'Can't a man kiss his own wife?'

'You never have done. Not till today.'

'I'm not going to make a habit of it, if that's what is worrying you. Tes just that I've got a devil in me and Brice always seems to bring it out.'

'So it *was* for Brice's benefit? I had a suspicion it might be.'

'I just wanted to stir him up. See the look on his face and maybe find out what he's made of. But Brice doesn't give himself away. He've got too much nous for that. He might be a block of wood sitting there for all you can see what goes on in his mind.'

'It seems you were disappointed, then.'

'Maybe. Maybe not.'

'What I don't understand is, why you should *want* to stir him up.'

'Because it amuses me, that's why, and because it's only what he deserves. He was in love with you – you know that – and yet he let that mother of his turn you out into the road and never lifted a finger to help although he knew what trouble you were in.'

'All that's in the past,' Maggie said. 'There was nothing Brice could have done for me. There was nothing I *wanted* him to do. And whatever he thought he felt for me was all over and finished with when he knew I was going to have a child.'

'If he'd had any gumption in him he would've married you just the same. I told him that myself at the time but he was so full of his own injured pride that he wouldn't hear of such a thing.'

'Of course he wouldn't! What man would? And I could *never* have married him. For one thing I didn't love him . . .'

'You didn't love me, neither, but you were willing to marry me.'

'That was different,' Maggie said. 'It was a business arrangement between us. You said so yourself. But a marriage like ours wouldn't do for Brice. He wants more from a wife than that and in time when he falls in love with some girl . . .'

'All right! All right!' Gus exclaimed. 'You don't have to defend him to me. Brice can take care of himself and he knows I don't mean him any great hurt. He *is* my brother's son after all. I'm fond of him, believe it or not, and I think in his way he's fond of me. Tes jus that sometimes when he's sitting there –'

'That's another thing,' Maggie said. 'The fact that Brice is your own kith and kin and that if I hadn't come along –'

'You troubled with conscience, suddenly, because

119

you're getting my property and Brice is getting nothing at all?'

'It's not so much a question of conscience – '

'Damme! I should hope not indeed! You're my wife before God and man and in my will I've made it clear that *everything* is to come to you. The property's yours by entitlement and tes no good getting a conscience now because that's the way I want it and that's the way it's going to be.'

'What I was going to say was, that Brice has been very good about it. There could have been so much ill feeling . . . just as there is on his mother's part . . . but instead he's always been friendly and kind.'

'Oh, yes, that's true enough. Brice has behaved very well. Never a word out of place. Always very proper and correct.' Gus's tone of voice was dry and his glance sardonic. 'Tes one thing you can depend on,' he said. 'Brice will always do the right thing.'

Maggie looked at him sorrowfully. Then she picked up her needlework.

'You make it sound like a fault,' she said.

She herself was grateful to Brice because he had made things so easy for her and one day when they were alone together she tried to express her gratitude. She spoke of it in much the same way that she had spoken of it to Gus but the words did not come so readily and Brice was obliged to help her out.

'You are thinking about the property? But I am not jealous – not in the least – and I hope you won't let it worry you. It's true I was taken aback at first when I heard you were marrying uncle Gus. It was a shock, I don't deny that, and people were very quick to point out how much I was going to lose by it.'

Brice paused, looking at her.

120

'That was the worst part of it, knowing what a lot of talk there was . . . Knowing that people were watching me, waiting to see how I would behave . . . But as for losing the property, except for the boat it means nothing to me, and I hope you'll believe me when I say that I'm glad things have gone the way they have.'

'That's what I mean,' Maggie said. 'Only a generous man could say that – anyone else would have hated me – and I want you to know I'm grateful to you for – for accepting me as your uncle's wife.'

Brice had called with a gift of fish and it happened that Gus had gone with Isaac to buy canvas in Polzeale. So Maggie and Jim were alone in the house and the little boy, now two and a half, was helping her to shell peas. Brice sat at the table with them and whenever Jim had difficulty in opening a peapod he would push it across to Brice and Brice would split it open for him.

'I could never hate you,' Brice said. 'I don't think I'm a hating man.'

'No,' Maggie said, 'I don't think you are.'

'You've done so much for uncle Gus. You've given him something to live for. And although he and I have our differences I like him enough to be glad of that.' There was a pause and then Brice said: 'He seems so much better nowadays . . . So much stronger in every way . . . I can't help wondering if perhaps . . .'

'Yes,' Maggie said, 'I wonder that, too, and it's what I pray for, constantly.'

'Is he still refusing to see Dr Sam?'

'Yes. He's very obstinate. *I've* been to see Dr Sam myself and I've told him how much better Gus is, but although he listened to all I said, he wouldn't say anything much himself, not without examining Gus. "It's in God's hands." That's all he would say. I told Gus that when I got home and he gave a loud snort and said,

"Well, I can only hope that God is a better doctor than Sam Carveth!"'

Brice smiled.

'My uncle Gus will have the last word right to the very end,' he said.

He got up, preparing to leave, and took his cap from the back of the chair. Little Jim snatched it from him and ran out through the open door. Brice and Maggie followed him and stood in the yard watching as he placed the cap upside down on the ground and, bending over unsteadily, tried to put his head into it. Something went wrong with this plan and instead he tumbled head over heels. He sat up with a look of surprise and gave a little bubbling laugh as he saw that his uncle Brice's cap had somehow got caught up on his foot.

'Can I have my cap?' Brice asked.

'No! Can't have it!' Jim said.

He scrambled to his feet and ran off again but Brice in three strides caught up with him, lifted him, chortling, into his arms, and wrested the dusty cap from him. The little boy struggled and squirmed and as soon as Brice set him down again he went running to Gus's empty wheel-chair, standing outside the porch, and began pushing it round the yard.

'The only time he's ever still is when he's in bed asleep,' Maggie said.

'You wanted a son.'

'Yes.' She laughed.

'Is he like his father?' Brice asked.

'Yes, he's the image of him,' she said. 'When he laughs . . . When he frowns . . . When he's thinking hard . . . Even the way he holds his head . . . It really is quite absurd that two people should be so alike.'

There was a sudden catch in her throat but in a moment she was calling to Jim, telling him to take more care and not push the wheelchair into the wall. Together she and

Brice watched as the child swung the chair round and pushed it in the other direction.

'He's like you, too,' Brice said. 'He's got your eyes.' He dusted his cap and put it on. 'I must be getting home,' he said.

He waved to Maggie and Jim from the gate.

Little Jim, out in all weathers, grew into a strong healthy boy, and by the time he was three years old he was full of boundless curiosity. He wanted to know about everything that went on in the sail-loft and barking-house and was always climbing onto the yard wall to look at the ships standing out to sea.

'What ship is that?'

'A schooner,' Gus said.

'And that one?' Jim asked.

'A barquentine.'

Where was the schooner bound for and what was she carrying, Jim would ask, and Gus, looking through his spyglass, would do his best to answer the boy.

'That's the *Aurelia*, out of Polzeale. She's probably carrying pilchards – hundreds of hogsheads, all salted down – and taking them to Italy. They're great ones for eating pilchards there. They can't seem to get enough of them and they're always crying out for more.'

'Why are they?' Jim asked.

'Because they're all Roman Catholics there and they've got a chap they call the Pope who tells them they've got to eat plenty of fish.'

'Why does he?'

'Because he's the Pope.'

'Does he eat plenty of fish himself?'

'Well, if he doesn't, he should do,' Gus said, 'cos otherwise where would he get his brains?'

Jim asked questions all day long and Gus answered them

patiently, but one day he turned the tables on Jim and the boy had to answer him instead.

'See that ship out there in the bay? The one with two masts and her sails half-reefed? I want you to tell me what she is.'

Jim looked at the ship in the bay and a deep frown wrinkled his brow.

'Is she a brigantine?'

'*You* just tell *me*.'

'Yes! She is! I know she is!'

'How do you know?'

'I know by her rig.'

'Bless my soul, but you're some smart! You can go to the top of the class for that!'

And as Maggie came out to the yard, to hang her washing on the line, Gus shouted across to her, saying how clever her son had been to answer his question about the ship. Maggie was inclined to smile. She thought it was just a lucky guess. But Gus would not hear of this and was highly indignant on Jim's account.

'He knows all right! You mark my words! He's smart as paint, this boy of yours, and getting smarter every day. A brigantine, that's what he said, and a brigantine she is, by God!'

But whether it was pure luck or not, the time came soon enough when Jim really did know which ship was which, and could tell you a great deal more besides.

'There's a full-rigger out in the bay. Handsomest ship I've ever seen. Such great masts she've got on her – '

'What flag is she flying?'

'I can't see.'

'Then you'd better look through my spyglass.'

Gus held the old, battered spyglass so that it rested on the wall and Jim, standing on a box, swivelled it round to look at the ship.

'She's putting another anchor down. There's sailors running about everywhere. One of them's stripped bare to the waist.'

'Can you see her flag?' Gus asked.

'Yes, it's the tricolour,' Jim said.

'Ah, French, I thought she was. Can you see what name she's called?'

'Yes, I can see it plain as plain.' Jim had not yet learnt to read but he knew his letters well enough and he spelt out the name on the great ship's bows. 'H.E.L.O.I.S.E..'

'The *Heloise*? Why, she's an old friend. I went aboard her once, years ago, when she was berthed in Plymouth Sound.' Gus now took the spyglass and had a look at the ship for himself. 'She's out there waiting for the tide so that she can get into Polzeale and unload her cargo at the pier. I wonder who's her skipper now . . . It used to be a chap called Pradell but that was thirty years ago . . .'

'Did you ever sail in her?'

'Only up the Sound, that's all.'

'I would like to sail in a ship when I'm a grown man,' Jim said 'Will you come with me, uncle Gus?'

'No, I shan't come with you,' Gus said. 'I'll have gone on a voyage all by myself, long before you're a grown man.'

'Why will you?'

'Oh, just because.'

'Do you have to go all alone? Can't I come too?'

'No, you'll be needed here at home, keeping your mother company.' Gus closed the old spyglass and lowered it into his lap. 'And that'll be a comfort to me, knowing she've got you to look after her, when I set out on this voyage of mine.'

'Do you *have* to go, uncle Gus?'

'Yes, when the time comes, I shan't have no choice.'

'When will that be?'

'Not yet, I hope.'

'Where will you go to?'

'I don't know. I'll be under sealed orders, as they say.'

'Will you be going in the boat?'

'What boat?'

'The *Emmet*, of course.'

'Well, now!' Gus said, and gave a laugh, reaching out with one big hand to ruffle the little boy's dark hair. 'That's how I would *choose* to go if I had any say in it. – Sailing out in the old *Emmet*, with a two mizzen breeze and not too much tide, making for Sally Quaile's, perhaps, when the pilchards are running nicely there . . . Yes, that would suit me handsome, that would, 'cos I should like to get my hand on her tiller again and feel her riding over the swell . . .'

'You'll have to ask uncle Brice,' Jim said. 'He'd let you go. I'm sure he would. After all, it *is* your boat.'

'Yes, that's right, the *Emmet* is mine.'

Gus sat looking out to sea, his eyes screwed up against its pale glare, and was lost for a while in his own thoughts. Then he turned towards Jim again and, thrusting out his bearded chin, spoke to him in a great hearty voice.

'And a good boat she've always been, too, right from the day I had her built. Old Tommy Laycock built her for me and he never did a better job in his life. Pure gold she is from stem to stern.'

'She's the best-kept boat in Polsinney,' Jim said. 'Uncle Brice sees to that.'

'H'mm!' Gus said. 'And so he ought!'

Later that same September evening, when Jim was in bed, Gus sat out in the yard watching the sun going down behind Mump Head. The evening was warm, with only the gentlest south-west wind beginning to breathe in from the sea, barely enough to disturb the gnats that hovered in the air above his head. Behind him the cottage had grown quite dark and Maggie had already lit the lamp. He could hear her moving about, closing the casements and drawing the curtains and speaking quietly to the cat, disturbed from its place on the window-sill. Then she came out with the cat in her arms and stood looking at the western sky, now a saffron-coloured glow streaked with bars of purple cloud.

'Isn't it time you came in?'

'Yes, it's high time,' he agreed, and slapped at the gnat that had settled on the back of his neck. 'I'll be eaten alive, else,' he said.

Maggie put the cat on the wall and wheeled Gus into the house. She went back to close the porch door and when she entered the kitchen again, Gus was at the table pouring himself a glass of rum.

'Well, that's another day gone!' he said. 'They seem to get shorter all the time.'

'Don't they always at this time of year?'

'I wasn't thinking of the time of year.'

'No,' she said gently, 'I know you weren't.'

He had been drinking heavily lately and it was a thing that worried her. She watched him empty his glass at one draught and reach out to fill it again.

'Do you think it's wise to drink so much?'

'I don't see what harm it can do me now. I'm already a dying man, or so I've been led to believe, anyway . . . Two or three years Dr Sam gave me and that was over four years ago. So I'm living on borrowed time now and I may as well make the most of it.'

Once again he drained his glass. Maggie drew out a chair and sat down. She looked at him with troubled eyes.

'I don't believe you're a dying man.'

'Come to that, neither do I!'

'Then why not see Dr Sam?'

127

'Where's the point in seeing him? He said there was nothing he could do, except pronounce sentence on me, and he've already done that, damn his soul!'

'But you've been getting better, not worse.'

'No thanks to him, is it?' Gus said. 'It's all your doing, not Dr Sam's, so where's the point in seeing him?'

'He knows you're better. I told him so. But he wouldn't say what that might mean without seeing you for himself.'

'An examination!' Gus said with a snarl. 'I've had enough of them in the past!'

'Yes. I know. But I thought perhaps, for my sake, you might be willing to face it again.'

'No doubt you're in a hurry to know when you'll be made a widow!' he said. 'Tes only natural, I suppose.'

Contrition followed immediately and he turned from her in self-disgust.

'Don't mind me – or what I say. I hit out at you – I'm a swine for that – but I don't mean the things I say.'

'I know that,' Maggie said. 'I know why it is and I understand.'

'Yes,' Gus said, looking at her, 'you are more understanding than I deserve.' And then, because he was still ashamed, he quietly gave in to her. 'All right, I'll see Dr Sam. No good putting it off, is it? The devil will get me in the end.'

Dr Sam examined Gus in his bedroom on the ground floor and the door of the room was kept bolted to stop little Jim from bursting in. Dr Sam was very thorough; the examination took half an hour; and at the end of that time he frankly admitted that he was astonished.

'The general improvement in your condition, since I last examined you, is nothing short of miraculous. If I hadn't seen it for myself I would never have believed it possible. Heart . . . lungs . . . digestive organs . . . I'd say they're working as well as my own . . . So, considering your disability and the strain it must put on your system as a whole, you are in pretty good health and I'd say you're a very lucky man.'

'Am I going to die or not?'

'Well, of course, we're all going to die – '

'The last time you examined me, you gave me two or three years, so you've already made one mistake.'

'Such things do happen,' the doctor said. 'You pressed me for a verdict then and I gave it to you in all honesty. It was based on your condition at that time and I'm sure that any other doctor's prognosis would have been virtually the same. You were neglecting yourself badly. You hardly ate. You slept in damp sheets. You'd lost heart in every way and were letting yourself go downhill. Now all that is changed – '

'What about the damned disease? You said the palsy would spread to my lungs.'

'That is the course it most commonly takes and it's usually only a matter of a few years from the onset of the disease. But your general health has improved so much that the palsy rather mysteriously, seems to have been completely checked. I can't explain it. I don't know enough. But if you would like a second opinion – '

'One doctor's enough,' Gus said. 'How long do you give me now?'

'I really wouldn't like to say. Having already been wrong once – '

'I'm willing to overlook that. You've gone over me pretty thoroughly. You've asked enough questions to fill a book. So what's your latest prognosis, based on how I am today?'

'Well, I can only do my best, but I'd say, judging from your condition now, that there's no very serious reason why you shouldn't live your allotted span.'

Gus stared. He drew a deep breath.

'Three score years and ten?' he said. 'That's another fourteen years!'

'You don't look exactly pleased at the news.'

'It takes some getting used to, that's why. Having faced up to death these past few years, then to be told you've got fourteen to go!'

'That was just a figure of speech. You mustn't hold me too firmly to it.'

'Damme! I'll hold you to *something*!' Gus said.

'Can I unlock the door now?'

'God, yes, let's get out of here!'

The door was unlocked and thrown open and Gus wheeled himself out into the kitchen. Maggie came forward expectantly but his face was difficult to read and Jim, clambering into his lap, was loudly demanding his attention. Dr Sam spoke to her, first remarking on Jim's healthy colour, then complimenting her on the appetizing smell of cooking that came from the Cornish slab. On reaching the door he paused, looking back at Gus in his chair.

'There is no doubt about it,' he said. 'Your wife is the one you have to thank for your amazing recovery.'

'Yes,' Gus said, quick as a flash, 'but *you're* the one that'll send in the bill!'

The doctor departed chuckling.

Gus now sent Jim out to play in the yard so that he and Maggie could be alone.

'It's good news, then?' she said to him.

'That all depends how you look at it.'

'But from what Dr Sam just said – '

'Damn fool doctors! They're no use at all! First they say you're as good as dead and then they say quite the opposite!' Gus scowled ferociously and in a voice not quite steady he said: 'He tells me I'm in such good shape that I *could* live as long as any other man of my age. Of course he dunt give no guarantee and he might just be talking widdle again but that's what he said, sure nuff, and he've gone over me with a fine tooth-comb.'

'Oh, Gus! You do sound so *angry*!' Maggie said, torn between laughter and tears. 'But surely, however you look at it, that can't be anything *but* good news?'

'Good news for me but not for you. I promised, when I asked you to marry me, that I should be dead within two or three years. That was the bargain we made, you and me, and I haven't kept my side of it. I've cheated you. Gone back on my word. I've got no *right* to be still alive '

'Yes, you have *every* right!' Maggie cried. 'And I *hate* to hear you talking like this when you've just been told such wonderful news! Do you think I *want* you to die?'

'No, I could never think that,' Gus said. 'The way you've looked after me these past four years – '

'Then why talk about cheating me?'

'Because tes only the honest truth. You're a young woman. No more than a girl. And it's all wrong that you should be tied to an old wreck of a man like me.'

'Have you ever heard me complain?'

'No, never, but that's not the point.'

'I'm happy. That's the point.'

'Are you?' he said, with a keen look.

'Yes,' Maggie said quietly. 'I have everything in the world I want, for myself and boy Jim, and I consider myself very lucky.'

'I'm the one that's lucky,' Gus said. 'You've kept me alive. You've made me well. You heard what Dr Sam said about that. But it's all wrong just the same and if I had known I was going to live I would never have married you.'

'And what would've become of me then?'

'You could've been my housekeeper. I'd still have left

131

you my property. But that way you would still have been free to marry some chap of your own age who'd have been a proper husband to you.'

'But I never wanted such a thing.'

'Not at first. I know that. Jim's father was not long dead and the way you felt at that time no one else could have taken his place. But that was more than four years ago. You've had time to get over his death – '

'Have I?' Maggie said tonelessly.

'Well, if you haven't, you will do in time. And then if you weren't married to me – '

'But I *am* married to you!' Maggie said. 'And I only wish I could make you believe that I am content in every way.'

'You may not always be content. You've got your life in front of you and it could happen, one of these days, that you find yourself looking at some young chap . . . and thinking of all the things you've missed . . . You might well turn against me then for standing in the way of your happiness.'

'I shall never turn against you.'

'How can you be so sure of that? You don't know what the future holds.'

'Come to that, neither do you,' Maggie said, with a smile. She came and stood close to his chair and put a hand on his arm. 'It seems to me we must just have faith.'

'I reckon I came off best all round, in that bargain of ours,' Gus said. 'The past four years have been good ones for me, even stuck in this chair, expecting death, and now I've been told I shall live after all! But what've *you* got out of it? I've led you up the garden path!'

'You don't understand what it means to me that Jim and I have a home of our own and are wrapped around in security. Jim is only a little boy and he doesn't know what we owe you. But *I* know it and I don't forget.'

Gus took her hand and gripped it hard. He looked up at her, searching her face.

'Some good've come out of it, then, eh?'

'Yes, and a great deal of happiness.'

'You don't feel I've played a trick on you, making a promise I couldn't keep?'

'It's a promise nobody wanted you to keep.'

'I never thought to see boy Jim grow up . . . but now it seems I may after all . . .'

'Yes, and it's what I've prayed for,' she said. 'A boy needs a man he can turn to, especially as he begins to grow up, and Jim thinks the world of you.'

'That's an honour I share with Brice.'

'Brice has been very good to him, too.'

'Naturally. He's your son.'

'It could have been very hard for Jim, having no father of his own, but he has you and he has Brice, and he's really a lucky little boy.'

'Maggie – ' Gus began to say.

'Yes? What?' Maggie said.

'Aren't you afraid of the future at all?'

'I thought we'd already settled it that the future could take care of itself.'

'It's bound to be hard for you, you know, whatever you say about having faith. You're a young girl. I'm an old man. There are bound to be problems, you must surely see that.'

'We shall face them together, as they come.'

'You've certainly got your share of faith! But yes, you are talking sense, of course. The future is hidden from all of us and nothing we say will change it one jot. Tes God who determines these things and if I'm to live another few years – '

'We shall give thanks for it. – Both of us.'

'You really mean that?'

'Yes. I do.'

'So be it, then,' he said, quietly.

Almost as soon as Brice entered the room, on the following Saturday evening, Gus was pouring him a drink.

'This is a drop of Jamaica's best that I bought specially to celebrate with.'

'Celebrate?' Brice said. 'Is it a special occasion, then?'

He caught Maggie's glance and she smiled at him.

'He's been celebrating for days – ever since he saw Dr Sam.'

'Ah,' Brice said. He understood.

'It seems I'm not dying after all,' Gus said in a loud voice, as Brice pulled out a chair and sat down, facing him across the table. 'At least, no more than anyone else . . . I might even live my allotted span . . . That's how the good doctor put it to me . . . And he was man enough to admit that his verdict was all wrong last time.'

'Why, that's wonderful news,' Brice said, 'and makes it a special occasion indeed.'

'Will you drink to it, then?'

'Yes, with all my heart,' Brice said, and touched the old man's glass with his own. 'Long life to you and all happiness – and I know the crew will say the same.'

He drank, half emptying his glass, and set it down on the table. Gus reached out to refill it but Brice covered it with his hand, and Gus, refilling his own glass, eyed him with a humorous, sidelong glance. Maggie now came to the table, bringing the *Emmet*'s account book, and Gus touched her on the arm.

'That's something you'll never see – Brice the worse for drink,' he said. 'I think tes a great pity, myself. It would make him more human. Approachable.'

'I'm human enough, surely?' Brice said.

Gus disagreed. He shook his head.

'Tes the sins of the flesh that make a man human,' he said, 'and what do you know about them?'

'As much as anyone else, I suppose.'

'Oh, is that so?' Gus exclaimed. He looked at Brice with rounded eyes. 'Are you going to tell us about them?' he asked.

'No. I think not.'

'That's just the trouble with you. Always close-reefed. Trimmed by the head. Hatches securely battened down. But you needn't be shy with us, you know. I'm a man of the world myself and Maggie, although she sits there looking so very prim, is only flesh and blood after all. She's no stranger to the sins of the flesh – '

Gus broke off. He had shocked himself. He stared for a moment into space.

'What in God's name am I saying?' he said, and, looking into his glass, he added: 'Seems I've had more than my full allowance.'

He slammed the glass down on the table and forced himself to meet Maggie's gaze. But she, though her cheeks were warmly flushed, merely looked at him with glimmering amusement.

'Yes, I think perhaps you have. It's the rum talking, not you.'

'The rum has got too much to say for itself!'

'It was only speaking the truth even so.'

'I'm damned if I touch another drop! Tes turning me into a drunken sot!'

But he was sober enough now. He had shocked himself into sobriety. His glance flickered towards Brice but Brice, no less than Maggie, it seemed, was inclined to be tolerant and amused.

'You young people, sitting there, letting an old man make a fool of himself!' Gus turned towards Maggie again. 'Tes all your fault!' he said to her. 'You are old beyond your years, my girl, and you've no right to sit there so calm, making me feel so small as a worm.'

'You will not pick a quarrel with me,' Maggie said, 'even if you try all night.'

'No, nor with me,' Brice said.

Gus suddenly gave a laugh and, leaning forward across the table, drew the *Emmet*'s account book to him.

'We may as well talk business, then, and see if we can fall out over that!'

Chapter 6

Jim, when he was not with Gus, was sure to be in the sail-loft, watching Isaac and Percy at work. He loved the big spacious room with its many windows and fanlights and he loved to see the way the sun, coming in at all angles, slanted in so many criss-cross shafts and made little pools of light and warmth here and there on the bare-boarded floor. The sail-loft floor seemed to stretch for miles; it was twenty paces from end to end and eighteen from side to side; and those were a man's paces, not a boy's.

Isaac, with a piece of chalk, drew his sail-plans on this floor. He was always full of importance whenever he came from the boat-yard, after measuring-up a new boat, and Jim, sitting crouched on his haunches nearby, would have to keep very quiet and still while Isaac, after consulting his notes, drew the appropriate mast-length on the bare boards of the floor. Isaac used a measure for this but when it came to drawing the sails he did it all by eye alone. He would stand deep in thought for a while, squinting this way and that, and then, bent two-double as he himself said, he would lick his piece of chalk and, moving backwards with short, shuffling steps, would draw the clean, faultless lines of the sail. Jim never ceased to marvel at this. The miracle of it was fresh every time.

'How do you know exactly what size the sails've got to be?' he asked.

'I've seen the boat, of course,' Isaac said. 'I've measured her and I've measured her masts and I'd be a poor sort of sail-maker if I couldn't schemey the shape and size of the sails that John Ellis d'want on her.'

At the end of the sail-loft, on deep wooden shelves, the bolts of new canvas were stored, and when the sail-plan had been drawn out, Percy would fetch one of these bolts and lay it down at Isaac's feet and Isaac, with a little kick, would send it unrolling across the floor. Jim liked to see the canvas brought out, so clean and new, a bluish-white, and to see it go rolling out like this, rippling across the sail-loft floor. He liked the peculiar smell of it and the feel of it, so thick and strong, and best of all he liked to watch as Isaac, with his big sharp scissors, went snip-snip-snip so courageously, cutting out the first 'cloth' of the sail.

'Supposing you was to cut it wrong?'

'Ess, you'd like to see that, I believe.'

'No, I wouldn't.'

'Aw, ess, you would. That's why you're geeking at me so close.'

'Did you ever cut it wrong?'

'No, I never did, not wunst. I'm a sail-maker, not a fool, and I don't *belong* to cut it wrong. But if I *was* to cut it wrong, that'd be your fault for prattling at me.'

Isaac at first did not approve of the little boy's presence in the loft and he grumbled about it to Percy Tremearne. 'Is this a sail-loft?' he would say. 'Or is it a blamed nursery?' And Percy Tremearne said once, 'Maybe the old man d'send him up here to keep an eye on the two of us.'

But one day when Isaac was cutting out a sail it happened that the lower point of his scissors kept catching in a rough bit of floor and Jim, who was crouching nearby, put out a hand and lifted the cloth so that it could be cut more easily. Isaac was impressed by this, for Jim was not quite five at the time, and, turning to Percy Tremearne, he said:

'Did you see that?'

'Ess, I did. He d'knaw like a 'uman, sure nuff.'

'Seemingly this tacker of ours is just about brave and smart enough to be a sail-maker when he grows up.'

Isaac was friendly to Jim after that. 'So long as you're good, you can stay,' he said. And often the little boy made himself useful, rubbing out old sail-plans, perhaps, or crawling under a great stretch of canvas in search of a thimble Isaac had lost.

Even when Jim began going to school, he always found time every day to call in at the sail-loft, and he would always try to be there when he knew that a new suit of sails was ready to be taken down to the barking-house. There was great excitement in this and he would be allowed in to watch. He enjoyed the smell of the boiling cutch, even though the fumes stung his eyes, and he liked to watch as the new white sails were lowered into the dark brown liquor seething and bubbling in the vat. The sails would have to be steeped for hours and Eugene, with his short wooden 'oar', would swirl them round every so often to make sure they were well 'roused'.

'How dunt ee take off your smock, young Jim, and dip it in the cutch?' he would say. 'That'd last you a lifetime, then, *and* it'd keep the weather out.'

This was a favourite joke of Eugene's because Jim wore a short canvas smock exactly like those the fishermen wore and many fishermen did indeed dip their smocks into the cutch at the same time that they dipped their nets. But Jim preferred his smock as it was. His mother had made it and it was blue, just like the one uncle Brice always wore.

'No! Shent do it!' he would say, whenever Eugene made his joke. 'My smock is weatherproof as it is.'

Uncle Brice never barked *his* smock and that was good enough for Jim,

As he grew older his world opened out, for his mother and his uncle Gus, although they imposed certain rules on him, allowed him to come and go as he pleased. They gave him his freedom; they trusted him; and because he felt that their rules were fair, Jim never betrayed that trust.

Released from school in the afternoon he would rush with the other boys to the shore and only when hunger gnawed at him did he think of setting foot indoors. There was always so much to do, always so many things to see, all round the little harbour town, that the days were over all too soon. Even the long midsummer days were never really long enough and always when he went to bed his mind would be seething with those things he had meant to do and had not yet done but would certainly do after school next day.

His world was full of activity. There was always something going on. The harbour, the fish-quay, the rocky shore, lured him from his own home and kept him away for hours on end. But Maggie never fussed over him. She had seen to it that he could swim; that he knew and understood the tides; and that he could handle whatever small boat he managed to beg the use of from some special 'friend' on the quay. He learnt these things early in life and the water had no terrors for him. He was sturdy and strong and sure of himself and when he went stepping from boat to boat, in the harbour pool at high tide, his feet, whether booted or bare, would move so quickly and confidently that a boat scarcely had time to rock before he was out of it into the next.

Sometimes, if he and his friends could borrow a boat, they would go rowing out of the harbour and make their way along the shore, whiffing for mackerel. Mackerel were very easy to catch; they would even snap at unbaited hooks; but it was a triumph all the same for a small boy of seven or eight to go home at the end of the afternoon with a string of them in either hand.

'Bless my soul!' uncle Gus would say. 'That's a brave lot

of mackerel you've got there. We shall all feast like kings at teatime today!'

And for Jim this was perfectly true because no fish was so good to eat as the fish you had actually caught yourself, and mackerel, whether fried in flour or marinated in vinegar with a bay-leaf and a few peppercorns, was indeed a dish for a king.

'There are twelve fish here,' his mother would say. 'We shall never eat them all ourselves.'

And Jim would know the pleasure and pride of calling on old Mrs Emily Newpin or some other solitary neighbour with a gift of two or three fish.

'My mother asked could you do with these?'

'My dear soul and body! I should just think I could! But where've they come from, I'd like to know? You surely never catched them yourself?'

'Yes, I did,' Jim would say, and then he would give a little shrug. 'You know how tis with mackerel. You always catch more than you can eat.'

'Your mother's a good kind neighbour to me and you're my bestmost boy in the world. And if you just wait there a minute I'll fetch you a slice of my new saffron cake.'

Almost everyone in Polsinney was young Jim's friend; the older people, especially, always had a kind word for him; but there was one exception and that was Mrs Rachel Tallack. She, if he passed her in the village, always pretended not to see him, and her face, so deliberately turned away, was always set in harsh lines.

'Why dunt Mrs Tallack like us?' Jim asked his mother one day. 'Is it something to do with the time when you was her servant up at the farm?'

'Yes, it is partly that,' Maggie said. 'Certainly that's when it all began. And then she didn't like it, you see, because I married your uncle Gus.'

'Why didn't she?'

141

'Well, because – ' Maggie began, but here she was interrupted by Gus.

'Because she's a jealous old crabpot, that's why, and have had her nose pushed out of joint. You needn't fret over her, young Jim. Just leave her to stew in her own sour juice.'

'Uncle Brice doesn't hate us so why should she?'

'You'd better ask him that yourself.'

But Jim never broached the subject with Brice. He sensed that such questions would bring a rebuff. Besides, when he was with uncle Brice, there were better things to talk about.

The sea and all things connected with it were the very breath of life to Jim, as to the other Polsinney boys, and together they talked of nothing else. In late summer, when the seining season came round, they would be out on the cliff at Porthvole, watching for the pilchard shoals which, from early August onwards, came closer and closer in-shore. At the sighting of a shoal, when the huer's great trumpeted cry, 'Hevva! Hevva!', rang round the harbour, the whole of Polsinney went mad and madness could last for days and weeks. The bay would be dotted with seine-boats and when a shoal was successfully netted the beach and the wharves and the fish-cellars swarmed with such activity that the noise of it could be heard for miles.

The work went on all day and all night and Polsinney was gripped as if by a fever. Pilchards were its meed and creed. For these small silver fish could be eaten fresh out of the sea; could be salted down for the winter; could be shipped in their millions to other countries, thus bringing the seine owners rich revenue; and, in addition, would provide the oil that lit the lamps in humble homes. 'Meat, money and light, all in one night,' the old Cornish saying went, and this was why, at this time of year, everyone,

142

whether rich or poor, whether they took an active part or were watching for the fun of it, was infected by the happy madness of this great pilchard jubilee.

The seining season was at its height in August and early September; in the following month it dwindled away and in November came to an end; the seine-boats were laid up again in Scadder Cove and the seine-nets were put into store. But the drift fishermen went to sea all the year round and when the pilchard season was over they would go after the herring; and for Jim, as for most young boys, there was no excitement so great, nor any sight so beautiful as when the luggers pushed away from the quay, in late afternoon or early evening, according to the state of the tide, and, their sails first flapping and rippling, then growing taut as they drew the wind, sailed out through the harbour entrance and went tacking across the bay, making for those fishing grounds that lay far out of sight of land. The harbour would be very quiet then and there would be a sense of loss but in the morning, on the flood tide, the boats would come sailing in again, each with its following of gulls, and this was a sight that never failed to bring a boy's heart into his mouth and set him dancing on his feet.

Jim, if he could manage it, was always out and about first thing, to see the fishing fleet return. However cold and dark the morning, he would not miss it for the world, and would stand with his little bunch of cronies, elbowing them, competing with them, eager to identify each boat as she came stealthily in from the dark and passed under the lamp on the quay-head. The *Speedwell*; the *Ellereen*; the *Rose Allan*; the *Boy Dick*; the *Emmet* and the *Trelawney*: these were always amongst the first, for their skippers were first-rate seamen and could get the best out of their boats; and this was a very important thing, for the first boats got berths at the quay, where the fish merchants were waiting for them, while the latecomers had to come in on the beach and would thus miss the best prices.

You could always tell when a boat had an extra good catch of fish in her by the way she sat low in the water and by the large number of gulls escorting her in, and as soon as Jim sighted the *Emmet* he would be on tenterhooks, reading the signs. Had she a good catch of herring in her? No need to ask. Of course she had! Everyone in Polsinney said that if there were any fish about Brice Tallack was sure to find them. He was a 'lucky' fisherman. Other skippers would follow him. But it was not only a question of luck. There was more to it than that. Brice was shrewd, energetic, alert. He knew the fishing grounds as well as though he carried a chart of them in his head and he had that extra bit of good judgment that told him which were the best grounds to try.

He was a good man with a boat: one of the best, William Nancarrow said; and this reputation Brice had among the older fishermen was a matter of great pride to Jim. He would try to look unconcerned as the *Emmet* slid in beside the quay. He would turn and kick at a stone and pretend it meant nothing at all. For in this, as in everything else, he took his cue from Brice himself. His uncle Brice never showed off, but was always quiet and businesslike, getting on with the work in hand; and although he could give and take a joke as well as any other man, he was never boastful or blustering.

All these things impressed young Jim. There was nobody like his uncle Brice. And he longed impatiently for the day when he himself would be old enough to go as one of the *Emmet*'s crew, learning the hundred and one things that a good seaman needed to know; learning the secrets of the sea; learning that quiet self-reliance he so admired in his uncle Brice. Then, perhaps, when he was a man, he would have a boat of his own: a new one, specially built for him in Martin Laycock's boatyard; and that would be the best thing of all because then he would really be equal with Brice, hailing him at the quayside, one skipper to another, exchanging a few words with him as each made ready to put to sea. They would move out of the harbour together, the two of them leading the rest of the fleet, and would sail away to those distant places where there was nothing to see but the sea. And then – the fish had better look out for themselves!

Isaac Kiddy was full of scorn when he heard that Jim meant to be a fisherman.

'I thought you were going to be a sail-maker.'

'I never said that. Twas you that said that.'

'Well, and what's wrong with it, I'd like to know?'

'Edn nothing wrong with it, I just don't belong to do it, that's all.'

Isaac sniffed. He took an immense pride in his craft and he felt Jim had cast a slight on it.

'A sail-maker, I'll have you know, is somebody special, a man apart. You could meet a hundred men – two or three hundred, come to that – and not one of them would be a sail-maker. That'll tell you how special we are. But a fisherman! Well! My dear soul! They're about as common as scads!'

Isaac's scorn left Jim unmoved. He merely turned away with a shrug. His father had been a fisherman; so had his mother's father, too; and that meant it was in his blood. Besides which, the sea was always there, and Jim had only to look at it to feel its restlessness in his heart; to feel something rising up in him, catching his breath in a little gasp; something that filled all his thoughts by day and got into his dreams at night.

Maggie knew and understood this. She had lived all her

145

days within sight of the sea and she knew what a powerful influence it wielded over the minds of boys and men. She knew the sea would be Jim's life. She saw it like a picture clear in her mind. And she knew it was something she had to accept.

Jim's thoughts often dwelt on his dead father and sometimes, especially at bed-time, he would ask his mother questions about him. No one else in Polsinney had ever known him, for he had been a Porthgaran man and Porthgaran was a long way away, thirty or forty miles down the coast. His mother had a picture of him in a locket she wore round her neck but this picture was so small that Jim, whenever he looked at it, would click his tongue in vexation.

'I wish you had a better picture than this. I can't even tell if he's dark or fair.'

'His hair was dark brown, the same as yours.'

'Was he tall?'

'Tall enough.'

'Strong?' Jim asked.

'Yes. Very strong.'

'Was he as tall as uncle Brice?'

'I think, perhaps, not quite so tall. But very strong and quick and brave . . . and always clever with his hands.'

'Was he a good seaman too?'

'I think he was,' Maggie said, 'but he was only nineteen when he died.'

'I wish he hadn't been drowned like that.'

'I wish it, too.'

'You must've been lonely, left all alone like you were. Grandad gone . . . Uncle David gone . . . You had nobody left after that.'

'Yes, I did, I had you,' Maggie said.

'But I wadn born then, was I?'

'No, you were just a secret then.'

'You brought me with you, didn't you, when you came to Polsinney?' Jim said. 'You carried me with you all the way, wrapped up in a bundle with your clothes, and nobody even knew I was there.'

'Who told you that?'

'Willie Wearne.'

'Did he indeed!'

'Why, edn it true?'

'Oh, yes, it's true enough. Or as near the truth as makes no odds.'

'Some old surprise you must've got when you opened the bundle and I was born.'

'Oh, no, it was no surprise. I knew you were there all the time.'

'How did you know?' Jim asked.

'Because,' Maggie said hugging him close, 'mothers always know these things.'

His uncle Gus had been a fisherman, too, before illness had struck him down, and his old white oilskins hung in the cupboard even now, after all these years.

'I know I shan't wear them again,' he would say, 'but I like to see them hanging there, to remind me of the old days.'

On cold evenings in wintertime Jim would often sit for hours listening to his uncle Gus yarning about the old days. It seemed there was never any end to the tales his uncle Gus could tell: of the great catches taken sometimes, that had filled the *Emmet*'s holds to the coamings and overflowed onto the deck; of terrible storms ridden out to a sea-anchor made of oars and spars with sails wrapped round them and of how, during one of these storms, the foremast had been snapped off; of how, once, a steamship had passed over the drifting nets and carried them all clean away; of the great whales the old man had seen, breaking

147

the surface of the sea and blowing water up in a spout forty or fifty feet high.

Jim never tired of his uncle's tales. They were so full of marvellous things. And he would sit very quiet and still, pretending not to hear the clock when it struck the hour for his bed-time, but knowing only too well that in another minute or two his mother would draw attention to it.

'I'm not tired. Honestly. Can't I have another half hour?'

He would open his eyes very wide to show how untired he was but although his mother laughed at this she rarely gave in to him.

'Off you go. No arguments. I'll be up in ten minutes to hear your prayers.'

Sometimes when the fierce south westerly gales came blowing in from the sea, the cottage would shudder most dreadfully, for it was built on the very edge of the old sea wall itself and had its back to the foreshore.

'Ho! We're in for it good and proper tonight!' uncle Gus would say at these times. 'Just hark at it thumping against that wall! We'd better put an anchor down!'

That was just a joke, of course; the little house was as strong as a rock; but in the morning, after a gale, coral, seashells and seaweed would be found strewn all over the yard and perhaps even big stones from the shore, evidence of the sea's angry power as it hurled itself over the sea wall. Sometimes, especially in winter, the gales would last many days and nights, keeping the fishermen fretting at home, thus bringing hardship and poverty. And sometimes, worse than this, a gale would blow up very suddenly, while the fishing fleet was at sea.

Jim, from an early age, knew just what the sea could do when it was whipped up into a fury. The knowledge was inescapable and came to him in a great many ways. He saw it in the eyes of the old men when they stood on the quay in the grey dawn, watching for boats that were overdue. He heard it in old Mrs Lewin's voice as she wept for her grandson, Billy Joe, swept overboard from the *Jenefer* on a dark December night in 1877. Even when the sea was flat and calm there could be death and danger in it and once, on a fine September day in 1878, a Polsinney gig, overloaded with mackerel, capsized and sank in St Glozey Bay, drowning all three of her crew.

Jim knew about these things and the knowledge of them got into his bones. You could never turn your back on the sea. You had to watch it all the time. His uncle Brice always said that. 'Rough or calm, lion or lamb, you can never take the sea for granted,' he said, and Jim never forgot those words.

Still, the sea had this fascination, somehow. The *idea* of it got a hold on you. Boys and men felt it the same and the danger was all a part of it. It was something you had to face; any seaman would tell you that; and most of them, in saying it, would give a little shrug. There were other sufferings, too, and fishermen's hands and wrists were scarred where saltwater boils had festered and burst and where the cuffs of their oilskins, wet with the sea and razor-sharp, had cut the flesh until it bled. They made nothing of these things. They would show you their scars and laugh at them. They said it was all in the night's work.

The only thing that embittered them was when bad weather kept them at home for days on end. There was no laughter among them then. They were angry and sick at heart because their livelihood was gone and their wives and children went hungry. Brice was all right; he had the farm; and often, when the weather was bad, he would be down on the seashore, loading seaweed into a cart to spread as manure on the fields at Boskillyer.

Sometimes Brice would persuade his crew that a little

money could be made by loading seaweed into the *Emmet*'s punt and taking it up the River Shill to sell to farmers on riverside farms. On these occasions Jim went, too, and it was a great adventure for him to row up the silent, sheltered river to these mysterious places inland. But the men got no joy from it. They felt they were demeaning themselves.

'Three shillings!' Ralph Ellis exclaimed, when Brice shared out the money they had earnt from one day's work of this sort. 'My family will get *some* fat on that!'

But poor though the reward might be, it was that or nothing, uncle Brice said, when the weather turned bad and kept them at home.

Every morning, summer or winter, Jim would be on the fish-quay to see the drifters coming in, and often, as he grew older, he would go aboard the *Emmet* and make himself useful there, helping to clear the last fish from the nets or counting them into the baskets. He was always reluctant to leave; he loved to be part of the busy scene enacted at the quayside in the early morning; but always there came a moment when uncle Brice took out his watch and held it up for Jim to see.

'Time you went home to breakfast now, otherwise you'll be late for school.'

'Aw, there's plenty of time yet!'

'I shall count up to ten,' Brice would say, 'and if you aren't out of this boat by then – '

'What will you do?'

'Try it and see!'

Jim, with an air of unconcern, would linger to the very last, but always, by the count of ten, he was out of the boat and on the quay. There, he would spin round on his heel, giving a little excited laugh, but he never tried anything with Brice; not with the crew looking on; there was something in Brice's blue eyes that somehow kept you up to the mark.

On Saturdays he was allowed to stay until the fish had all been sold and the boat had been thoroughly cleaned out. One Saturday morning in late summer, at the height of the pilchard season, Rachel Tallack, driving the milk-float, came onto the crowded quay to collect a basket of fish that Brice had put ready for her. It happened that Jim was standing nearby and when Brice beckoned to him, he went forward immediately and helped to lift the basket of fish into the float, beside the churns. Rachel, as always, ignored him, even though he was standing so close that he could have reached out and touched her skirts. She merely glanced down at the fish and made some remark on their quality.

'This is Jim,' Brice said, putting a hand on the boy's shoulder. 'He's been helping us in the boat.'

'I know quite well who he is,' Rachel said, and before Brice could say any more she was already moving away, pulling on the nearside rein to bring the pony sharply round.

Brice and Jim went back to the boat, where the crew were busy with buckets and brooms, cleaning out the fish-hold. Neither the man nor the boy spoke of the incident, for there was an understanding between them that Mrs Tallack should not be discussed, but Brice, on getting home, spoke to his mother reprovingly.

'What's past is past,' he said. 'Jim's only a boy, just eight years old. Surely you could find something to say to him?'

'That boy is his mother's son and for his sake she's robbed you of your rights.'

'Maggie has robbed me of nothing.'

'Well, she will do in time,' Rachel said, 'and the only comfort to me is that *she* thought your uncle was going to die and it must be a sore disappointment to her that the awkward, obstinate old fool is lingering on as long as he is.'

'That's not true and you know it,' Brice said, 'Anyone in Polsinney will tell you that it's Maggie who's kept uncle Gus alive.'

'More fool she, then,' Rachel said.

All seamen were heroes to Jim, and Brice, being skipper of the *Emmet*, was the biggest hero of them all. His name was always on Jim's lips and everything he said or did was reported in detail at home.

'Uncle Brice says we're in for a cold snap – the gulls are flying inland,' he would say, or, 'There won't be no mackerel catched for a while – uncle Brice says they go down deep when the weather's as cold as this.'

'That's nothing,' Gus said. 'Any fisherman knows that.'

'The herring season starts next week. Uncle Brice is going to try the Bitts. He says that's always a good place to start. Better than Coggle's Deep, he says.'

'They're all good places – when the fish are there,' Gus said with a little growl, and afterwards, when Jim was in bed, he said to Maggie: 'The way that boy talks some-times, you'd think my nephew Brice was maker of all heaven and earth.'

'Yes, I know,' Maggie said, with a smile, 'but you surely aren't jealous of him, I hope?'

'Of course I'm blamed well jealous of him!'

'Why?'

'Because he's a young man, healthy and strong, and got two good legs he can walk with, and because he can do a man's work, the kind I'd still be doing myself if I wasn't stuck in this damned chair.'

'Yes, I know,' Maggie said. 'It's natural you should feel like that.'

'Still, there tis, and can't be helped.' Gus turned back to

his bible again. He was re-reading the Book of Job. 'I daresay, if the truth were known, Brice is a lot more jealous of me than I am of him, and with very good reason, too,' he said.

For a brief season in spring or summer Brice and two or three of his crew would go crabbing in the *Emmet*'s punt and sometimes Jim was allowed to go too. He would take his turn at sculling, and was glad of a chance to display his skill, but he always took great care that no trace of pride should show in his face. When, one day, without hesitation, he took the punt through the narrow gap between Ennis Rock and Scully Point, he pretended not to notice the smile that passed between Brice and the other two men, or to hear the quiet remark that Jacky Johns made to Clem Pascoe later.

'He's a born seaman, edna, you? I wouldn't mind a son like he in exchange for the three maids I've got at home.'

Sometimes, in the school holidays, Jim was even allowed to go out in the *Emmet*, and these were special occasions indeed. A whole night at sea, like a grown man, right out beyond the Oracle Rocks in search of the great pilchard shoals as they came sweeping madly down the Channel.

Jim was turned nine by now. He had good sea-legs and was never sick. If there was a swell he exulted in it; his head remained clear; his stomach steadfast. But that was only half of it; the bad part came when you reached home; because, as soon as you stepped ashore, the solid ground would not stay still! The land went lurching from under you and landmarks heaved this way and that, tilting and swaying drunkenly, so that you felt giddy and sick. Your legs went like jelly under you and you had to hold on to something firm to keep yourself from tumbling over.

The feeling passed off after a while but it could return unexpectedly as Jim found when he got home and was washing himself in the scullery. The instant he bent over the sink, it swung away from under him, and there was a terrible sickly blackness reeling and rolling inside his head. He gritted his teeth and clung to the sink, staring at the water in the bowl until it became steady again. Washing himself was no easy task but in time he learnt the trick of it and did it without bending too low and without properly closing his eyes.

It was some comfort to Jim to know that even grown men suffered the same reeling sensation after long hours on a heavy sea and this he discovered quite by chance. One morning he and a few other boys were passing Scrouler Tonkin's cottage when Scrouler, just home from a night's fishing in the *John Cocking*, was about to wash himself, stripped to the waist, at a tub on a stool in the back yard. The yard door stood open wide and Scrouler, bending over the tub, clinging to it with both hands, was bellowing to his wife indoors.

'Emmeline! Come and hold this plaguey tub so's I can get myself washed in it! Tes swingen like the pit of hell!'

The eavesdropping boys were in transports and soon passed the story on at school, which meant that poor Scrouler, for months afterwards, had only to walk down the streets of Polsinney to be followed by a group of children crying:

'Emmeline! Come and hold this tub! Tes swingen like the pit of hell!'

Scrouler never lived it down; the joke became common property, enjoyed by young and old alike; and in Polsinney the chances were that it would follow him to the grave.

'Do you ever feel queer, uncle Brice, when you first step ashore?' Jim asked.

'Everyone does,' Brice said. 'At least, if there's been any

154

kind of sea. But you get used to it in time and then you no longer notice it.'

'Scrouler Tonkin still notices it.'

'Yes,' Brice said, solemnly, 'Scrouler's a bit on the delicate side.'

Jim hugged himself at this because Scrouler was six and a half feet tall and almost as powerful a wrestler as the champion Hitch Penter himself. But, as uncle Brice said, it was not always your big strong man that had the strongest stomach at sea. That was a gift bestowed chancelike and if you were one of the lucky ones, the gift was worth more to you than gold.

'Have I got a good sea-stomach?' Jim asked.

'I would say so, yes,' Brice said.

'Tes nearly six weeks since I last went out.'

'Six weeks? Surely not!'

'Well, a brave long time, anyway.'

It was a day at the end of September, a bright sunny day, very warm, and the *Emmet* was laid up on the beach at Porthvole, supported by the wooden 'legs' that kept her upright on her keel. The pilchard season had been a disappointment that year, both for the seiners and the drifters, and for almost three weeks now the *Emmet* had caught no fish at all. Brice and his crew therefore had decided to call it a day; the pilchard nets had been put into store and the mackerel nets had been overhauled ready for taking aboard; and it seemed to Brice a good opportunity to give the boat an extra 'paying'. The crew, however, were not there; they had gone with their families to the Michaelmas Fair at Polzeale; so Brice and Jim, on the beach, were cleaning and scraping the *Emmet*'s hull in preparation for tarring it.

Brice, on a ladder against the boat's side, was working with scraper and brush while Jim, with a hammer and chisel, was knocking off the barnacles that clung below the

155

waterline. Nearby, on a fire of driftwood burning between four flat stones, stood a large iron pot filled with tar and the smell of it, with the smell of the woodsmoke, was hot and rough and rather pleasant, drifting on the fresh sea breeze. There were ten or twelve other luggers dotted about on the beach but because it was Polzeale Fair Day only a handful of men could be seen working on them.

'Can I come mackerel driving with you?'

'One day, perhaps. I'll have to see.'

'How can I ever learn anything if I never get the chance to go out?'

'You *have* been out.'

'Three times, that's all.'

'You'll have your fill of it soon enough when you leave school and join the crew.'

'That won't be until I'm twelve.'

'And how long is that?'

'Two years and a bit.'

'It will soon pass. You mark my words.'

'Georgie Dunn and Denzil Grose were only ten when they went to sea.'

'They come from poor families, that's why. Georgie's father is laid up sick and Denzil's mother, as you know, is a widow with five other children to raise. So they had to leave school and go to work.'

Jim, with a smart blow of his hammer and chisel, knocked a barnacle from its place on the hull.

'I wish I was poor like Georgie Dunn.'

'Do you indeed?'

'Yes, I do!'

'Well, if you were to ask him,' Brice said, 'perhaps he'd like to change places with you.'

Jim looked up with a sheepish smile that spread over his fresh-skinned face and then slowly faded again. Georgie

Dunn was poor indeed. His family lived on parish help and this meant that the boots he wore were branded on the inside to show they were parish property.

'I shouldn't have said that, should I? About wishing I was poor?'

'Nobody heard it, only me.'

'I didn't mean it.'

'No, I know.'

'Shall I put some more wood on the fire?'

'Yes, if you think it needs it.'

While Jim was thus occupied, poking bits of dry wood into the fire under the tar-pot, his mother came along the wharf and down the slipway onto the beach. She had a piece of paper in her hand and Jim, guessing that he would be sent on an errand, glanced up at her with a mutinous scowl. Couldn't she see that he was busy, helping uncle Brice with the boat?'

'Your uncle Gus wants you to go to the boatyard with this note. Wait for Mr Laycock's answer and then bring it home to him.'

The boatyard. That was different. Jim was always pleased to go there and, taking the note from his mother, he paused only long enough to exchange a quick word with Brice.

'You'll wait for me, won't you, before you begin tarring the boat?'

'Yes, all right, I'll wait for you. – So long as you're not gone all day.'

Brice, left alone with Maggie, stepped down from the ladder and picked up the tools Jim had dropped on the sand.

'He's growing up fast, that boy of yours.'

'Much too fast,' Maggie said. 'He's very independent sometimes.'

'Finding his feet.'

'I suppose so.'

'He's quite determined to be a fisherman.'

'Yes, he can talk of nothing else. It's always the fishing, the boat, the sea . . .'

'It must worry you very much, after what happened at Porthgaran, but I notice you never try to discourage him.'

'I know it wouldn't be any use. I'd keep him from the sea if I could, but I know I can't. For one thing, it's in his blood and there's no going against that. For another thing – '

'What?' Brice said.

'He models himself on you,' Maggie said.

'Does he?'

'Yes, of course. You are his hero. Didn't you know?'

'In that case you must wish I was anything but a fisherman.'

'No,' Maggie said, absently, 'I don't wish that.'

There was a long silence between them. Maggie was thinking about the past. But she was thinking of Brice, too, and there was something she wanted to say.

'My father took terrible risks. He went to sea time and again in a boat he knew to be unsound and in the end he drowned himself and five other men besides. But you are a different kind of man from my father and you never take any risks except those that can't be helped. That's why I'm glad that when the time comes, Jim will go to sea with you. You're a good seaman. One of the best. I've heard Gus say so oftentimes.'

'Does he say that?' Brice was surprised. 'Well, whatever I know of the sea, I learnt it all from him, and *he* was a seaman if you like. There was no one to touch my uncle Gus in the days when he was fit and strong. Anyone will tell you that.'

'I know what they say about Gus and I know what

they say about you. No young boy, going to sea, could be in better hands than yours. Jim is intelligent. Quick to learn. And I know he'll learn nothing but good from you.'

Brice stood looking at her. Not a muscle moved in his strong, lean face. And when in a while he answered her it was with a certain formality that kept his voice toneless and flat.

'I shall do my best, I promise you, to see that it is always so.' And then, because of the way she looked at him, he asked: 'Is there something troubling you?'

'Yes, I'm often troubled,' she said, 'when I think back over the past . . . Of how I first came to the farm and persuaded your mother to take me in . . . I'm not surprised she hates me when I think how I came, a perfect stranger, and caused such an upset in your lives.'

'That was ten years ago. You are scarcely a stranger now. And uncle Gus at least has cause to be thankful for you coming. You saved his life.'

'But you have no such cause,' Maggie said.

'Haven't I?'

'You know what I mean.'

'We talked like this once before. Years ago. Do you remember? I said then – and I say the same now – that being cut out of my uncle's will meant less than nothing to me.'

'You said you did mind about losing the boat.'

'Did I say that? Perhaps I did.' Brice looked up at the *Emmet* and with a quick, mechanical movement, scraped at a patch of moss with his scraper. 'But I haven't lost her, have I, not yet? I'm still her skipper – so far at least – and will continue so, probably, until Jim is old enough to take over from me.'

'And then?' Maggie asked.

Brice smiled.

159

'Jim is not quite ten. We don't need to think about that yet.'

'No, perhaps not,' Maggie said.

But afterwards, as she walked slowly home, she was thinking about it a great deal.

Chapter 7

The year 1879 was a bad one for the Cornish fisheries. The pilchard fishing had been poor everywhere and in most areas the mackerel fishing turned out little better. Catches were slight throughout the season and already, by early December, many boats were coming back 'clean'.

The *Emmet* was no exception. Night after night she shot her nets, only to take them up empty, or to draw in a few rabblefish, which, when divided among the crew, were 'scarcely enough to feed the cat,' as Ralph Ellis said with great bitterness.

'I hope to God the herring season will turn out better than this!'

'Tes all we *can* hope for, edn it?' Billy Coit said snappily.

Tempers were often short aboard the *Emmet* at this time, as they were on all those boats whose crews, having suffered two bad seasons, faced hardship and poverty.

During the first week in December the mackerel nets were put into store and the herring nets were taken aboard and early on a calm Tuesday afternoon the *Emmet*, with the rest of the fleet, set sail for the herring grounds thirty or forty miles up the Channel.

The season began well enough. Catches were not big at first but that was only to be expected, for the weather continued soft and mild, and it wanted a good steady breeze to set the herring shoals running. In the new year there was a change; a cooling and freshening of the air;

catches improved accordingly and the drifter crews, with high hopes, talked of it being a good season. One night the *Emmet* caught ten thousand fish; on another twelve and a half thousand.

'Seemingly your good luck haven't deserted you after all,' Ralph Ellis said to Brice. 'None of the others have done so well as us so far.'

But luck was something you could never take for granted; not if you were a fisherman; and sometimes it happened that what appeared to be good luck could suddenly turn into bad, all in the space of a couple of hours, as Brice and his crew discovered one night early in February.

They were fishing that stretch of the English Channel which Cornish fishermen called the Dings and which lies some ten to fifteen miles due south of Kibble Head. It was a fine clear night with a brisk wind from the south east and the moon just entering her last quarter. With Brice and Clem Pascoe sharing the watch, the *Emmet* rode to her fleet of nets, rocking rhythmically on a sea that murmured busily to itself and slap–slapped against the boat's hull.

Brice and Clem stood in the bows, looking along the line of floats stretching away into the distance. In the bright moonlight they could see a large number of gulls gathered on the surface of the sea, all along the line of floats, and this was a sure sign that the herring were coming into the nets.

'We've found'm tonight, sure nuff,' Clem said, and put up his nose to sniff the air which was strong with the smell of fish–oil. 'I wonder how the rest are doing, you.'

Astern of the *Emmet*, away to the east, could be seen the lights of the rest of the fleet, like tiny stars in the distant darkness, Brice turned and studied them and saw that a few of the lights were on the move.

'Some of them are giving up. Four of five of them at least. So plainly *they've* got no fish tonight.'

'Poor souls,' Clem said, contentedly.

By six o'clock in the morning, the wind had freshened appreciably and there was a big sea running, causing the *Emmet* to roll badly. The assembled crew were now at work, shifting ballast in the holds and getting the bank-boards and roller in place, ready for hauling in the nets. They were all in high spirits, for they had let down a sample net and, having found it full of fish, knew they were in for a record catch.

'We've struck it rich tonight for sure. There's a herring in every mesh, very nearly, and all prime maties at that. And if we're the only ones that've found'm we'll be able to ask what price we please! We shall make our fortunes tonight, boys, and not before time, neither.'

Brice, though he shared their jubilation, was cautious in expressing it because, with the wind and sea as they were, he feared they would have a difficult haul.

By half past six, all was made ready; the men took a pause for food and drink, then put on their oilskins and big sea-boots; and, as the first light grew in the sky, prepared for the long task of hauling. Brice went forward into the bows and, lying back on the spring rope, began pulling the lugger close up to the nets. Clem Pascoe and Martin Eddy wound in the warp on the capstan and as the first net came splashing up out of the water, Billy Coit and Jacky Johns reached out with eager hands to ease it in over the roller.

A great many fish fell out of the net and rained down into the sea and the frenzied gulls, flapping and screaming, swooped on them and snatched them up. But the bulk of the catch was firmly enmeshed and at sight of the glittering silver mass the men gave vent to a shout of excitement. This was a splendid catch indeed and although Billy Coit

163

was in his sixties even he had to admit he had never seen anything like it before.

'If this is what the first net is like, how will it be with the rest?' he said, and Jacky Johns answered him, 'Billy, my handsome, tes three shoals in one!'

As the net was pulled in further, however, a change came over these two men, and over the rest of the crew, for, in spite of the heavy bags of ballast carefully stowed on the boat's port side, she was listing badly to starboard, pulled down by the weight of the nets. Billy Coit gave a shout and the capstan men stopped work at once but even so, such was the list, that when a big sea came rolling at them it broke clean over the gunwale, immersing the men for a moment or two and washing some of the fish from the net, sending them spinning and slithering all along the waterways.

Brice, his earlier fears not only confirmed but magnified a hundred times, hurried to join the two net-hands and, looking down at the laden net sloping so steeply into the sea, knew at once there was danger in it. He turned towards Billy Coit.

'Are you thinking what I'm thinking?'

'Yes,' Billy said, in a grim voice, 'we shall never be able to get them in.'

Ralph Ellis now came up with a face as black as a thundercloud.

'What do you think you're talking about? Of course we can damn well get them in!'

'The nets are too heavy. We've got too much fish. You can see what's happening to the boat.'

'Once we've got some fish in the holds, that'll soon steady her,' Ralph said.

'No, it's too dangerous,' Brice said. 'We shall have to cut away the nets.'

Another sea came rolling at them and again they shipped

it over the bow. The men bent their heads to it and when it had passed they stood in silence, shaking the water out of their eyes. Each, as he hung on to the nets, was sick to the heart with disappointment.

Every fisherman, being human, dreamt of taking a record catch that would put extra money into his pocket, but this night's catch was so big that instead of gain it meant heart-breaking loss. Their fleet of nets was one mile long and, with hundreds of thousands of fish enmeshed in them, formed such an enormous weight that if they attempted to haul them in the *Emmet* would almost surely capsize. All the men knew this. Ralph Ellis knew it as well as the rest. But the bitterness of the loss they faced made it a difficult thing to accept.

'Tedn just *your* nets you're talking about, tes ours as well!' he said to Brice. 'And two of mine were new this year!'

'Better to lose our nets than our lives,' Brice said.

'Skipper's right,' said Billy Coit, and Ralph Ellis turned away, kicking savagely at a fish that floated in the scummy water frothing along the edge of the deck.

So the *Emmet*'s nets were cut away and quickly sank to the bottom of the Dings and in a while, as the crew watched, large numbers of dead fish floated to the surface of the sea and were swooped upon by the ravening gulls. The men turned their backs on this sad sight and set about cleaning the boat, gathering up the few scattered fish and putting them into a basket. Bankboards and roller were stowed away, ballast was redistributed, and the punt was put back into place. They then heaved up the foremast, made sail and headed for home, and, having a good strong wind behind them, reached Polsinney at half past ten.

On the quay, as usual, the fish merchants and jowsters were waiting, but even before the *Emmet* berthed they could see that she had no fish in her. A few other boats lay at the quayside but they had all been unlucky too.

'They've all of'm come in clean so far,' one old jowster said to Brice, and Ralph Ellis, leaping ashore, said with spluttering anger: 'At least they've still got their nets, haven't they?'

He strode off towards the village, leaving Brice and the rest of the crew to explain the loss of their herring nets to the sympathetic crowd on the quay.

On his way home, an hour later, Brice called at his uncle's cottage, where the old man and Maggie were expecting him.

'I hear you cut away your nets,' Gus said without preamble. 'I've just had Ralph Ellis in here. He was feeling pretty sore.'

'We're none of us over the moon about it but it was something that couldn't be helped.'

'You are quite sure about that, I suppose?'

'I wouldn't have done it otherwise.'

'Ralph seemed to think different from you.'

'Yes,' Brice said tersely, 'he always does.'

'He said, if you'd only given it a chance, you could've got that catch aboard, or part of it at any rate.'

'Since when, might I ask, have you or anyone else taken any notice of Ralph?' Brice was suddenly very angry and, looking down at his uncle, he said: 'I've skippered the *Emmet* for thirteen years but perhaps you feel the time has come when you would like to make a change? If so I would prefer that you said so straight out in plain simple words!'

Gus made a gesture of impatience.

'Now you're talking plumb foolish,' he said. 'I'd back your judgment against Ralph's any day and well you know it. That's why I made you skipper in the first place – not because you're my nephew but because you're a first-class seaman. It just seemed, from what Ralph said, that you'd been a bit over-cautious, perhaps, when you decided to cut away.'

Brice, although mollified, would not for one instant agree with this.

'By the time we had known for sure, it would've been too late,' he said. 'Plenty of boats have gone that way.'

Maggie, who was standing nearby, now spoke for the first time.

'There's no such thing as being over-cautious,' she said. 'Not when men's lives are at stake.'

Gus looked at her for a while in silence. Then he looked at Brice again.

'Yes, well,' he said at last. 'You've made your point, both of you, and there's nothing more to be said. Except to discuss the nets, of course . . . How many are there in the store?'

'Five or six new ones, perhaps,' Brice said, 'and three or four old ones, but they're badly shrunk.'

'Then you'd better take the horse and cart and get what you need from Steeple Lumbtown. The sooner the better. Today if you can. Then Eugene can bark them this afternoon.'

Brice nodded and turned towards the door.

'I'll go straight away after breakfast,' he said.

The new nets were fetched and barked and put aboard the following Monday and that night, though their catch was small, there were few complaints from the crew.

'I shall never pray for big catches again,' Billy Coit said, shaking his head. 'Not after that strike in the Dings. I'm content to take what comes. I leave it in the hands of the Lord.'

Not all the crew were as philosophical as this. The loss of a whole fleet of nets, together with an exceptional catch, still rankled with Ralph Ellis and a few weeks later he left the *Emmet* to go as skipper in a new lugger built by John Lanyon of Penlaw. Brice was not sorry to see him go; there had been friction between them for years; and Ralph, now that he had been lucky enough to get a first-class boat like the *Bright Star*, was even disposed to be friendly, hailing Brice at the quayside and exchanging good-humoured banter with him.

'How're you getting along without me?'

'Oh, we muddle along, somehow.'

'Cut away any nets lately?'

'No, but I hear you lost your jib.'

'Ess, we had some old weather out there, fishing the Cowlings last night. – While you were skulking in the Chawls!'

Ralph's place in the *Emmet* was taken by Clem Pascoe's son Reg. Brice was well pleased with the change and so were his crew. And it happened that from that moment on, until the season ended in March, the herring catches were much improved.

Some weeks after the loss of the nets Maggie decided to speak to Gus about an idea that had lain in her mind for a long time: that he should, by process of law, make the *Emmet* over to Brice; but although she used all possible tact in putting forward her suggestion, Gus's reaction was hostile.

'Your conscience playing you up again, because you'll inherit my property?'

'Yes, I suppose you could say that. We've got so much, you and me . . . Not only of worldly goods, but so many other things besides . . . And over the boat it seems to me that you could afford to be generous.'

'I'm not in the habit of giving things away like that.'

'Not even to please me?'

'Why *should* it please you? That's what I should like to know. Because when I'm dead the boat will be yours and you want to spare Brice's feelings at having a woman employing him?'

'I wasn't looking so far ahead as that.'

'It can't be all that far ahead. I've lived thirteen years with this disease and that in itself is a miracle. But my luck can't hold out for ever and it's only right, I suppose, that you should look ahead a bit and make plans for the future.'

'I'm not thinking about the future. I'm thinking of now. Brice is your own kith and kin and if it hadn't been for me – '

'Brice has said often enough that he doesn't care tuppence for the property. Why don't you take his word for that?'

'But the boat is different, isn't it? The boat really means something to him – '

'Don't you think it means something to *me*?' Gus's anger now came to the boil. 'The *Emmet* is mine! My very own! Tommy Laycock built her for me and I sailed in her for thirty years. That's something you seem to forget!'

'Yes,' Maggie said, in a small voice, and was vexed with herself for her lack of wisdom. 'I shouldn't have tried to interfere. It was wrong of me. I see that now.'

Gus leant forward in his chair and poked the fire in the stove. It burnt up bright immediately and the red glow lit his bearded face. For a moment he sat watching the flames, broodingly, his face creased with thought. Then he dropped the poker into the hearth and leant back in his chair again.

'I don't need to give Brice the boat. He'll get it anyway in the end. *And* everything else as well.'

'What do you mean?'

169

'I mean, when I'm dead, you'll marry him. He will have everything then. Boat . . . business . . . cottage . . . wife . . . I daresay he've got it all worked out.'

'That's a terrible thing to say. Why do you say such terrible things? Brice isn't that sort of man at all.'

'Oh, it isn't so bad as I've made it sound, bearing in mind the important fact that he's been in love with you all these years.'

Maggie looked down at her hands, at the piece of needlework, so far untouched, that lay meaninglessly in their grasp. Absently, she turned it over; stared at it in a blank way; then allowed it to fall again. Gus watched her closely and shrewdly.

'You're not going to say, as you did once before, that all that was over years ago when he found out you were having a child? Because we both know that isn't true. Oh, he hides it well enough! He certainly never makes a fool of himself. But it's there all the same, no doubt of that, and if *I* can see it, so can you.'

'Even if what you say is true, I don't think we ought to talk about it, if only for Brice's sake.'

'Brice! Brice! Never mind about Brice! I *want* to talk of it!' Gus exclaimed. 'This is something that needs threshing out. We've always been honest with each other, you and me, and we must try and keep it so. That means facing up to facts.'

There was a long, difficult silence and in it he watched her consideringly. But at last, in a dry tone, he said:

'You'll run into some trouble, of course, when it comes to marrying him, owing to affinity. "A man may not marry his father's brother's wife." But you can always get round that. Others have done, often enough. The parson will soon sort it out for you.'

'It seems,' Maggie said, haltingly, 'that you've given the matter a lot of thought.'

'Yes, well, so I have. I want your happiness. You know that, I hope. So of course I've given it a lot of thought. Brice is a good enough chap in his way. He's grown up in the past few years. You'll be in good hands, married to him, and I've got no worries on that score. It will all work out well enough, I'm sure, once I'm dead and out of the way . . . I can see you together, plain as plain . . . and in my more Christian moments, I ask God's blessing on you both.'

Maggie tried to speak but could not, and he saw that there were tears in her eyes.

'No need to get upset,' he said gruffly. 'My Christian moments are all too rare and there *are* times when I'd damn him to hell. I know I've no right to be jealous, but I *am* jealous all the same, knowing that when I'm out of the way Brice will step straight into my shoes.'

'I wish you wouldn't talk like that.'

'I'm just facing up to facts.'

'But you've got no *cause* to be jealous of Brice, because I never think of him in that way.'

'Don't you?' Gus said, with a keen look. 'Are you certain sure of that?'

'I wouldn't lie to you,' Maggie said.

'Don't talk so foolish! Of course you would! You'd lie to me with your last breath if you thought it would only spare my feelings. And the lies would come easy to you because you believe in them yourself. Not that I have any claim on you – our marriage being what it is.'

'Those vows I made when I married you . . . they were not without meaning for me, you know, whatever sort of marriage it is.'

'You don't have to tell me that,' Gus said. 'You'll be a loyal wife to me, whatever it costs you, I know that. But it's hard on you all the same and I did you a grievous wrong when I married you and tied you down. You're a

171

young woman, not thirty yet. You've got warm blood in your veins – Jim is living proof of that – and with Brice always so close at hand, a handsome young man, devoted to you, you wouldn't hardly be human, else, if you hadn't come to feel something for him with the passing of the years. As for boy Brice himself, well, he's only human, too, and I can't say that I blame him if he wishes me out of the way.'

'You don't really think that, knowing Brice as you do?'

'I only know what I should feel if I was him,' Gus said. 'And that's something I'd like brave and well – a chance to change places with Brice. To be a strong man again and walk about on my own two legs. *I'd* soon show you a thing or two if I was in boy Brice's shoes, cos I couldn't suffer to stand by and see the one woman I loved tied to a useless old hulk of a man more than twice her own age. *I* should've upped a good while since and carried you off across the sea, to Jersey or Guernsey or some such place.'

'Would you indeed?' Maggie said. 'And supposing I didn't want to go?'

'If *I* was boy Brice, my girl, I'd damn well *see* that you wanted it! But that's Brice all over as he is. – Just enough sin in him to covet another man's wife but not enough to do something about it!'

'Why do you always speak of him in that disparaging way?' Maggie asked. 'Even when you say something good about him, it always comes grudgingly, with a sneer.'

'*You* won't grudge him nothing much, once I'm out of the way, will you?'

'Gus!' Maggie said beseechingly.

'Oh, I know, I know!' he exclaimed. 'I ought not to talk like that. It's hard for a young woman like you to understand an old man's feelings and you mustn't take too much heed of me if I burst out in a temper sometimes.'

'I suppose it's only what I deserve. I had no business

172

trying to tell you what to do with your own property and I can only say I'm sorry.'

'Yes, well, never mind, we'll say no more about it,' he said. 'It's over and done with and wiped off the slate. We've said what we think, both of us, and that's an end to it, once and for all.'

But that was not the end of it and during the next two or three days it became only too obvious that the matter was still very much on his mind.

It happened just then that the weather was bad and he was obliged to keep indoors. This always produced choler in him and now, in his present brooding mood, he would sit in front of the window, often silent for hours at a time, looking out across the harbour and watching the great wind-vexed seas breaking over the far quay-head. At meal-times, when Jim was present, he made some effort to talk, and whenever Maggie spoke to him he answered her readily enough; but his manner and tone were cold and abrupt and Jim soon noticed it.

'What's the matter with uncle Gus? Isn't he feeling too clever just now?'

'He's got something on his mind. I expect he'll get over it quite soon.'

But Gus's mood only got worse and, as always at such times, he was drinking heavily. It was something that worried Maggie and she felt she had to speak of it.

'Why do you drink so much? Dr Sam said it was bad for you and surely you've proved it often enough?'

'I shall drink as much as I choose! And if it kills me, so what of that? — You'll be your own mistress then and all your problems will be solved!'

'Oh, dear!' Maggie said, distressed. 'And all this has blown up because of what I said about giving Brice the boat.'

173

'Damme! That boat is mine! Why in hell's name should I give it away?'

'No reason at all,' Maggie said. 'I wish I'd never mentioned it.'

'Brice is her skipper. What more should he want? I'd change places with him like a shot if it meant I could go to sea again. And *I* wouldn't skulk at home days on end just because of a blow of wind!'

'It isn't only Brice,' Maggie said. 'All the boats have stayed in ever since the gale on Monday night.'

'No, not all of them,' Gus said. 'Two or three have been out since then.'

'Two or three mad ones, that's all.'

It was now early April; the long-lining season had begun; but strong south-westerly winds, coinciding with spring tides, had kept the fleet at home all the week. The skippers and crews could be seen on the wharf, shoulders hunched and caps pulled well down, sheltering from the worst of the wind in the space between the coopers' sheds; chatting together and smoking their pipes; constantly watching the sea and the sky and discussing every subtle change.

Brice was not among them because, however bad the weather, there was always something to do on the farm, and he was particularly busy just now, repairing the damage caused by the gales. So it happened that he did not come for his usual Saturday evening visit but came on Sunday afternoon instead. Maggie and Gus were alone together; Jim had gone to Sunday school; and the moment Brice walked into the kitchen it was plain that Gus had it in for him.

'Where did you get to yesterday?'

'I was mending the barn roof. We lost a lot of slates in last Monday's gale. The cowshed door was damaged too. I only finished repairs this morning.'

'Seems you're more of a farmer than a fisherman these days.'

'I'm afraid that's true,' Brice said. 'Not that I've got much cause to complain. It means I can catch up with all the odd jobs. But it falls hard on the crew when we lose so many nights in a row.'

'Shares worked out two and tuppence a man. None of them was best pleased at that. You'll find yours up on the mantelshelf there.'

Maggie, who was standing on the hearth, took down the money and gave it to Brice. He looked at her enquiringly, hoping for some guidance as to the cause of his uncle's mood, but there was little she could convey in a glance, beyond her own anxiety, and he turned away with a puzzled frown, slipping the money into his pocket.

'Don't spend it all at once,' Gus said, 'cos dear knows when the next lot'll be coming.'

'That's nothing new in fishing, is it, especially at this time of year? But luckily the weather is on the mend. The glass is rising steadily and now that the spring tides are slackening off I'm hoping with a bit of luck we shall maybe get out tomorrow night.'

'Wonderful! Wonderful!' Gus said. 'If you haven't lost the knack of it!'

Brice, trying hard to keep his temper, looked the old man straight in the eye.

'Would you have had us go out, then, in spite of conditions all this week?'

'Not for me to say, is it? You're the skipper, not me. I'm just the owner, no more than that. But a few boats did go out, didn't they, unless my old eyes were playing me false?'

'Four boats went out,' Brice said, 'out of a fleet of thirty-three.'

'Ralph Ellis was one, I believe, and even managed to get a few fish.'

'Yes, that's right,' Brice said, and this time it was his turn to be sarcastic. 'He got all of two stone of hake, I heard.'

'Better than nothing,' Gus said. 'More than *you're* likely to get, kiddling about up there on the farm.'

Brice, tight-lipped, walked to the door. He felt he had been patient enough. He paused and looked back at Maggie.

'It seems I'm not welcome here today so I may as well take myself off. I'm sorry I couldn't wait to see Jim. Tell him I ran into a squall.'

As soon as the door had closed on him Maggie rounded fiercely on Gus.

'Are you proud of yourself, I wonder, for driving him away like that?'

'You don't need to fight Brice's battles for him. He can stand up for himself. Else, if he can't, tes high time he could!'

'But he doesn't even know what it's all about!'

'Maybe you'd like to tell him?'

'Yes,' Maggie said, 'that's a good idea!'

She took her shawl from the hook on the door and went out into the wind.

Brice, having walked at a furious pace, was well on his way up the steep cliff road when Maggie, calling out to him, at last managed to make him hear. He turned in surprise and stood watching her but then, seeing her toiling up the hill, fighting against the boisterous wind, he began walking down towards her and they met just as an extra strong gust came in over the sea wall, bringing a skitter of spray with it.

For a moment she was unable to speak; wind and hill had defeated her; and she stood before him, quite breathless, giving a little choking laugh as she clumsily rearranged her shawl, pulling it tight over her head and twisting her hands into its folds so that the wind should not whip it away. Brice stood in silence, too. Under the peak of his close-fitting cap, his face was clenched in angry lines and there was still a look in his eyes that made them glint, a cold, hard blue, yet failed to hide the hurt in them. Maggie, seeing this look in his eyes, and the bitter lines about his mouth, felt the hurt in her own heart as though a knife had twisted there. At last she found enough breath to speak.

'You mustn't mind what Gus says to you. He doesn't mean it most of the time. It's just that he's – he's feeling under the weather these days.'

'Yes, the weather's to blame for a lot just now. If it doesn't let up pretty soon – '

'You won't take any risks, will you? You won't let him goad you into it?'

'Is that what he wants by any chance?'

'Oh, Brice!' Maggie exclaimed. 'I don't know which of you is the worst, you or your uncle Gus, for saying things you don't mean.'

'I can guess what things he says about me and I daresay he means them sure enough.'

'No, no, that's where you're wrong! It's only the mood he's in at the moment and I'm the one who's to blame for that.'

'You?'

'Yes. It's something I said.'

In a few words Maggie explained about her suggestion concerning the boat. Brice listened. He understood. But it did nothing to soften his mood.

'You certainly made a mistake there. What made you think that uncle Gus would ever do such a thing? The way he feels about the boat, he'd just as soon give his soul, and most seamen would feel the same.'

177

'I know! I know!' Maggie said. 'And oh, how I wish I had thought more clearly before speaking about it to him! But anyway, it's my fault, as you see. It isn't anything you've said or done and I wanted you to know that.'

Where they stood, on the narrow road that wound its way steeply up from the harbour and skirted the edge of the rising cliff, they were some half mile out of the town and it lay below them, grey in the wind, an irregular jumble of slate roofs and smoking chimneys, the houses and the narrow streets all sunk in their Sunday afternoon stillness and quiet.

But Polsinney, even on the Sabbath, was never completely deserted and down on the far side of the harbour, overlooking the fish–quay, a number of fishermen leant on the rail, gossiping and smoking their pipes and watching the luggers that curtseyed and bobbed, moored close together in the harbour pool. Outside the shelter of the harbour there was still a big sea running and although it was not yet high tide, the waves already covered the foreshore and reached as far as the undercliff, where they reared themselves up against the revetment, fifteen or twenty feet high, and sought to hurl themselves over the edge.

Brice turned and leant on the parapet and Maggie did the same. The wind was now full in their faces, blowing in from the open sea, and below them, at the foot of the cliff, the green and white water seethed and tossed. Brice glanced sideways at Maggie's face; then he looked straight ahead again, across the bay to Struan Point. A kind of angry detachment was slowly taking possession of him, and, in a spirit of defiance, he yielded himself up to it.

'It isn't just your idea about the boat that has made uncle Gus the way he is. It's because he knows I'm in love with you.'

Maggie remained perfectly still. She too was looking straight ahead.

'Did you *have* to say that?' she asked, and her voice, though quiet, was like a cry. 'Where is the *point* in saying that?'

'Foolish, isn't it?' Brice said. 'After keeping it secret all these years, to go and blurt it out like that! I suppose it's the sort of mood I'm in. – I'm taking my revenge on uncle Gus.'

'You mustn't think of him like that. I know he can be provoking sometimes, and he was specially so today, but surely I've explained why that was?'

'I've loved you all along,' Brice said. 'Right from the start, more than ten years ago, when you first came to us at the farm. I think you must have known that because I didn't try to hide it then.'

'Yes, I knew you felt something for me . . . but I thought it would change when you knew the truth . . . when you found I was having another man's child.'

'I thought so, too, but I was wrong. I soon found I loved you just the same and I could do nothing to alter it. I did my best to hide what I felt but I think uncle Gus has known all along. That's why he's always making these jokes about my finding myself a wife.'

'Yes, he knows,' Maggie said.

'Has he spoken about it to you?'

'Yes. Twice.'

'So you knew I still loved you, if only from him?'

'I did my best not to believe it. I hoped you'd find somebody else. But yes, in my heart, I knew all along.'

'No doubt my uncle Gus thinks it's a judgment on me because I did nothing to help you when my mother turned you out of the house. He's always despised me for that and of course he's right. I was a paltering, spineless fool. But God knows I've paid for that, over the past ten years, by loving you and longing for you and not being able to speak of it.'

'You are speaking of it now.'

'Yes, there's no going back on it now. Somehow there's relief in that.'

Still leaning over the parapet, he turned his head to look at her, and, for the first time in his life, allowed his feelings to show in his face, so that Maggie, when she met his gaze, found herself almost overwhelmed. Just for an instant their eyes held but then abruptly she bent her head and stared blindly down at the sea boiling over the rocks below.

'Brice, don't look at me like that. Please.'

'Why not?' he said harshly. 'What have I got to lose – now?'

'People might be watching us.'

'They're too far off to see us plain.'

'If you love me – '

'If! Dear God!'

'Then please don't make things difficult for me.'

'But you've known about it all along, so why should it be difficult now?'

'That's a foolish question to ask. Things are always more difficult once they're – once they're out in the open.'

'You'll put it out of your mind in time. That's what you did before. You'll say to yourself, "Poor Brice," and then you'll put it out of your mind.'

'No, I shan't. Not after today. That will be impossible now.'

'Why? Does it mean something to you, then?'

'That's another foolish question,' Maggie said impatiently. 'I'm a woman, not a stone, and to have a man look at me and speak to me as you're doing now – ' Her voice failed her. She took a deep breath. She was careful not to look at him. 'Of course it means something to me but it happens that I'm married to Gus.'

'You don't have to remind me of that.'

'No, I know I don't,' she said, 'but perhaps I have to remind myself.'

Her words, spoken so quietly, were almost drowned in the noise of the surf, but Brice heard them all the same. They were words that took him by the throat.

A big sea came running in, hurling itself against the cliff and rearing up in a great folding curve that licked its way up the granite wall and broke over the parapet. Brice and Maggie leant back on their heels but the spray caught them even so and they tilted their faces away from it, eyes closed while the stinging drops skittered and splashed over them.

The green and white wave curled back and sank, teeming at the foot of the cliff, and Brice and Maggie, standing together, their hands on the cold wet parapet, could feel the sea's mighty power pulsing vibrantly in the granite blocks. Brice turned and looked at Maggie's face; it was wet with spray, as though with tears, and he watched her as she wiped her cheeks with a corner of her knitted shawl; then he looked out to sea again.

'So,' he said, very carefully, 'if things were different and you were free, you would be willing to accept my love?'

'If things were different,' Maggie said, still in the same quiet voice, 'I would be in your arms by now.'

Another big sea came in and Brice watched it as though in a trance. Outwardly he was perfectly calm; his eyes were half-hidden under their lids and his face might have been carved in wood; and only by the quickening of his breath did he betray the tumult within as his heart leapt with the leaping wave.

The wave rose, higher and higher, climbing the wall with slow-seeming swiftness, and this time Brice and Maggie held their ground, letting the spray break over them, each glad of its cold sharp sting. They glanced at each other, blue eyes meeting grey, and then turned again into the wind; and so careful were they to keep their faces expressionless that nobody, seeing them there together, could have guessed what message had passed between them in that one quick, deep glance.

Brice felt that his lungs would burst and when, in a while, he spoke again, his voice was not quite under control.

'You chose wisely, didn't you, saying that here and now, in this public place where you are safe? Otherwise . . .'

'No,' Maggie said, firmly. 'There can never be any "otherwise". It must always be like this. And I didn't choose the time or the place. It was something that just happened to me. But always, in future, after today – '

'We must be as we were before. Do you think I don't know that? But what you've just said . . . you can't take it back . . . it's mine now till the day I die. But you don't need to worry, you know. When we meet, in the ordinary way, I shall keep my feelings to myself. I've had plenty of practice in the past. As for my uncle Gus, I know he has a down on me, but – '

'Brice, I must tell you something he said, only a few days ago, when I spoke to him about the boat. He was talking about dying – no, wait, let me finish – and he said he knew that when he was dead you and I were bound to marry.'

'He knows that you care for me, then?'

'He knew it before I did myself.'

'No wonder he hates me the way he does.'

'He doesn't hate you,' Maggie said. 'It's just that you're young and he's not. You can walk and he can't. And sometimes he thinks you wish him dead.'

'You don't think that?'

'Of course I don't. Neither does he, in his heart of hearts.'

Away in the town the church clock struck three.

'Brice, I must go. I really must. He'll be wondering what's become of me.'

'Maggie, wait,' Brice said. 'Maggie, I want you to understand – it's what I was trying to say just now – that I am not the sort of man . . . I mean, whatever I feel for you, and whatever I said about uncle Gus just now, I wouldn't ever do anything that would hurt his feelings in any way.'

Maggie smiled at him with her eyes.

'You don't have to tell me that. I know what sort of man you are.'

Drawing her shawl more closely about her, she turned and walked away from him, the wind now whirling behind her, sending her hurrying down the hill. Brice, resisting the impulse to watch her all the way down, leant further over the parapet and stared at the water seething below. The cold spray came up into his face and he tasted its salt tang on his lips.

'You haven't gone off with him, then?' Gus said as Maggie, coming in on a gust of wind, struggled to close and fasten the door.

'No, not yet!' she answered lightly. She hung her shawl up on its hook and faced him with a resolute smile.

'No, you wouldn't do that, would you, cos that'd mean losing all those things you married me on purpose to get?'

The extreme bitterness of these words drove the smile from Maggie's lips. She stood before him, silent and still, and he, seeing the look in her eyes and the way the colour drained from her cheeks, was suddenly stricken with angry shame.

'God! Why do I say such things?' he said in a voice that was wrung from him. 'And why do you always take it so meekly, without ever hitting back at me? I suppose it's because I'm a crippled old man and you can't help feeling sorry for me. But you shouldn't be so considerate and kind. You should damn well give as good as you get and let me have it hot and strong.'

'Well,' Maggie said, recovering, 'when I've thought of something, perhaps I shall.'

'Surely that isn't so difficult? There's plenty of things you could throw up at me that'd catch me amidships if you liked. You could scuttle me in no time at all.'

'Is it to be a sea-fight, then?'

'Damme! Why not? Tes what I deserve!'

Suddenly he waved his hand.

'For pity's sake sit down in that chair,' he said. 'You make me feel so small as a worm, standing over me like that.'

Obediently Maggie sat down, and they looked at each other across the hearth, the firelight glimmering in their eyes.

'Hadn't I better get the tea?'

'No, I want to talk to you.'

'Jim will be in presently.'

'Then I'd better get a move on with what I've got to say to you.'

For a little while longer, he looked at her. His mood of the past few days was quite gone. He could read a great deal in her face and because he knew her very well he could guess what had happened between her and Brice. It was only what he himself had foretold, after all, but now that it had come to pass and he saw the sadness of it in her eyes, he found he was able, once and for all, to put his own feelings aside and accept it without jealousy.

'I suppose you've sorted things out with Brice? Begged pardon for my bad behaviour and made peace with him on my behalf?'

'Well,' Maggie said, uncertainly.

'And I would say, by the look of you, that you got your own feelings for each other sorted out at the same time.'

Maggie, speechless, looked down at her hands.

'You don't need to feel guilty,' he said. 'It was bound to happen sooner or later and if it's happened today, well, I have only myself to blame. I drove you together, didn't I, by picking on Brice the way I did? And tes only where you belong after all. If anyone should feel guilty it's me. And I *do* feel guilty. That's just the trouble. Tes because my conscience is troubling me that I've been behaving the way I have.'

Maggie looked up.

'Why should your conscience be troubling you?'

'You know well enough what I mean. Tes because of what I've done to you. Such a mess I made of things when I tied you down all those years ago! I thought it was such a clever plan – to marry you and provide for you and learn Brice a lesson at the same time. I felt sure that you and him would come together in your own good time but I thought I'd be out of the way by then and that everything would go suant for you. But my clever plan went astray and here I am, still alive, nothing but a wretched hinderment, getting in the way of your happiness. But tesn't no good railing about it. We've got to schemey to put it right.'

There was a pause. He studied her.

'What I said to you just now, about you going off with Brice . . . that was just a bit of spite but I'm not being spiteful now . . . I've thought about it oftentimes and I reckon that's what you ought to do.'

'Go off with Brice?'

'That's what I said.'

'You surely don't mean it?'

'I surely do. Look at me! – I'm as tough as old boots! I could live to be old as Methuselah and what chance of joy will you have left by the time you've seen me into my grave? But if you and Brice and young Jim were to go clean away from here – Guernsey would be a good place to go – you could start a new life together there and nobody would ever know but that you and Brice were man and wife and boy Jim your son by him. Your name's Mrs Tallack right enough so you wouldn't have to tell lies about that. Twould all be as simple as ABC. And as for my bit of property, I should see Frank Rogers about that and come to some arrangement whereby – '

But here Maggie broke in on him.

'Do you think I would do that to you?' she asked in a tone of sad reproach. 'Go off and leave you alone like that, after all you've done for me?'

'I thought if you knew you had my blessing, you would find it easy enough.'

'No, it only makes an impossible thing even more impossible.'

'You mean, if I was to beat you, you would leave me soon enough.'

'Perhaps,' she said, with a little smile, 'but it's no good your beginning now, because I should know it was just a trick.'

'Perhaps I should have spoken to Brice, not you.'

'He would only say the same. You've told me often that Brice would always do what's right, so how could he ever treat you like that? And how could he ever leave his mother?'

'You and Brice should think of yourselves. You're still young, the pair of you, and got your own lives to live, but Rachel and me are both grown old, and if you and Brice've got any sense, you'll leave the dead to bury the dead.'

'And what about Jim in all this? What would he say to such a plan, that he and I should go with Brice to some strange place, goodness knows where, and leave you here all by yourself? It's out of the question. You must see that. It's so much out of the question that I don't know how you can talk of it.'

'So you won't allow me to set you free?'

'No, never,' Maggie said. 'I am your lawful wedded wife and you will just have to put up with me!'

'I suppose, if I was to tell you the truth, I knew all along what your answer would be.'

'Of course you did,' she said, gently scoffing.

'I had to say it all the same and if you should ever change your mind – '

'I shall never change my mind.'

'H'mm,' Gus said, and was silent a while, still looking at her intently as he pursued his own thoughts. At last he came to a decision. 'Well, if you won't let me set you free, at least there's one thing I can do. – Give Brice the boat, as you asked me to.'

'But I ought never to have asked you that. I told Brice I'd suggested it and he said at once that I had done wrong.'

'No, you did right. Tes a good idea. Oh, I know I've said this and that, and been dragging my anchor about it all, but that was the devil at work in me. I've been wrestling with *him* for days but I've thrown him brave and fitty at last. Why should I hold on to the boat? *I* shall never sail her again. Tes just my selfishness, no more than that. Much better fit if I give it to Brice and that's what I intend to do. – For *your* sake, since it's what you want, and for boy Brice's sake, too, so that he knows I mean well by him in spite of the way I treat him sometimes.'

'You've made up your mind, then?'

'Yes. Fair and square. I'll send for Frank Rogers first thing tomorrow morning. But I don't know what boy Jim will say when he hears I'm giving the *Emmet* away'

Jim, however, though surprised, showed nothing but pleasure on hearing the news and had only one question to ask.

'Uncle Brice will still take me into his crew just the same, won't he?'

'Of course he will!' Gus said. 'And if so be you should ever fall out with him, why, I'll build you a new boat of your own! – A bigger and better boat, even, than the old *Emmet!*'

The next day, true to his word, Gus sent for Frank Rogers, who came in the early afternoon and drew up the deed of gift whereby that lugger known as the *Emmet*, registered PY 19, with all her gear and tackle and everything pertaining to her, was given up by the present owner, Edward Augustus Tallack, and became the personal property, without let or hindrance, of the donor's kinsman, namely nephew, Brice Henry John Tallack; 'this gift being made in a spirit of goodwill, affection, and esteem; signed in the presence of witnesses this day, the twelfth of April, in the Year of Our Lord 1880.'

Chapter 8

The weather had improved during the night; the wind had gone round to the north, and although there was still plenty of sea, the waves were no longer breaking; and all morning, around the harbour, there was much bustle and noise as the lugger crews made ready for going to sea with the afternoon tide.

At half past two Brice and his crew were at the net-store under the sail-loft, loading their bait-nets and baskets of line onto a handbarrow, when Gus appeared in the cottage doorway and called Brice inside.

Brice, with the events of the previous day very much in his mind, entered the kitchen with mixed feelings, but, as he stood before Gus and Maggie, not knowing what to expect, he had little time to speculate, for the old man, without preamble, put the deed into his hands and bade him read it.

As he read the deed of gift, Brice was not only surprised but deeply moved, and when he looked at the old man he found it difficult to speak.

'I don't really understand.'

'No doubt you think I'm off my head. Nothing but needling yesterday and today I'm giving you the boat. You must put it down to senility.'

'Uncle Gus – '

'Never mind about thanking me. It's more Maggie's doing than mine. As you know, it was her idea, so she's the one you have to thank.'

'I thank you both,' Brice said simply.

Maggie was standing nearby; he knew he would have to

look at her; and just for a moment he was afraid. What had passed between them the day before was too disturbing, too immense, and he felt he would give it away in a glance. Yet when he did look at her, her gaze was so steady, so serene, that the weakness he feared he would betray passed completely out of him and he felt instead a renewal of strength, warm, quiet, reassuring.

Still, there was constraint all the same, and he was relieved when his uncle Gus suggested calling in the crew, to hear the news and to celebrate it 'with a nip of something warm.'

The crew were called and came clumping in, in their great stiff leather sea-boots. On hearing the news about the boat, there was a murmur of approval among them, and when a bottle of rum appeared, together with a proper number of glasses, there was only a modicum of protest, delivered for the sake of form. Being staunch Methodists, they were teetotallers to a man, but, as Gus dryly observed, were always willing, with a little persuasion, to set their principles aside.

'Seeing how tes a special occasion . . .'

'And a celebration, you.'

'Don't want to be a wet blanket, do us, and spoil it all for everyone else?'

'Not too much for me, skipper. Just to the top of the glass, that's all.'

'I'd like to give the toast if I may,' said Billy Coit, raising his glass. 'To the old boat – and her new owner.'

The toast was echoed with a warmth that took Brice by surprise. Plainly the crew were pleased for him. And of course, although it hadn't been mentioned, they were pleased for themselves, too, since it meant that in future the *Emmet*'s profits would be shared between six men instead of seven. The glasses were drained and put down. Gus leant forward and filled them again.

'So you're going out?'

'Yes,' Brice said. 'The whole fleet's going out tonight. We thought we'd try the Bara Breck.'

'Good place for pollack.'

'Yes, and hake.'

'Might even get the odd turbot there.' Gus cocked a bushy brow. 'I haven't had turbot for many a day.'

'Right. We'll see what we can do.'

Brice emptied his glass and set it down and the crew, catching his eye, did the same. Together they moved towards the door, each man nodding politely to Maggie, and young Reg Pascoe, staring at her, stumbled against a small stool. His father, Clem, apologized for him.

'Reg edn used to strong drink, you see, especially tip-top stuff like that.'

'Went down handsome!' Reg said with a grin.

'Straight into his feet,' said Billy Coit.

'He'll be all right when we get to sea.'

'Aw, that'll sober him up, sure nuff.'

Brice and his crew went back to their task of loading bait-nets and baskets of line onto the old handbarrow. The crew were all in good spirits; the rum ran merrily in their blood; they had an item of fresh news to pass on when they got to the quay; and in another few hours would be out at sea after fish for the first time in a whole week.

'This'll be a good trip for us, I seem,' said Martin Eddy, confidently. 'I can feel it in my bones.'

At three o'clock Brice went home to collect the big bag of provisions his mother had filled ready for him. He told her the news about the boat and gave her the deed of gift to read.

'Well!' she exclaimed, having read. 'To think that after all these years he's done something decent for you at last!' She laid the document on the table and put away her spectacles. 'And what about her? That wife of his? Does she know he's given you the boat?'

'Yes, it was Maggie's idea,' Brice said.

'Was it indeed?' Rachel said, and then, recovering from her surprise: 'Well, I suppose it's the least she could do, seeing she's robbed you of everything else.'

'Have you no charity in you at all? Do you still feel the same about her, even now, after all these years?'

Rachel looked at him long and hard.

'*You* still feel the same about her. It's just that your feelings are different from mine.'

'Yes, that's true, I love her,' Brice said.

'Does she know it?'

'Yes, she knows.'

'And does she care tuppence what you feel?'

'Yes, she cares more than I deserve.'

He slung his crowst bag over his shoulder, took up his oilskin smock and sou'wester, and left the house. Rachel followed him out through the yard; his tidings had given her food for thought; and at the gate she did her best to put her thoughts into words.

'If, as it seems, your uncle Gus is trying to make some amends for his meanness to you in the past, then I think perhaps it's only right that I should go down and call on him. In other words let me say, my son, that I am willing to do my own part in putting things right between us all.'

Brice looked at her with understanding. He knew what this speech must have cost her pride. And on an impulse of the moment he did a thing that was rare with him: he bent towards her and kissed her cheek. Then he went striding out of the gate.

When he arrived at the fish-quay he was hailed from all sides by the other skippers and their crews who had heard the news from Billy Coit. There was banter from some of them and especially from Ralph Ellis whose boat the *Bright Star* was berthed immediately next to the *Emmet*.

'So now you're owner as well as skipper? No wonder you look some pleased with yourself! But dunt that feel queer to be in a boat after sticking at home so long? Maybe you'd better follow us, else you might get lost in the bay!'

Brice merely flashed him a glance, jumped down into the *Emmet*, and stowed his gear away in the cuddy. He then went to help his crew, who were lashing the baskets of line to the bulwarks, for although there was only a slight swell in the bay, it would be a different matter 'outside'.

'We'll get it out off Burra Head,' Clem Pascoe observed to his son, 'and the motto on this boat is "never leave anything to chance."'

From all along the quayside now came the krik–krik of masts being stepped, the grunting of men as they strained at the falls, and the cheep–cheeping of blocks and pulleys as sails were run up and made secure. A flapping of canvas here and there; men's quiet voices talking, sometimes interspersed by a shout; and the first boats moved away from the quay, gliding towards the harbour mouth. No sweeps were needed today; they had all the wind they required; and first the *Speedwell*, then the *Swift*, followed by the *Sea Horse* and the *Minette*, passed out of the harbour into the bay.

The *Emmet* was the next boat out and Brice, at the helm, turning his head, saw Maggie and his uncle Gus and young Jim, just home from school, watching from the yard above the old quay. They waved to him and he waved back and his uncle Gus called out something that he failed to hear.

'He says to remember and bring him a turbot,' said Jacky Johns, who had sharp ears.

Behind the *Emmet* came the *Bright Star* and, the wind coming down hard upon them the instant they left the shelter of the harbour, they were soon beating swiftly across the bay, standing out on the first tack that would carry them past Struan Point. The *Bright Star* was keeping close – 'Too blamed close,' Clem Pascoe said – and Ralph Ellis, enjoying himself, wedged the tiller between his legs so that he could put up his hands and cup them about his mouth to shout.

'This'll take the creases out of your sails!' he roared, and then, as he bore away from them: 'I suppose you still know what a fish looks like? If not I'll draw you one on the slate!'

The *Emmet*'s crew, with fine dignity, swallowed these jibes and said nothing. And it happened quite soon that they had their revenge.

They were two hours south of Crockett Lighthouse, a distance of some fifteen miles, and the sun was going down dimly in a misty greyness that hid the sea-line. As it vanished from sight completely Brice gave orders to heave-to and here, with the early twilight settling about them, they shot their four drift nets for pilchards to use in baiting their lines.

As darkness grew they lit their lamps and all around them, mistily, other lights began to glimmer, showing the rest of the fleet strung out like a necklace of stars afloat on the sea. With the coming of darkness the wind had changed and now blew straight from the west. There was less tide now and the sea had settled to a slow swell.

Hauling took less than an hour and soon they were getting under way, beginning at once to cut up the pilchards and fasten the bits to the hooks on their line. Some of the fleet had already gone; most of the others were making sail; but a few boats still remained, having so far failed to get their bait, and the *Bright Star* was one of them. Brice, with a word to his crew and a touch of helm, altered course just enough to bring them within hailing distance of her and this was when they had their revenge.

'Not got your bait yet, *Bright Star*?' he asked.

'No, not a sniff of'm!' Ralph called back. 'But no need to ask if you've got yours, I suppose?'

'Yes, first shot, no trouble at all. Ten or twelve stone. Just enough and no more.'

'Where did you shoot?' Ralph asked.

'We shot where the fish were!' Brice replied, and aboard the *Emmet* as she went on her way there were chuckles of satisfaction because the score had been evened out and because surely, with such a beginning, the night was bound to go well for them.

Four hours' sailing brought them to the Bara Breck where, already, the sea was dotted with boats from Carnock, Polzeale, and Porthcoe. This meant that the Polsinney fleet had to press on, further west, and it was almost midnight when the *Emmet* at last found a berth, well clear of all other boats, and shot her line before the tide, which was now running from west to east.

By this time there was fog coming up, blowing in swirls before the wind, and the lights of the boats eastward of them were slowly dwindling and fading away.

'West wind, best wind, when fishing the Bara Breck, but why did it have to bring this fog?' Martin Eddy asked gloomily.

'Aw, you can't have it all ways,' Jacky Johns said, 'and there's fish down there, I'm sure of that.'

While they ate a bite of food and drank the hot tea Reg Pascoe had made they drew lots and settled the watch. It fell to the two Pascoes so Brice and the other three men made their way into the cuddy, stretched themselves out on their narrow bunks and, with the ease of long practice, fell asleep instantly, lulled by the motion of the boat rocking gently on the swell.

When they emerged, an hour later, they found that the fog had gathered and thickened. It pressed up into their faces in dense, blinding swirls and surged about them, impatiently, cold and wet and enveloping. The *Emmet* was completely enclosed, cut off from all other sight and sound of life except that every now and then there was a faint mew, mew, from the gulls that floated, unseen, on the sea around them. No other boats' lights were visible now. The fog had swallowed them utterly. Even their own masthead light could not be seen from below, and the big lantern on its spear amidships cast only the dimmest glow, in which the fog twisted and squirmed.

'Some old skew,' Clem remarked, as Brice and the others joined him. 'You won't have seen many worse than this.'

'No,' Brice agreed, 'it's as thick as cheese.'

'Thick as Grammer Opie's breath,' said Jacky Johns, close behind him. 'We shall need our magic specs on if we're to see the fish tonight.'

Dark shapes in the swirling fog, the crew came together around the lantern, shrugging themselves into their oil-skins and strapping on their sou'westers. There was no time wasted that night and they were soon ready to begin their task of hauling in the three miles of line.

'Tedn no night for hanging about,' Billy Coit said to Brice. 'We shall have some old job of it, as it is, getting home in this old skew.'

'I'm hoping it will have cleared by then.'

'No harm in hoping, I suppose.'

But although the wind blew steadily, keeping the fog on the move, it still came pressing up in waves, closer and denser all the time. It was like flannel, Billy said, and wrapped them round, cold as a shroud, in a silence as of the grave. Somehow the boat felt very small, shut in as it was by the fog, and every sound the men made as they prepared for the night's main work was muted and muf-fled and made unreal by the fog's close density.

The noise of the hatches being removed, the squeak of the capstan as it wound in the warp, and the tramp, tramp of the men's feet as they trudged stolidly round and round, all had a dim, dead quietness as though falling on ears gone deaf. And when, as the first length of line came aboard, bringing the first few fish, and the waiting gulls rose from the sea and came floating pallidly out of the darkness, the cries that issued from their throats were small and thin, almost pathetic, as though they were nothing but the ghostly echoes of cries they had uttered in the past.

By now the tide had turned again, thus lifting the line from the bed of the sea and making their task that much easier. Some lengths of line came in without any fish on the hooks but if this caused disappointment at least it meant less work. At the end of two hours the whole line was in and they had, at a rough estimate, a hundred and ten stone of fish. It was mostly skate and ray, with some conger, pollack, and dogfish, and a small number of cod and ling. There were also three sizeable turbot and these were carefully put on one side.

'Could've done better, could've done worse,' Billy Coit said to Brice. 'But tedn a bad catch, I suppose, for your first catch as owner, eh? At least it came in without a hitch and you've got the old skipper's turbot all right. He can take his pick of three.'

'Yes, we haven't done badly, all things considered,' Brice agreed.

The baskets of line were stowed away, blood and fish-slime were swilled from the decks, and hatches were replaced over the holds. Reg had been sent to make tea and was taking a long time over it and now that the others had finished their tasks they were beginning to grow impatient.

'Drat the boy! Where's he to with that tea? I reckon he've fallen asleep down there.'

197

'Tell him if he don't hurry up, we shall go without'n!' said Jacky Johns.

In his own good time Reg came and the men, now gathered in the stern, ate their food and drank their tea. The fog was just as thick as ever and nothing much could be seen beyond a distance of ten feet. It would be a difficult journey home and although they talked cheerfully enough they were acutely aware of it. Seamen feared and hated fog; it preyed on their nerves; and Billy Coit spoke for all when he said:

'Give me a gale of wind any time. At least you can *see* what you're up against then.'

The crew, as they ate and drank and talked, kept glancing towards Brice, who had lit the lamp in the binnacle and was closely studying the compass. They were aware of the tension in him; could sense the deep concentration of thought as he took his bearing and worked out his course; and they knew that all his faculties were keyed up to the highest pitch as he faced the task of getting them home. He, as skipper, would take the helm; on him would lie the responsibility of guiding them through the fog; and they knew what a strain that put on a man.

But they had complete faith in him. He had brought them through fog many times and never once in thirteen years had he failed to make a perfect landfall. He was like his uncle Gus in this. There was a particular quality to be found in certain seamen, as though they had some special knowledge, implanted in their very bones, and although it was a difficult thing to define, it was always quite unmistakable. Gus Tallack in his prime had had it, and Brice Tallack had it too. The *Emmet*'s crew recognized it in him; acknowledged it without question; and, to a man, put their faith in it.

Brice, having finished his deliberations, stood erect. He

finished his food and drank his tea. Although keyed up, his senses alert, he was at the same time perfectly calm, with the calmness of self-confidence, and, finding that his crew were watching him, he said:

'I'm setting our course east by north. That way we don't run any risk of overshooting Crockett Light.'

'Two man watch?' Billy enquired.

'Yes, and eyes well skinned,' Brice said. 'There's a good hundred sail of boats out there.'

'For as much as I can see tonight, I might so soon keep my eyes tight shut.' Billy, coming to stand beside Brice, tapped the glass on the compass-case. 'Tes a blessing that needle can see in the fog. I'd say we owe more than a groat or two to the man who invented the North Pole.'

'Cousin of yours, wadn he?' Clem Pascoe said sarcastically.

'Ess, that's right, on my mother's side.'

The men, chuckling, began to move, handing their empty mugs to Reg and piling their crowst bags into his arms so that he could take them below, and as they did so they teased him, telling him not to get lost in the fog.

'Think you can find the cuddy all right or shall us come with you to lead the way? Well, don't you fall asleep again, cos we'll want your help with heaving the mast. And remember, if you're gone too long – '

'Quiet! Listen! What's that?' Jacky Johns said suddenly, and turned his head, straining his ears to catch again whatever sound had come to him faintly out of the fog, over on their port bow.

All six men became very still, heads cocked identically, mouths fallen slightly ajar. Brice, standing with his hand on the tiller, listening for he knew not what, felt the cold, creeping sensation of hairs rising on the nape of his neck; but although he strained his ears to the utmost he could hear only the wind in the stays and the cheeping of the

199

halyard blocks. And he saw that the others were just as perplexed.

'I can't hear nothing,' Billy Coit said, in a hollow whisper. He turned sharply towards Jacky Johns.

'Hush! Listen!' Jacky said. He put up an urgent, imperious hand.

Suddenly it was heard by them all: a loud swishing noise, getting louder and nearer, coming at them from out of the fog; growing so loud that it filled their ears. Brice felt his head would burst with it; burst with the knowledge of what it meant; for the noise was of a great sailing-ship cutting swiftly through the water. And with the knowledge he found his voice.

'Look out, she's coming straight for us!' he roared. 'For God's sake save yourselves if you can!'

But even as he shouted his warning the oncoming ship loomed out of the fog, her tall masts, crowded with canvas, towering greyly over them. The six men cowered away, instinct making them throw up their arms, as though the great ship could be warded off. Her prow passed clean over them and her bows caught the *Emmet* broadside on. There was a terrible splintering crash, a screeching of wood against wood, and, as the *Emmet* broke in two, the loud, angry, sibilant rush of the sea pouring in between the halves and spreading out to engulf her.

Brice, jarred in every bone, was sent hurtling through the air, and his right shoulder, close to the neck, struck the toppling mizzen mast. Then he was in the cold churning sea and the waters were closing over his head. The pain in his shoulder and neck almost robbed him of consciousness but the cold shock of the seawater, sucked in at nose and mouth, flashed its message of danger at the centre of his brain and he fought his way up to the surface, spewing out water and gulping in air.

* * *

The great ship had gone on its way and in the tumult of broken water caused by its passing a few of the *Emmet*'s timbers and spars tossed and bobbed and clashed together, amidst a strewn-out tangle of cordage, amongst which floated a mass of dead fish that brought the gulls swooping in, no longer quiet, awed by the fog, but restored to their normal boldness, clamouring raucously in their greed.

The seething of the water gradually lessened, the sea flattened out and became smooth again, and a spar bumped gently against Brice's head. He got his left arm over it and, thus supported, trod water until he had managed to kick off his boots. Through the crying of the gulls he could hear the voices of his crew calling out to one another and as he paddled his way towards them he heard Reg Pascoe crying shrilly: 'Feyther! Oh, feyther! Are you there?' But he could not be quite sure whether he heard Clem answering.

A dark shape loomed out of the fog immediately in front of him and his heart gave a jolt as he saw that it was the *Emmet*'s punt, right way up, undamaged, and with two of his crew clinging to it, Martin Eddy and Billy Coit. He swam closer, let go of his spar, and reached up to grip the gunwale. He and Billy remained where they were, steadying their side of the punt while Martin splashed his way round and climbed in at the other side. He then gave them a helping hand, but as they clambered into the punt it canted over dangerously, shipping a fair amount of water and a few dead fish. Martin, splashing about on his knees, groped in search of the boat's dipper which, together with the rowlocks, was fastened with twine to one of the thwarts. He wrenched it free and got to work, bailing out water and fish.

Brice and Billy, peering into the fog, cupped their hands about their mouths and set up a long, loud halloo that scattered the rabble of squabbling gulls and sent them wheeling and crying overhead. There was an answering call from nearby and very slowly, out of the fog, came floating the punt's four oars, still lashed together in a bundle, and with Jacky Johns swimming beside them. They hauled him inboard, bleeding from a gash in his cheek, and then hauled in the oars. The rowlocks were slotted into place, the oars were untied and put into them, and the four men settled themselves on the thwarts. The two Pascoes were still missing but young Reg's voice, faint and despairing, could be heard not far away and in a short while they were pulling towards it.

To their surprise they found that the two shattered halves of the *Emmet* were still floating, only partly submerged, a space of fifteen feet between them, but tethered together and borne up by a great tangle of nets and cordage and by the floating mizzen sail which, still attached to its splintered mast, lay out flat on the sea's surface. And in the midst of this terrible tangle, made worse by the fishing line floating in coils out of the baskets, they found Clem Pascoe and his son.

Clem was caught up in the coils of line and young Reg, with a knife in his hand, was desperately trying to cut him free; but in their frantic struggle together they had become more and more embroiled, the line coiling itself about them, the barbed hooks sticking in their clothes and their flesh; and all about them, as they struggled, the screaming gulls flapped and swooped, gorging themselves in a frenzy of greed on the dead fish floating everywhere. Reg, with sobs of fear and frustration, hit out at them with wide sweeps of his arm, for in their frenzy the ravening gulls took so little heed of the two men struggling in the water that they kept buffeting them with their wings.

Father and son were close to exhaustion, but strong hands now reached out to them, the tangle of line was cut away, and they were hauled safely into the punt. For a time Clem lay on the boards, his whole body shaken in spasms as he fetched up water from stomach and lungs, helped by Billy Coit who was squeezing his sides. Then, at last, it was over; Clem gave a protesting groan, humped himself over onto his back, and raised his head to look about him.

'Are we all here?' he asked weakly.

'Ess, one and all,' Billy assured him.

'I thought my last hour was come.'

'So it would've done, sure nuff, if it hadn't been for boy Reg.'

Clem, with an effort, struggled up and was helped to the seat in the stern. The other men resumed their places, unshipped the oars, and, with cautious strokes, because of the tangle, began pulling away from the wreck. It was scarcely a moment too soon, for the two halves of the *Emmet* were now sinking rapidly.

When they had got well away from danger, and well away from the noise of the gulls, they took a rest and leant on their oars, allowing themselves not only a breather but time to absorb what had happened to them. In silence they followed their own thoughts. Then Billy Coit spoke.

'To think that a great smart ship like that should come all the way from America just on purpose to run us down!'

'She've certainly made a good job of it!' Jacky Johns said bitterly. 'And where was her look-out, I'd like to know?'

'Think she'll come back and look for us?' Reg Pascoe asked.

'Not she! Oh dear me no! All these merchantmen think about is getting where they've got to get and God help those who get in their way. Anyway, if they did come back, they'd never find us in this fog.'

'Anyone see what she was called?'

'Don't talk so soft as you are, boy. Wadn no chance of seeing that.'

'She must've got some damage, surely, sheering clean through us like that.'

'Ess, I daresay, and serve her right.'

'Poor old *Emmet*,' Billy said. 'She was a good old boat to us. She didn't deserve to end that way.' He turned his head and spoke to Brice. 'Only yesterday she was given to you and now, this morning, she've been taken away. Tes some queer old mysterious job, the way things belong to be sometimes, and I don't understand it at all.'

'No more do I,' Brice said.

'The old skipper'll have something to say when he hears she've been all scat up like that.'

'My uncle's first concern will be to ask what shape her crew are in.'

'Well, you can tell him we're middling, then.'

'Ess, that's right,' said Jacky Johns. ''Twill take more than a barquentine to sink us old Polsinney boys!'

'I could do with a change of clothes, mind,' Billy Coit said wistfully.

'You can change with me and welcome,' said Clem Pascoe's voice from the stern.

'I'm sticking to mine,' Martin Eddy said, ''cos when the water inside'm gets warm, that'll keep me warm as well.'

'You're right there, Martin, sure nuff. Edn nothing like saltwater for keeping you warm, I believe.'

'Or for bringing you up in boils.'

'Or for drowning you,' Reg Pascoe said.

'You haven't been drowned yet, have you, boy?'

'No, just practising for it, that's all.'

Sitting hunched in the open boat, coldly blanketed by the fog, the six men, by joking together, defied the danger they were in and sought to keep their courage alive in a mixture of faith and obstinacy.

Underneath their oilskin smocks, their sodden clothes were icy cold upon flesh that cringed and shrank on the bone, and each man had to fight, with all the willpower at his command, to still the spasms that swept over him and brought teeth clicking together in rigor-clamped jaws. All of them had lost their sou'westers and all except Clem Pascoe had kicked their boots off in the sea. But at least they were still alive; at least they had the punt and the oars; and if they had been spared this much, surely they could hope for more? And so gradually, by degrees, and always with a touch of grim humour, they came to a discussion of their plight.

The *Emmet*, when they had shot their line, had been seven hours south west of Crockett Light and had made eight knots almost all the way. So now, in the little twelve foot punt, they were more than sixty miles from Burra Head, their nearest landfall; had no compass to guide them, nor any glimpse of the stars; and were on a westward going tide which would not turn for another two hours.

Their only present guide was the wind, which had blown all night from the west. But if it changed – and it probably would – they could, as Billy Coit said, row themselves to Kingdom Come 'and be none the wiser in this skew'. But row they must, to keep themselves warm, and, being all of one accord, they brought the boat cautiously round till the oarsmen had the wind in their faces and Clem had it on the back of his neck. The boat rose and fell on the long-backed waves and the oars creaked and splashed in unison.

'Good practice, this, for the June regatta.'

'Ess, so long as we get there in time.'

'What are the chances,' Reg Pascoe asked, 'of coming up with one of the fleet?'

'What do you think they are?' Jacky Johns asked.

'Well,' Reg said, and gave it some thought, 'there's a brave lot of boats out here, counting the ones from Carnock and all.'

'Ess, and a brave lot of open sea, too.'

'Not much hope, then? Is that what you mean?'

'There's always hope, boy,' said Billy Coit.

They pulled for a time, then took a rest; pulled again and rested again; and when they rested they shouted together, sending a long hallooing call, hopefully, into the fog. But fog and darkness swallowed their shout and all that came back to their listening ears was the cold heave and surge of the sea.

'Nobody home, seemingly.'

'No, not even Sally Quaile.'

'I keep thinking about my crowst. I was saving the best to eat going home. Now they old gulls will've had it all.'

'There's a few fish down here, somewhere, floating about round my feet.'

'Ess, and we might be glad of them, some time before we're done.'

'Raw?' said Reg Pascoe in disgust.

'Aw, you're some faddy, boy!' Jacky Johns said.

They pulled again, two hundred strokes, and Brice counted them to himself. The pain in his shoulder and neck had grown intense and the upper part of his arm was swollen, filling the sleeve of his guernsey so that it pressed tight and hard on his flesh; and although he shared his oar with Reg Pascoe, the effort it cost him was such that the sweat poured from his forehead and dripped down into his eyes; and this time, when they stopped for a rest, he was glad to yield his place to Clem, who, perceiving the pain he was in, crept quietly from the stern and edged him off the thwart.

'You sure you're all right now?' Brice asked.

'Ess, fitty,' Clem said, 'but could as a quelkin, just about, and got to do something to warmy myself.'

Brice, now sitting in the stern, took off his oilskin smock and dipped his arm in its tight guernsey sleeve into the cold sea water, leaning over to plunge it in right up as far as the armpit. This brought him some relief, the coldness gradually quenching the fire that raged up and down his muscles; and when, in a while, the arm became numb, he withdrew it, dripping wet, and shrugged himself back into his smock.

The men began pulling again; the oars creaked hollowly; and the fog licked and curled about the small boat as though trying to devour it.

They had hoped, with the coming dawn, that the fog would lift and clear away, but instead it persisted, thick as ever, so that even when daylight whitened the sky, the sun itself remained in recession, yielding no trace of its orbit to guide the watchers in the punt.

'The fleet'll be on their way home by now.'

'So are we on our way home. Tes just that we're more behinder than they.'

'Tes all very well saying that,' said Reg Pascoe despondently, 'but in this durned old blinding fog we don't even know for sure whether we're even going the right way.'

'No, that's perfectly true, my son. We can only hope for the best and maybe say a word of prayer.'

To some extent they lost count of time but when at last the fog did lift they saw by the height of the sun in the sky that it was well after ten o'clock. To their dismay they saw, too, that the wind had gone northerly and they watched as the fog drifted before it, rising to form a dusky bar that gradually fell away to the south.

As the pale daylight grew they searched the sea with hungry eyes; with gaze that ranged about swiftly at first, skimming impatiently over the surface and all around the clearing skyline; but then more slowly, meticulously, searching the dark patches of sea as well as the light, watching every rise and fall, always hoping that out of some trough a sail would be revealed to them. But there was nothing. Not a sign. From one horizon to another they had this stretch of the sea to themselves. And those horizons were utterly bare. There was no slightest smudge to suggest a landfall.

'Silly, I know,' said Billy Coit, in a voice grown husky with tiredness and thirst, 'but when that old fog began to clear, I thoft to see Crockett just over there and Burra Head rising handsome behind it.'

'I was the same,' said Jacky Johns, 'only I thoft to see the *Ellereen* or maybe the old *Betty Stevens*, perhaps, cos they were the last two boats we passed before we got a berth of our own. But there, twas only a foolish dream and I did know it all along, cos the fleet'll be just about nearly home by now. Twas all a sort of mirage in my mind. Wishful thinking, as they say.'

The men's disappointment was bitter indeed; their screwed-up faces were grey with it and had a shrivelled, defeated look; but in their eyes as they scanned the sea there was at the same time a steely glint, showing keen minds at work, weighing up the odds against them. Tired men, chilled to the bone, out in a small open boat in the Channel, without food or water, unable even to tell how far they were from land: they knew only too well what peril they were in; and yet about each man's mouth there was a certain grim twist that seemed to say to the sea: 'You have not seen or heard the last of me yet!'

'Anyone like to guess where we are?'

'A pure way from home, I can tell you that.'

'I fancy the Bay of Biscay myself.'

'Why, have you got a cousin there as well?'

'Ess, that's right. Cousin Frog, he's called.'

'Jacky, you're nearest. – Give Billy a clip.'

'We're certainly too far south and west. We took a wrong turning somewhere back there.'

'That old wind played us false, going about like that,' Billy said. 'I knowed it would, sure as fate, but I can't forgive'n all the same, cos that've put another few miles between us and the breakfast we deserve.'

'Breakfast!' Reg Pascoe said hollowly, and looked with loathing at the dead fish lying in the scummy pool at his feet. 'We shall miss more than our breakfast, I seem, before we make harbour and home again.'

'Yes,' Brice said, still scanning the sea, 'we've got a long pull in front of us.'

But at least they now had the blessed daylight and could take a bearing from the sun, and this they now proceeded to do, debating the matter quietly and pooling the knowledge of many years. Together they then studied the waves, which, with the wind obliquely behind them, were just beginning to break a little, curling delicately at the crests. The tide was now running from west to east, which meant a strong drift southward, and to counter this they judged it best to set their course north east by east. And so, guided by the sun and the set of the sea, they brought the punt gently round and, at a word from Brice, began once again to straighten out.

While they were easing the boat round, one of the long, low-backed waves came at them in such a way that they shipped the top of it over their bows and as the water swirled round their feet, Brice reached for the dipper and bailed it out. He had to use his left hand, for his right arm had stiffened completely, all the way from shoulder to wrist.

'Can you manage all right, skipper?' Clem Pascoe asked.

Brice, sitting up again, made a wry face.

'This is all I'm good for,' he said.

'Well, we're bound to get a few more of those, so you won't lack employment, you may be sure. Anyway, tes *your* job to keep us clean on our proper course.'

'Keep a look-out for ships, boys,' Jacky Johns said hopefully. 'Any old sort, it don't matter which, so long as there's Christian men in them.'

They needed no telling; their eyes were skinned; but even if they spotted a ship, what were their chances, young Reg asked, of being seen in this small craft, sitting so low in the sea, without any sail sticking up from her?

'Chances, my son? Only God knows that. Tes up to us to have faith in him. But if the worst should come to the worst, well, our chaps'll be out again tonight and *they'll* be looking out for us. Trouble is, twill be dark then, and if we get another foggy night – '

'Seems to me,' Reg said, 'we'd better put our backs into it.'

As the sun rose in the clear sky the men lifted their faces to it, gratefully, this way and that, so that the faint warmth of its rays should play over their stiffened skin and penetrate their weary flesh. But gratefully though they lifted their faces, the sun's faint, teasing warmth only made them more keenly aware that their bodies were chilled through to the bone, and when they gazed out over the sea they felt its unending coldness and greyness flowing in their very veins.

Shivering, they bent to the oars.

Chapter 9

On the quay at Polsinney that Tuesday morning, the fish merchants and local jowsters had resigned themselves to a long wait, for the fog lay thick on the sea and at ten o'clock showed no sign of clearing. By half past ten it was shifting, however, and soon the greater part of the fleet could be seen, lying-to outside the bay, waiting until it should be safe enough to venture close inshore. By eleven o'clock the fog had quite gone, the April sun was shining thinly, and the first boats were drawing in to the quayside.

Gus, sitting out in the yard, watched them through his spyglass. *Speedwell. Trelawney. Ellereen. Cousin Jacky. Samphire. Sea Breeze.* These were the first boats to come in and each had its escort of hovering gulls, showing that the fishing had been good that night. He saw Bob Larch of the *Ellereen* throw a good-sized dogfish to Dicky Limpet on the quay and, watching Dicky's wild efforts to catch and keep hold of his slippery prize, he quietly joined in the laughter that floated across the harbour pool.

At half past eleven Maggie brought him a mug of cocoa. She stood looking across at the fish-quay, where the boats were now berthed two and three deep.

'Has the *Emmet* got a good catch?'

'The *Emmet* haven't come in yet.'

'Not come in?' Maggie said. She put up a hand to shield her eyes and looked out across the bay. 'It isn't like Brice to lag behind.'

'He's not the only one late in today. There are quite a few to come yet. The fog must've been pretty bad out there.'

211

Gus swung his spyglass round until he too was looking across the bay. Four boats were rounding Struan Point. The spyglass dwelt on each in turn.

'Is the *Emmet* among them?' Maggie asked.

'No,' he said.

He put the spyglass into his lap, took the mug of cocoa from her, and blew on it with noisy breath.

'They seem to have had a good fishing last night. *Speedwell*'s got a pretty good catch. So have *Trelawney* and *Ellereen*. And I heard Watty Grenville shouting the odds that he'd got half a stone of turbot aboard.'

'Then there's a good chance that Brice will have got a turbot for you.'

'If he haven't,' Gus said, 'I shall have something to say to him!'

Maggie went back indoors, leaving Gus sipping his cocoa. But the instant he knew he was alone he put the mug on the bench beside him and took up his spyglass again. Two more boats had appeared off the headland, *Maid Molly* and *Little Hob*, and these were soon followed by three more, *Betty Stevens, Pintail* and *Swift*. Gus gave an anxious sigh and counted the boats in the harbour pool. All except the *Emmet* were accounted for. Once again he looked out to sea.

When next he picked up his mug of cocoa, it had gone quite cold. He emptied most of it onto the ground. And then, as he moved to set down the mug, he saw that Maggie had come to the door again and was standing quietly watching him.

'You're worried about them, aren't you?'

'Yes,' he said, 'tes time they were in.'

'You think they've missed their way in the fog? Gone aground somewhere, perhaps, like the *Samphire* did last year?'

'Any skipper can miss his way in bad fog but I've never

known Brice to do it yet. Even the *Maid Molly* is in and if Sam Cox can make harbour any fool can!'

The *Maid Molly* had now come into the harbour and, there being no room at the quayside itself, she was berthing beside the *Shenandoah*. Gus, through his spyglass, was watching her, and he saw that her skipper and crew, instead of setting to work at once to unload their catch, were talking to the men on the other boats. They then crossed the *Shenandoah* and stepped ashore, and something in the way people gathered, coming from all over the quay, confirmed the old man's growing fears. He closed his spyglass with a click, thrust it down into the chair, and swung himself round to face Maggie.

'Wheel me down there, will you?' he said. 'Something's happened. Something's wrong.'

They were seen coming, of course, making their way round the harbour road, and as they turned onto the fish-quay, Sam Cox and his crew, with a number of other fishermen, came forward to meet them. Their faces showed that they had bad news. There was some con-straint among them and all looked towards Sam Cox. Sam carried something in his arms, which he laid on the ground in front of Gus. It was one of the *Emmet*'s hatches. It bore the number PY 19.

Gus, in silence, looked up at Sam, and Sam, haltingly, told his tale. They, like the rest of the fleet, had been out fishing the Bara Breck. They had started for home at five o'clock and at half past five, still in thick fog, they had found themselves amongst the floating wreckage of what they judged to be a fair-sized lugger.

'There were broken timbers and spars and all sorts, bobbing about everywhere, and there were a few baskets, too, with the lines all trailing out of them, so we knowed twas a fishing boat straight away. Then we got the hatch

213

inboard and there was her number painted on it. That told us who she was. The old *Emmet*. PY 19.' Sam paused. Cleared his throat. 'Seems she was run down,' he said, 'and that must've been a pretty big ship, cos some of those timbers had been smashed right through.'

Gus and Maggie both stared at the hatch and its white-painted number, PY 19, but what they each saw, in their mind's eye, was the helpless lugger at sea in the fog and the six men caught up in that moment of horror as the ship came at them to smash and destroy.

Maggie still stood behind Gus's chair and he turned himself round to look at her. Pale with shock, she met his gaze and then, with eyes full of pain and pity, she looked towards a group of women standing nearby, at the edge of the crowd. These were the women whose menfolk made up the *Emmet*'s crew and they had already been told the news. Martin Eddy's young wife, scarcely more than eighteen and soon to give birth to her first child, stood with the tears streaming down her face, and the older women, no less stricken, were gathered about her protectively.

Gus began questioning Sam Cox.

'I take it you didn't find any bodies?'

'No. We'd have brought them home if we had.'

'What about the *Emmet*'s punt? Was that broken up along with the rest?'

'I don't know. Tes hard to say. Everything was so scat to bits – '

'Easy enough, I should've thought, to tell bits of lugger from bits of punt.'

'We didn't *see* no sign of the punt, neither whole nor in bits,' Sam said, 'but more than likely she was sunk.'

'What makes you say that?'

'On account of how everything looked.'

214

'Did you search around at all?'

'Ess, we did. Of course we did. But what with the fog being so bad, there wadn no chance of seeing much.'

'What time did you say that was?'

'Half after five, near enough.'

'Daylight, then.'

'Just about. But what with the fog being so bad – '

'If you had waited for the fog to clear, you'd have stood a better chance of seeing something.'

'Ess, we might've done, I suppose. – If there'd been anything to see. But us should have had some good long wait cos that didn't clear till well after ten and we'd got a catch of fish to get home.'

There was a silence after this and the *Maid Molly*'s crew looked uncomfortable. One of them, Amos Saundry by name, muttered something under his breath. Then Sam Cox spoke again.

'That was a nasty shock to us, finding the *Emmet* wrecked like that, and we all thought the best thing was to come on home as fast as we could and let folk know what had happened to her.'

'No wonder bad news travels fast,' Gus said. 'Tes because people like you are always in such a hurry–all to spread it around. But if only you had waited a while you might've brought good news instead of bad.'

'What good news?'

'You might just have found the punt and maybe the crew alive in her.'

'I understand how you d'feel, Gus Tallack, but if you'd seen that wreckage for yourself, and the way those timbers were splintered and smashed, you wouldn't pin much faith on the punt coming out of it in one piece.'

'If you'd had a nephew on board of her, you'd pin your faith on *anything*.'

'Tedn fair to say that,' said Sam Cox, 'cos Brice was

always a good friend to me and Jacky Johns was my brother-in-law.'

'Was? Was?' Gus exclaimed. 'You said you didn't find any bodies.'

'No, that's true, there wadn no sign – '

'Then how do you know they're not alive?'

Sam Cox shifted uncomfortably and his glance kept straying, in a meaningful way, towards the missing fishermen's wives who had drawn close and were listening.

'Seems to me you do wrong to raise poor people's hopes like that.'

'Don't worry about us,' Betsy Coit said to him. 'If there's any hope at all, we d'want to know about it. And the next thing we d'want to know is – what is there to be done about it?'

'Well, I reckon the first thing we should do,' said Tommy Bray of the *Ellereen*, 'is to send a message round to Polzeale for the lifeboat to go and search for them.'

'I've got a better idea than that,' said another voice from among the crowd, and Ralph Ellis of the *Bright Star* elbowed his way forward until he stood in front of Gus. 'Why waste time sending round to Polzeale when we can send a boat ourselves?'

'What boat had you got in mind?'

'The *Bright Star* of course.'

'You mean you're willing to go out and search?'

'That's what I mean, sure nuff, and I speak for my crew as well.'

'Why you more than anyone else?'

'First, cos the *Bright Star*'s a good fast boat. Second, because when we went out last night, we didn't manage to get our bait. We shot three times without a sniff and at midnight we decided to come back home. So we're all fresh men – we slept in our beds – and we haven't got any fish to unload.' There was a pause and then Ralph said:

'Besides, they're all old shipmates of mine, and I know they'd do the same for me.'

'How soon can you be ready to go?'

'Twenty minutes. No, say half an hour. We shall need to put plenty of food aboard – '

'Then we'd better get a move on, I seem.'

'We?' Ralph said.

'Yes, I'm coming with you,' Gus said.

News that the *Emmet* had been lost at sea was already spreading fast and as Maggie and Gus returned home they were watched by little groups of people who had gathered along the harbour road. One or two tried to question them but Gus gave only the briefest answers and ordered Maggie to wheel him on.

On entering the cottage kitchen, Gus went straight to the cupboard under the stairs and got out his old white oilskin smock and sou'wester, his old brown leather sea-boots, and two big hessian bags which he handed to Maggie. Into one bag, as instructed by him, she put all the food the larder offered, together with two bottles of rum; and into the other she put blankets and shawls and all Gus's spare warm clothes.

While they were thus occupied the door burst open and Jim came in. He had heard the news on his way home from school. He looked at Gus with anguished eyes.

'Do you really think they might be alive? Out there somewhere? In the punt?'

'I don't know, boy. I aim to find out.'

'You're going out in the *Bright Star*?'

'Yes.'

'Can I come with you?'

'No,' Gus said. 'You must stay at home and look after your mother. But there *is* something you can do.'

'What?' Jim asked.

'We haven't got nearly enough food and I want you to go to Mrs Beale's.'

Gus, busy with pencil and paper, wrote these brief words: '1 Whole Cheese. 4 Quartern Loaves. Butter for Loaves. Jar of Jam.' He gave the note to boy Jim and found him another hessian bag.

'Don't bring the things back here. Take them straight down to the quay. I want you to be as quick as you can, so don't let anyone hinder you.'

For an instant the boy hesitated. There were things he wanted badly to know. But then, with a nod, he turned and ran.

Gus was now ready to go. The two heavy bags lay close to his chair. He gave a little sign to Maggie and she lifted them into his lap where, already, his oilskins and boots were stowed together in a bulky bundle. She stepped back and stood looking at him.

'Gus, is it wise for you to go?'

'You want me to find Brice, don't you?'

'You're not really fit,' Maggie said. 'And you haven't been to sea for years. Leave it to the crew of the *Bright Star*.'

'Brice is my nephew. My own kith and kin. I *belong* to go out and look for him. And if he's out there, still alive, I swear by Almighty God I shall find him and bring him back to you. As to my being fit, I'm just about as strong as a horse! Tes just that my legs aren't much use to me and that won't matter much in a boat.'

'You're an obstinate man.'

'Yes. Maybe.'

'You *will* take care?'

'Be sure of that.'

'Very well. I'll wheel you down.'

When they returned to the fish-quay, they found that two or three boats had moved, thus making room for the

Bright Star at the farthest end of the quay, the best place for getting away. The mast had been stepped and the sails hoisted and Ralph Ellis and his crew were carrying casks of fresh water aboard, together with the blankets, clothes and provisions which Betsy Coit and the other *Emmet* men's wives were hurriedly bringing to the quayside. Ralph Ellis's wife was there, too, and so were the wives of some of his crew; and altogether such a crowd had gathered at the far end of the quay that Jim, arriving with his bag of provisions, had difficulty in getting through.

Just after one o'clock Pony Jenkin, the *Bright Star*'s first hand, lifted Gus from his wheelchair, carried him aboard in his arms, and put him to sit on a straw pallet placed on a coil of rope in the stern. In another few minutes the boat had cast off; there was a regular creak and splash as her great sweeps were brought into play; and, with the floodtide strong against her, she was moving slowly and cumbrously towards the narrow harbour mouth. Maggie lifted a hand to wave and Jim beside her did the same. Gus touched the peak of his cap in response, then turned his bearded face to the sea.

The watching crowd were almost silent, perhaps because many people there felt the boat's mission to be forlorn, but as it slowly drew away, Betsy Coit, at the quayside, called after it in a clear voice that carried across the harbour pool.

'The Lord bless you, *Bright Star*, and grant you find our men alive.'

And everywhere along the quay the voices of two or three hundred people, who had heard Betsy Coit's prayer, quietly said 'Amen'.

For a while longer the crowd remained, watching as the *Bright Star* moved from the harbour into the bay and stood out to sea. Then people began to disperse; the fishermen returned to their work of unloading their catches; a few jowsters, already supplied, drove away in their carts. But one fisherman, Matthew Crowle, came over to where Maggie was talking to Betsy Coit and the three other *Emmet* wives.

'Tedn only the *Bright Star* that'll be looking out for that punt,' he said. 'Tes all of us. The whole fleet. We'll be out at the Bara Breck again tonight and we shall be sailing well spread out so that if she's there we shall surely see her. Of course it'll be dark by the time we get there and if there's fog like there was last night we shan't see nothing at all. But tomorrow we shall wait till it clears – we're all agreed on that – and we shall be keeping a sharp look-out. The whole lot of us. One and all.'

He touched his cap and walked away and Maggie, absently watching him, found herself thinking of Rachel Tallack. She turned to speak to Betsy Coit.

'Has anyone seen Mrs Tallack? Has she been told what's happened?'

The four women eyed one another. None knew the answer. They shook their heads.

'I'd forgotten all about her,' Ann Pascoe said, 'and, wicked or not, tes only the truth.'

'Yes, so had I,' Maggie said, and was filled with shame. 'I'd better go and see her straight away.'

Jim, with Clem Pascoe's two younger sons, had gone aboard the *Maid Molly* and was talking to Sam Cox and his crew. Maggie went to tell him that she was going to Boskillyer and the boy looked at her with a frown.

'Shall I come with you, mother?'

'No, there's no need,' Maggie said. 'Go home when you're ready. I shan't be long.'

She pushed the empty wheelchair home and left it in the yard. She spoke briefly to Eugene Kiddy and walked up to Boskillyer Farm.

Rachel was in the kitchen, busy preparing the midday meal. She had seen the first boats coming in more than two hours before and, assuming that the *Emmet* had been among them, she expected Brice home at any moment.

When she opened the door to Maggie, her face at first was blank with surprise, but slowly it darkened with instinctive foreboding.

'Mrs Tallack, there's bad news,' Maggie said.

Rachel was silent, absorbing the words. Bad news meant only one thing; there was no need to ask the nature of it; only the details remained to be told. For a moment she stood with her hand resting on the door. Then, with a gesture, she stepped aside.

'I think you'd better come in,' she said.

On getting home from Boskillyer, Maggie revived the fire in the stove and put the mutton stew on to heat again. While she was laying the table Jim came in.

'Did you see Mrs Tallack?'

'Yes, and I'm very glad I did. She hadn't heard the news at all. It was a terrible shock to her.'

'Did you tell her uncle Gus had gone out in the *Bright Star* to look for the punt?'

'Yes.'

'Some of the folk out there seem to think he's wasting his time.'

'Did they say so?'

'Not straight out. But I heard Dicky Limpet and Skiff Annear talking about other boats that've been run down by ships. They said there'd been a good few of them, though never one from Polsinney before. They said they could think of five at least. And I heard Dicky Limpet say – ' here Jim took a tremulous breath – 'that out of those five boats only two men were saved.'

Mother and son looked at each other.

'We must just have faith,' Maggie said, 'like your uncle Gus.'

Jim went off to wash his hands. He had carried fish home for old Horace Wearne. When he returned and came to the table he found his bowl filled with hot mutton stew. He sat down and stared at it numbly.

'I'm not hungry.'

'You must eat what you can.'

'Horace Wearne said if the punt *is* out there, there edn much chance of the *Bright Star* finding it today. Only by a miracle, and that's too much to expect, he said. So when it gets dark the *Bright Star* will heave-to for the night and start looking again in the morning.'

'Yes, and the fleet will be out there by then. They will be searching, too. Matthew Crowle told me that.'

'I wish there was something *we* could do.'

'Yes, so do I,' Maggie said.

Jim picked up his spoon; fished a piece of meat from his stew; blew on it; put it into his mouth. Maggie, too, began to eat, glancing up at the clock on the wall. The *Bright Star* had been gone an hour.

It was a typical April day that day, with the wind veering between north and west, bringing a skitter of rain now and then, short and sharp and rather cold. These showers came down from the moor, 'off the top of Teeterstone Hill' as folk in Polsinney always said; they darkened the slate roofs of the houses for a few minutes at a time; then blew away out to sea and were seen like dark patches of smockwork puckering the flat grey surface.

The fishing fleet left early that day and there were more people than usual gathered on the quay to watch. Maggie was among them, having been to Mrs Beale's for food to replenish the empty larder, and although it was only three o'clock, Jim was there, too, for the schoolmistress, Miss

Trembath, finding the children restless, had closed the school early and sent them home.

'Cissie Birch kept crying,' Jim said. 'She said her grandfather was drowned and would only come back as a seagull.'

Cissie Birch was barely six. Her grandfather was Billy Coit.

'Do you think it's true,' Jim asked, 'that when seamen drown they come back as gulls?'

'I don't know,' Maggie said. 'It's what people say, but I don't know.'

Out in the bay the fishing fleet was standing boldly out to sea, each boat under full sail and 'keen as mustard to do ten knots' as one old retired fisherman said, leaning over the harbour rail.

'Handsome wind for them,' said another, 'and let's hope it d'hold as it is, cos they won't be hindered with fog, not while it do blow like this.'

The boats sped away over the sea, growing smaller all the time, and at last vanished beyond Struan Point. Maggie began walking home and Jim, without being asked, took her basket and carried it for her.

''Tis strange to think uncle Gus is at sea. I can't get over that at all.'

'Yes, it is strange,' Maggie said. 'And the house seems terribly empty, too, without him in it.'

'Mother, when you think of uncle Brice . . . out there, on the sea, I mean . . . do you see him dead or alive?'

Maggie hesitated. She had already told Jim that they must have faith. She could not possibly tell him that she was filled with dread for Brice; that, having lost three men to the sea, she had little room in her heart for hope; so, after thought, she told a lie.

'I see him in the punt, alive.'

223

'With Billy Coit and the rest of them?'

'Yes, I see them all,' she said.

'That's how I see them, too,' Jim said.

Jim could not bear to stay indoors. He had to be out and about the harbour. And Maggie, having given him his tea, did not attempt to keep him back.

It was no good expecting news that day because even if the *Bright Star* found the *Emmet*'s crew at once, say forty miles or so from home, she would not be back until well after dark. Jim was well aware of this but the harbour was the place to be all the same and he, with other boys of his age, was drawn more than ever to the company of those old retired fishermen who leant on the wall and looked out to sea.

Jim and Clem Pascoe's two younger sons could not have enough of the seamen's talk as they argued out the chances of the *Emmet*'s crew being found alive. And Jim persuaded William Nancarrow, now eighty-four and long retired, but once the most respected skipper all along that stretch of coast, to tell again the familiar tale of how, as a young man of twenty-six, he had been swept overboard in a gale, some twenty miles off Kibble Head.

'The old *Sea Owl* I was in at the time, and the crew soon turned back to look for me. But there was some old sea that night and Wally Davey said afterwards the only reason they found me was because I'd got white oilskins on. They'd never have seen me else he said, cos the night was just so black as a shaft, and of course I was too far gone to shout. But that's how twas in those days. – A lot of us always swore by white oilskins because we knowed they showed up in the dark.'

'My uncle Gus has got white oilskins. He've taken them with him in the *Bright Star*.'

'Ess, and he'll be glad of their warmth, out there on the

sea tonight, even though tis April month and we've got a touch of spring in the air.'

Once Jim and the other boys climbed the cliff above Porthvole because from there they could see out as far as Burra Head and the wide stretch of open sea beyond. There was nothing to be gained from seeing thus far; it would not bring the *Bright Star* back any sooner; it was just something to do.

And yet, even so, the sight of a sail, out there abeam of Crockett Lighthouse, was enough to bring their hearts to their mouths. It was only an old hooker, making its slow way into Polzeale, and they told one another they had known *that* the instant she had hove into sight. And so they *had* known it, sure enough, for what else could she be? But they felt disappointed all the same.

They made their way down to the harbour again; helped Dick Geach and Figgy Tregenza to unload lobsters from their gig; and were still loitering on the slip when the sun went down behind Mump Head and the harbourmaster came out of his cottage to light the lamp on the quay-head. Lights were showing in the houses, too; the boys knew they would have to go home; they separated and went their ways.

On his way home, thinking of his mother alone all these hours, Jim felt guilty and hastened his step, for his uncle Gus had told him that he was to take care of her. But his mother was not alone. She had Martha Cledra with her, her old friend from those days long ago when they had both worked in the fish-cellars. Martha worked in the cellars still, in the summer seining season, but she was Martha Jenkin now and her husband was the giant, Pony Jenkin, who was one of the crew of the *Bright Star*.

'I've been keeping your mother company over a nice cup of tea. Tes lonesome for us women, you know, when our menfolk are all away. And *you'll* be off yourself, I daresay, not many years from now, though it won't be in the *Emmet*, will it, now she've gone to the bottom of the sea?'

Jim did not know how to answer this but Martha, heaving herself from the chair, was already preparing to leave.

'I'd better get back to my children, I suppose. They dunt much care for Granfer Dark. They'll be wanting a candle to go to bed.'

The door closed. Martha was gone. And Jim, shivering, drew near the fire, spreading his hands close to the flames. Evening and the fall of darkness had banished his bright optimism and touched him with fear. A cold, cruel fear that squeezed his heart.

'I suppose *she* thinks, like all the rest, that uncle Brice and his crew are drowned.'

'I don't know what she thinks,' Maggie said. 'I don't know what to think myself. All we can do is pray for them.'

'Even praying won't help,' he said, 'if they're already dead, will it?'

His voice broke and he bowed his head, and Maggie, with a little cry, drew him fiercely into her arms.

Maggie did not go to bed. She sat fully clothed in a chair by the fire, listening for footsteps in the yard and a knock at the door that would mean news of the *Bright Star*'s return. But the night passed without bringing news and towards morning she fell asleep.

She awoke to a loud noise of wind and knew at once it had changed direction by the way it blew down the chimney and flue, keeping the embers alive in the stove. She got up and poked at the ashes; put more wood on the fire; swung the kettle onto the hob. Dawn was a greyness at the window. It was nearly five o'clock.

Jim came downstairs, barefoot, in his nightshirt.

'Wind've gone sou'westerly. Tes getting up rough by the sound of it.'

'Did you manage to sleep?' Maggie asked.

'Yes, but I'm not going back to bed.'

'No. Well. You can fetch me some more coal. There'll be hot water soon for you to wash.'

Just after six Jim was on the quay. There were red streaks in the eastern sky and as the sun rose above Goonwelter it made a crimson splash on the sea, all around Black Pig Rock, and a red rippling path across the bay. There were quite a number of people about, some going to their work, some standing in groups on the wharf and the quay. Most of these were women and girls and, huddled against the wind as they were, their heads and shoulders rounded by shawls, they looked, Jim thought, like the grey seals that sometimes came ashore at Porthmell.

He hurried past them, awkward and shy, for he knew that they, like himself, were out watching for the *Bright Star*, and if they were to speak to him he would not know what to say. Martin Eddy's wife was one and he was afraid of seeing her tears. He walked out to the end of the jetty, stayed for an hour looking out to sea, and walked back again. There was no sign of the *Bright Star*. He went home and ate his breakfast.

'Do I have to go to school?'

'Yes,' Maggie said. She thought it best. 'You'll hear at once if there's any news.'

All morning the wind blew hard from the south west, bringing black ragged clouds up with it, but no rain.

'That won't come till the wind drops,' Isaac Kiddy said to Maggie, 'and there edn no sign of it dropping yet.'

Neither he nor Percy Tremearne were doing much work in the sail-loft that day. They kept coming out on the

227

stairs, the better to see across the bay. Eugene, too, was on the watch, from the door of the barking-house, and once Maggie heard him say:

'I dunt like the sound of that wind. There's more than a mite of spite in it. Twill get a lot worse before tes finished.'

Maggie tried to keep herself busy. There were plenty of chores to do in the house. But she could not make herself concentrate and when she heard the sound of the tide beginning to slap at the sea wall immediately below the house, she abandoned all thought of work and, putting on her shawl as she went, hurried out to join the people waiting and watching all round the harbour. The wind was now blowing ferociously and on the fish-quay itself the watchers stood close in under the wall or sheltered behind the fish-merchants' carts. It was after ten o'clock. The fleet was expected imminently.

'They said they would stay out all day and help to look for the *Emmet*'s punt but with this gale blowing up – ' William Nancarrow shook his head. 'They will have to think of themselves,' he said to Maggie, with simple directness, 'and that goes for the *Bright Star*, too.'

At eleven o'clock the first boats appeared, running swiftly before the gale, and William Nancarrow and Peter Perkin, watching them through their telescopes, called out their names to the waiting crowd: *Speedwell; Jenefer; Ellereen; Little Hob; Midge* and *Minette;* and these six were soon followed by others: *Starfish; Sea Breeze; Betty Stevens; Trelawney; Swift; John Cocking; Boy Dick.*

As the *Speedwell* came in beside the quay, closely followed by the *Jenefer*, their skippers and crews were besieged at once.

'Did you see the *Bright Star*?'

'No, not a sign, neither hide nor hair. But visibility was bad. There were black squalls on the Bara Breck. We didn't like the look of it so as soon as we'd hauled we ran for home.'

Prosper Geach looked around. His gaze came to rest on Betsy Coit and the rest of the *Emmet* wives.

'About the *Emmet*'s punt,' he said, and had to take a deep breath before he was able to go on. 'I hate to have to say it, midears, but if the *Bright Star* haven't found them by now, there edn no hope for them in this.' He glanced towards the black south west. 'Ralph Ellis will be on his way home by now. Else if he edn he ought to be cos there's worser weather to come yet.'

The women said nothing in reply. They were already watching the other boats drawing in beside the quay. But the question eagerly put to their crews brought the same answer again and again: No one had seen the *Bright Star*.

The first boats began to unload. Their catches were all fairly small and the merchants and jowsters were soon driving away. Three boats had no fish at all. Alarmed by the weather, they had cut away their lines.

Just before twelve o'clock Rachel Tallack drove onto the quay in the milk-float and Maggie went to speak to her.

'There's no sign of the *Bright Star* yet. Nor any news of her.'

'How many more boats to come?'

'Another fifteen,' Maggie said.

For a while Rachel waited and watched. The *Shenandoah* and the *Rose Allan*, the *Pintail*, the *Samphire*, the *Sea Horse*: these were coming in across the bay and their names were called out by William Nancarrow; but still the *Bright Star* did not come.

'I must get home,' Rachel said. 'I can't keep the pony standing here. I'll come down again later on.'

By twenty past twelve all the boats were in. People

counted. There were thirty-one. Out in the bay there was nothing to be seen except the grey blur of the rising sea. The wind was blowing harder than ever. It had a loud whining note in it. And as Maggie walked home many people who lived along the harbour road were fastening shutters across their windows.

On getting home she made up the fire and began preparing the midday meal. The little house shuddered and rocked, for the tide was well in on the foreshore now and, with the full force of the gale behind it, was pounding high against the sea wall. In her mind she heard Gus saying with relish, as he so often did in rough weather, 'Ho! We're fairly getting it now! We'd better put an anchor down!' But Gus was out on the sea in this gale and suddenly, seeing his empty wheelchair standing in the corner by the door, she was overcome with dread.

'Oh, Gus,' she whispered helplessly, 'I should never have let you go.'

In a little while Jim came in. He had been talking to the men on the quay.

'They say the gale is going to get worse. They're worried about the *Bright Star*.'

'Yes. I know.'

'She's a good sea-boat. She'll be all right. She *will* be all right. I *know* she will.'

'Yes, of course she will,' Maggie said.

She put a plateful of fried hog's pudding in front of him. Usually it was his favourite meal but today he looked at it with indifference.

'There's no school this afternoon. Miss Trembath spoke to the vicar and he said we were all excused.'

'Well, when we've had our dinner, then, we'll go down to the quay,' Maggie said.

She brought her own food to the table and sat down.

Together they ate, mechanically, listening to the wind thumping in the chimney.

Although Polsinney, with its stout-built harbour, made a safe anchorage in most conditions, it lay directly open to the fierce south westerly gales that swept in clean past Burra Head with nothing whatever to break their force. And all through that afternoon the gale blew with increasing venom. Huge seas came rushing in, hurling themselves over the quay-heads and causing such waves in the harbour pool that the thirty-one luggers, moored strake to strake along the wharf, were often washed over with foam.

By three o'clock, the greater part of Polsinney was out watching for the *Bright Star*. All the fishermen were there, numbering nearly two hundred men, and so were most of their families. And in the midst were the two groups of wives, the *Bright Star* wives and the *Emmet* wives, standing on the same part of the quay, sheltering in the lee of the wall, yet never quite mingling together.

Rachel Tallack was also there, but kept herself aloof as always. She would not seek comfort from anyone nor, when Maggie spoke to her, had she any comfort to give.

'Men talk about the harvest of the sea but the sea always takes more than it gives,' she said with angry fatalism.

Jim, at the outer end of the fish-quay, climbed into one of the look-out gaps in the ten foot thick wall and looked down onto Porthvolc beach, at the tide surging in over sand and rocks. When he put his head right out, past the shelter of the recess, he felt the full force of the wind cutting along the wall like a knife and when a big sea came in, rushing all along its base, the spray came up off the rocks and stung his face with the sharpness of gravel.

The strength of the wind took his breath away and the sharp spray hurt his eyes but he bore it all for a count of one hundred because of a superstitious feeling that by

231

enduring these hardships he would bring the *Bright Star* in. At the end of the count he climbed down. There was still no sign of the *Bright Star*.

A handful of watchers stood on the cliff above the beach, blurred figures in the grey wind, leaning against it to keep their balance. Jim had an itch to be up there too; to see out, beyond and beyond; but he wanted to be everywhere at once and it seemed more important to stay on the quay. For one thing, his mother was there somewhere, and he felt he must not stray too far from her; for another, he wanted to be near the seamen, to hear what they had to say to one another; and anyway, he very much doubted if the watchers on the cliff could see past Burra Head today, for the sea beyond it was storm–dark.

He stood with his hands in his pockets, staring at the ground, and again began counting up to a hundred. If he did not look out to sea, the *Bright Star* would come, he told himself. And if he counted very slowly . . .

But supposing the *Bright Star* came without uncle Brice and the rest of the *Emmet*'s crew? His mind seemed to swing dangerously, refusing to fix itself on this thought; finding it impossible to understand how life could offer two such extreme alternatives: on the one hand a thing so miraculous; on the other a thing so unthinkable. Had he reached one hundred yet? He didn't know. He had lost count. He would just have to start again.

Restless, he turned and walked a few paces. Then back again, kicking the ground. An old man stopped him and spoke to him but the words were whipped away by the wind and before the old man had time to repeat them there was a stir among the crowd and a great throbbing cry went up from half a dozen throats at once:

'*Here she comes!*'

Jim spun round and stared out to sea. It took him a

232

troubled moment or two before his eyes could focus again on that distant grey swirl of sea and wind so ferociously mixed together. But yes! *Yes!* There she was! The *Bright Star* was coming, sure enough, although scarcely more than a black speck out there in the turbulent greyness; a speck that appeared and disappeared, moment by moment, with the heave of the sea.

'Here she comes! Here she comes!'

The cry, taken up by all the watchers, became a roar like the roar of the wind. People hurried this way and that and some of them went to speak to those women whose menfolk made up the *Bright Star*'s crew. There were tears and a sort of hushed laughter among them. But there was awkward concern, too, because of that other group of women who stood in stillness and silence nearby, not yet knowing the fate of their own menfolk. Hoping. Praying. Yet fearing the worst.

Jim sought his mother among the crowd.

'Uncle Gus is coming! I knew he would!'

'Yes, I knew it, too!' she said, in a voice he had never heard before, and she caught hold of both his hands, squeezing them hard between her own.

But what of the *Bright Star*'s mission? That was the question in every mind; the question that now brought a hush on the crowd; drew all eyes seaward again.

Slowly the lugger was coming nearer, keeping well clear of Struan Point, one small jigger sail set on her foremast. But it was still impossible to see how many men were in her. William Nancarrow and Peter Perkin had their telescopes trained on the boat and a great many eyes were trained on *them*. Seven men had gone out, in search of six. How many were coming back?

The boat rose on a great running wave; seemed to hang there, eternally; then sank and vanished into the trough. A heart-stopping moment that lasted for ever and then she rose again to the sea, lifting, climbing, humouring the wave, balancing on it and riding it down.

'How many men?' people asked. 'William? Peter? Can you see?'

'I think I can see . . . ' William Nancarrow said, and his deep voice had a quiver in it, 'I think I can see . . . nine men.'

'I make it ten,' Peter Perkin said.

The boat disappeared. Reappeared. William Nancarrow spoke again.

'I can see eleven . . . Wait . . . Twelve!'

'I can see thirteen!' Peter Perkin roared. 'Thirteen men! They've found them all! The *Emmet*'s crew – they're all alive!'

This time the roar from the crowd was louder even than sea and wind. The two groups of women most closely concerned moved together and became one, wives of the rescuers and the rescued all weeping and laughing together, touching one another with eloquent hands. And part of the crowd surged about them, jostling them, sharing their joy.

Maggie still had hold of one of Jim's hands. She was squeezing it to the very bone. She turned to him with radiant face and gave a little broken laugh.

'Oh, Jim, they're coming! They're all alive! Was there ever anything so wonderful?'

They looked out again at this miracle, the *Bright Star*, with her one brave sail, coming to them out of the storm. William Nancarrow and Peter Perkin were letting their telescopes pass among the crowd, but those with keen eyes could now count for themselves the figures, seen each as head and shoulders, sitting tight in the boat as she rose and fell.

'Thirteen men, sure nuff. No doubt of that. I can see them plain.'

'Thirteen men – that's unlucky,' a voice said behind Jim and he turned with hatred in his heart for the man, Skiff Annear, who could say such a thing at such a time.

For Jim knew, quite as well as anyone there, that the danger was by no means past. That in fact the worst was yet to come. The gale was blowing as hard as ever and huge seas were breaking on the harbour walls; and the *Bright Star* faced the one task more dreaded than any other: that of coming in on a lee shore, driven before a living gale.

Rachel Tallack knew the dangers too. That was why she did not rejoice but stepped aside and stood alone as the crowd thronged round the waiting wives. Someone came up to her. It was the vicar, Mr Rowe.

'Well, Mrs Tallack! Our brave men are coming and your son among them. We must thank God, all of us, for showing his goodness and mercy to them.'

'I shall only thank God,' Rachel said, 'when I've seen our brave men come safe ashore.'

Jim had moved away from his mother and was once again drawing close to William Nancarrow and the other seamen as, with the first excitement over, they talked in grave, quiet voices, all watching the boat as she came, all speculating on the helmsman's intention. It would be madness, the watchers agreed, for her to attempt to come in at the narrow harbour entrance, with such seas breaking there. Her best chance – indeed her only chance – would be to come in on Porthvole beach.

Even that would be fraught with danger because of the many sharp-ridged rocks, some now covered and hidden by the tide. It would take skilled seamanship to bring her in, avoiding those rocks, and to beach her successfully on the shelving sand, and although no one said it in so many words, there were serious doubts in many minds as to whether Ralph Ellis was seaman enough.

'He'll need to keep a cool head,' – not something Ralph was noted for – 'and he'll need the judgment of Solomon,' said William Nancarrow soberly. 'But I will say this for him – he's doing very well so far. He's riding those big seas like a cormorant riding a bit of a lop.'

William Nancarrow's telescope was now in the hands of Albert Grose and he was narrowly watching the boat.

'Ess, he's doing a brave handsome job, but tedn Ralph at the helm,' he said.

'Who is it, then? Brice Tallack, I suppose. Well, of course, that explains it, and thank God Ralph's got more sense than conceit, to hand over to the better man.'

'No, tedn Brice, neither, cos I can see him in the bows and seemingly he've hurt himself, cos his right arm is hanging down at his side.'

'Who is it, then?' Peter Perkin asked.

'Just a minute. She've gone again.'

The boat disappeared; reappeared; and Albert made a strange sound in his throat.

'God in heaven, tes Gus Tallack!'

'Are you sure?'

'Here, see for yourself.'

'Damme, you're right!' Peter Perkin exclaimed and he in turn passed the telescope on. 'Tes Gus Tallack at the helm or I'm a Dutchman and can't say fish!'

There was a ripple among the crowd as this fresh piece of intelligence was passed along and William Nancarrow, in his deep voice, said:

'Well, if anyone can bring her in safely, Gus Tallack is that man.'

Jim felt that his heart would burst. His uncle Gus was at the helm and was bringing the *Bright Star* in, which meant that twelve men, including Ralph Ellis, had chosen to put their trust in him. And soon Jim could see for himself the thick, squat figure in white oilskin smock, sitting hunched in the stern like a graven image, one arm lying along the tiller, bearded face stolidly set under the peak of his seaman's cap, and with eyes staring steadily straight ahead.

The *Bright Star* was coming nearer. She was almost abeam of Craa Point. Would she make for the harbour mouth? Or would she make for Porthvole? Which, from out there, seemed most perilous? The boat rose and fell; her nose seemed to point; and soon the helmsman's intention was plain.

'He's putting her in onto the beach!'

Most of the crowd turned at once and surged back along the quay, round past the coopers' huts on the wharf, and down the slipway onto the beach. For, however skilful the seamanship that was bringing the *Bright Star* in, she would nevertheless need help as she made her way into shoalwater and came cutting through the boiling surf. And already, at the water's edge, many of the younger fishermen were tying ropes round their waists, ready to act as the moment required. Women and children were also there, willing and eager to play their part, and William Nancarrow directed them all, bellowing to make himself heard above the great noise of wind and sea.

The tide now reached that part of the beach where shingle gave way to sand, and as the pounding waves receded, shingle and sand were sucked down together in an almighty rushing roar. Here, too, were the first of those rocks that made the beach dangerous at high tide.

Some of the flatter rocks were covered already with water deep enough to hide them while other, taller, more jagged rocks were only partially surrounded, and on these the great waves broke, sometimes rising in spirals of spume twenty or thirty feet high. As these waves sank down again, the water swirled around the rocks and flung itself out shallowly, further and further up the beach, to lick with a kind of angry snarl at the feet of the people gathered there.

The *Bright Star* was coming in fast, with plenty of way on her, and she would certainly need it to carry her safely past the rocks and up onto the shelving sand far enough to prevent her, steep-sided boat as she was, from toppling over and broaching-to.

'She's coming! She's coming!' William Nancarrow said. 'Stand by, boys! Any minute now!'

The lugger came in at a place nicely judged, midway between two reefs of rock, where the water shoaled innocently over clean shingle and sand. The men could be seen crouching in her, bracing themselves against the shock, alert for all the possible dangers that would threaten them as the boat grounded. Ralph Ellis crouched in the bows with a rope, one end of which was fastened to the stemhead, the rest coiled in his right hand, ready to fling to the men ashore.

On the boat came, a big wave running behind her, and as she was now well into the shallows, the wave broke completely over her, running full length from stern to stem like a moving escarpment of water which, as it spread and flattened out, seethed over her decks in a mass of white foam. Out of this welter of broken water Ralph Ellis stood up in the bows and the rope, uncoiling, went snaking shorewards. There was a scramble on the sand and the rope was seized by many hands.

But the weight of the sea swamping the boat had caused her to lose way and as the underwave receded, so the boat receded too, sucked back with the yielding shingle and sand. The men on the rope were dragged down the beach, some into the water itself, and before they could regain their footing, the boat, caught by a smashing cross-sea rebounding from the harbour wall, had tilted sharply over to starboard, flinging all thirteen men headlong into the boiling surf.

The hawsemen dug in their heels. More men had come to help them now. And before the boat could broach-to completely, she had been hauled far enough up the beach for her keel to cut a path in the sand, making a bed into which she sank, still tilting at an ungainly angle, but resting unharmed on her starboard bilge. The end of the rope was passed through a ringbolt in a rock above the high water mark and a number of men stayed there to maintain their pull on the boat as the tide came further in around her.

Meantime those men who had stood by with ropes round their waists were already going forward, breast-high into the surf, where thirteen of their brotherhood were fighting desperately for their lives.

Brice, tossed about in the turbulent waters, with only his left arm to help him, was thrown onto his left side against a partly submerged rock. He tried to grip it with his hand but the sea was too strong for him and a fresh wave tore him away. Feeling the rock under his feet, he kicked himself vigorously up from it and rose, head and shoulders, above the sea. It was only two or three seconds before another wave engulfed him, but in those brief seconds he had seen his uncle Gus's white oilskins in the water ten or twelve yards away.

Again his feet touched rock and again he kicked himself up from it, striking out towards his uncle who, having no power in his legs, was unable to swim. The sea, however, was too much for him; he was soon overwhelmed; but this time, when a fresh wave caught him, it took him and carried him up the beach, where three or four rescuers quickly reached him and hauled him to safety.

One by one, all thirteen men were pulled from the sea

and carried up to the top of the beach, where there were plenty of helpers willing and able to minister to them. Dr Sam Carveth was there and to those who were tending Brice he said:

'He'll be all right, but he's got a dislocated shoulder. I'll come back to him when I've seen the rest.'

Maggie and Jim had got separated but both, from different parts of the beach, saw Gus taken from the sea and laid upon the dry sand well above high water mark.

By the time they reached the place, his rescuers had removed his smock and were giving him artificial respiration. He lay on his stomach on the sand and Matt Crowle, crouching astride him, was strenuously squeezing his sides. His bearded mouth was open and water was trickling out of it but in a while the trickling stopped and with a terrible heaving shudder Gus's lungs filled with air.

Matt Crowle and Scrouler Tonkin turned him over onto his back. Matt thrust a folded jacket underneath his shoulder-blades, so that his head lay well back, and Scrouler worked his arms up and down. Soon Gus gave another heave; his eyes flickered open; his lips moved.

Scrouler now made him more comfortable by removing the folded jacket and placing it under his head. Matt said something under his breath and the two men stood up. They turned towards Maggie, who stood nearby, and she came and dropped on her knees beside Gus, stifling a quick indrawn cry as she saw the deep wound in his temple, from which the blood ran streaming down, reddening his wet grey hair and beard.

'Gus, don't try to speak. Dr Sam is coming.'

If Gus heard, he did not obey. His dark gaze was on her. His lips moved again.

'Others?' he said. 'Are they all right?'

'Yes,' Maggie said, 'they're all safe now.'

'Boy Brice?' he asked.

'Yes,' Maggie said. 'You don't have to worry. He's alive and safe. I saw him myself just a moment ago –'

'I told you,' Gus said, in a hoarse whisper and gave a short, exhausted cough. 'I told you I'd bring him back to you.'

Somebody touched Maggie's shoulder. She rose and gave way to Dr Sam. But Dr Sam could do nothing for Gus, and Maggie knew it. She saw the dark eyes close, the wet bearded lips part slightly, and the shaggy grey head fall sideways as though he had turned to kiss the sand.

Jim, beside her, saw it too. His young face was white with the knowledge of death. She reached out to him with enfolding arms and he hid his grief against her breast.

Chapter 10

On a hot sunny morning in July, Maggie and Jim rode in
the cart with Isaac Kiddy to Martin Laycock's boatyard,
situated on 'the bank' up behind the fish-cellars. In the cart,
neatly rolled, lay the new suit of sails that Isaac and Percy
Tremearne had made for Brice's new boat which, caulked,
tarred, and painted, stood on the stocks in the boatyard.
When the cart drew up, Martin Laycock and two of his
men came at once to help Isaac unload the sails, so well
barked by Eugene that even now, after six days' drying,
the cutch came off brown on the men's hands.

'Ess,' Isaac said, complacently, 'they've been barked to
within an inch of their lives.'

As soon as the sails had been unloaded, Isaac drove off in
the empty cart, leaving Maggie and Jim behind. Jim had
brought her to see the boat and now, in a great state of
excitement, he escorted her across the yard, between the
piles of pitchpine planking, past the sawpit and sheds and a
half-built gig, to where his uncle Brice's new lugger stood
ready for launching the following day. It was the first time
Maggie had seen the new boat and as she stood under the
big black hull her gaze instinctively went to the bows and
dwelt on the boat's name and number painted boldly and
clearly in white: *Gus Tallack*, PY41.

Although she had known from the beginning what the
boat's name was to be, the sight of it affected her and
brought the quick tears to her eyes. Jim perceived this
immediately and put his hand into hers.

'Don't be upset, mother. Don't be upset. Uncle Gus – '
The boy cleared his throat. 'Uncle Gus would've been

pleased at having the boat named after him. And such a brave handsome boat she is, too! Just you wait till you've seen all round!'

Maggie smiled at him through her tears. She gave his hand a warm, hard squeeze. And in a few minutes more he was persuading her to climb the ladder and board the boat so that she could inspect its marvels with the thoroughness they deserved.

Jim, of course, knew everything there was to know about the new boat. He had been in and out of the boatyard at every opportunity ever since the morning, early in May, when the elmwood keel had been laid on the stocks. The boat was modern. She was also big. And everything about her was of the best.

Jim showed his mother the roomy cabin, with its neat little lockers and bunks for six men and its cooking-stove fixed to the bulkhead. He showed her everything everywhere: fish-hold, net-hold, capstan, pumps; and he pointed out how beautifully finished everything was inboard: the decks and bulwarks all painted a dazzling white, with just the right amount of blue used to pick out the coamings, the cleats, and the chamfered edges on the stanchions.

At last Maggie was allowed to descend and Jim, preceding her down the ladder, watched over her anxiously lest, encumbered by her skirts, she should catch her foot and fall.

'Careful, now, on this next rung. – It's the one that's got a split in it. And watch out for your hands. – There's some lot of splinters in this old ladder, you.'

On the ground there were more things to see: the two stout masts, of Norwegian larch, and the hatches stacked in a neat pile, all varnished to perfection; the lugger's punt, fifteen feet long, painted white, with a blue gunwale; and the two shiny black anchors, each weighing

243

forty-five pounds, delivered a few days before from the Carnock foundry.

These things, and many more, lay on one side in orderly fashion, all moveable gear and fitments having been taken off to lighten the boat ready for moving down to the slipway early next morning. As Jim was explaining this to his mother, the boatbuilders came and set down the sails. There were eight of them altogether: foresail, two mizzens, two jiggers, one jib, a mizzen topsail and a spinnaker; and now, as Martin Laycock said, every last bit of tackle and gear was assembled for carting down to the slipway.

'All excepting the ballast, of course, and that's already down there, loaded into hundredweight bags.'

'Yes, I know,' Jim said. 'I helped uncle Brice and the crew to shovel the shingle into the bags.'

'And shall you be here tomorrow morning to see us haul the lugger down?'

'Yes, I'll be here at six o'clock.'

'Honour bright?'

'Cross my heart!'

'And what about the launching, you? You won't be there for that, I suppose? You'll have something better to do than hang about all day just to see a new boat launched?'

'I *shall* be there,' Jim began and then, perceiving his mother's smile, realized that he was being teased. 'I shan't only see her launched,' he said. 'I shall be going out in her, on her first trials round the bay.'

On the wharf, as they walked home, Maggie and Jim met Brice, who had been to see the harbourmaster to discuss arrangements for the launching. – Always a Herculean task, with a boat of the *Gus Tallack*'s size, and one that required all available help.

'I hear you've been delivering the sails?'

'Yes. And Jim has been showing me the boat.'

244

'What do you think of her?' Brice asked.

'Oh,' Maggie said, and spread her hands, looking at him with a smile that said, What do women know of such things? 'She's very big. Very beautiful. And I know she's the finest boat in the world because Jim keeps telling me so.'

'Tes only the truth,' Jim declared.

'Gus always said that Laycock's yard built some of the best boats ever to sail out from this coast.'

'Certainly the *Emmet* was one of the best,' Brice said. 'She'd have sailed another thirty years if that barquentine hadn't done for her. And if the new boat turns out as good as the old – '

'She will do!' Jim said. 'Of course she will!'

'Then I shall be well pleased,' Brice said. He glanced up and around the sky. 'It'll be a fine day for the launch, I believe. A day pretty much like today, I would say, with the wind going nicely round with the sun.' He turned to face Maggie again. 'The crew are all down at Enery Trennery's, getting their hair cut,' he said. 'They mean to make a smart come-out of it tomorrow, be sure of that.'

'I'm glad the new boat will have the same crew.'

'Yes, so am I,' Brice said.

Since the loss of the *Emmet*, the crew had got work where they could, 'filling in' on other drifters that happened to be a man short, perhaps, but often obliged to go to Carnock and earn what they could on the quay there, helping to unload other men's fish.

Billy Coit and Clem Pascoe had in fact been offered permanent places on certain boats where they had filled in but, knowing that Brice was building a new boat with the insurance money from the *Emmet*, they had chosen to wait for the chance of crewing with him again. And they, like young Jim, had spent all their spare time at the boatyard, watching the *Gus Tallack* grow and sometimes giving a hand with the work.

245

'I reckon that's a good idea, naming her after the old skipper,' Billy Coit had said to Brice, 'cos he was a good old sort in his way, and I've got a funny old feeling that whenever we put to sea, he'll be watching over us, seeing we dunt come to no harm.'

As Maggie and Jim and Brice walked together along the wharf a number of people passed by and each had something to say to them, for everyone in Polsinney knew that the *Gus Tallack* was due to be launched the following day and, the launching of a new boat being always a great occasion, young and old alike looked forward to it with pleasure and interest.

'Handsome weather you'll have for it!' said old Horace Wearne, and Annie Tambling, touching Brice on the arm as she passed, said: 'There's my good luck on you, my son, but dunt say nothing back to me or that'll only send it away!'

Everyone had some special word and many, as they passed by, turned to look at Maggie and Brice with lively curiosity. In the three months that had passed since Gus's death, they had been closely observed, the subject of much speculation, and because they were well aware of it, they had throughout that time conducted themselves with great correctness.

Their feelings were in accord over this and had never needed to be put into words. They loved each other and in time they would marry; it would cause a good deal of talk and people would say they had known all along just how it would turn out; but there would be no undue haste for the more spiteful gossips to fasten on. Maggie was in mourning for Gus and it was no mere formal display; she mourned for him quite genuinely and knew that Brice did too; and much as they might long for each other, neither of them wanted marriage while Gus's death was still fresh in their minds.

That morning, early, Maggie had been in the churchyard, trimming the grass on Gus's grave. She liked to go there very early, before anyone else was about, and she liked to keep the green mound well trimmed because Gus had respected neatness and order above all other things. On the headstone, above his name, was carved, in the simplest fashion, a boat under sail. 'I am the Lord,' said the text, 'which maketh a way in the sea, and a path in the mighty waters.'

She had been to the grave many times but on that particular morning, as she knelt beside the mound, she had received a strong impression of Gus's presence close beside her. This feeling was with her still and although it filled her heart with sadness, it also brought a sense of peace and a sense, somehow, of being protected. She spoke about this now to Brice, as they reached the gate of the barking-yard, and he told her what Billy Coit had said about Gus watching over the new boat and keeping it safe from harm.

'Uncle Gus was a seaman and spent his last hours at sea. He was happy doing that. And I know even the way he died will have been more to his liking than dying slowly in his bed. These things, and the way we remember him, are enough to bring peace to his soul, I think, don't you?'

'Yes,' Maggie said, quietly, 'his soul is at peace with itself, I'm sure.'

At three o'clock the next afternoon, watched by a huge crowd that thronged the fish-quay and the wharf, Maggie launched the *Gus Tallack* from Laycock's slipway at Porthvolc.

The day, as promised, was fine and sunny, with a hot south easterly wind giving a sea that was deep blue and calm, with just a bit of a lop on it. The boat had been hauled down to the slip without any mishap just after six that morning and from then until midday men had swarmed all over her, crew and boatbuilders working together, rigging her out ready for sea.

At one o'clock, washed and shaved, and wearing their best dark serge suits, they had gathered again at *The Brittany Inn* for the special launching feast, where cold roast beef and pickles, followed by apple tart and cream, had been washed down by beer or cider or, in the case of the teetotallers, by Mrs Kemp's special lemonade.

At half past two, out on the slipway, the crewmen were joined by their families. Maggie and Jim were already there, with Rachel Tallack; Isaac Kiddy was there with his wife and son; and Percy Tremearne was there with his new sweetheart from St Owe. These, together with the boat-builders and all the other stout-armed men standing by to help with the launching, almost filled the slipway; and everywhere about the harbour, wherever there was a piece of ground that commanded a view of the proceedings, the onlookers were thronged in their hundreds, the young girls in their summer frocks, some carrying parasols, making splashes of bright colour among the men in their sober blacks, under the red and green bunting fluttering gaily overhead.

The *Gus Tallack*, with her stern towards the sea, stood with her keel resting on rollers, well and truly chocked underneath and supported all along her sides by struts of timber firmly wedged under bilge-keels and strakes. Jim, gazing up at the boat, which was forty-four feet in length and weighed sixteen tons, thought how immense she looked, standing here on the slipway, and yet how small such a boat could seem once she was out on the open sea. And he thought, too, with a tingle of pleasure, of the silver shilling which, earlier that day, watched by uncle Brice and the crew, he had placed underneath the foremast as a token to ensure the boat's good luck.

All around him on the slipway the launching party, in

high spirits, were chatting with one another and with a few privileged persons, including the vicar, Mr Rowe, the Methodist minister, Mr Hoskins, and, representing the 'parliament' of old retired fishermen, the stalwart William Nancarrow. The boat was inspected, discussed, admired; compared with famous boats of the past; and made the subject of predictions concerning the speed she might achieve and how she would most likely behave in a lively seaway.

But Brice and his crew, though they chatted, had one eye on the time, and promptly at five minutes to three they boarded the boat, with young Jim and Martin Laycock. The ladder was taken away and the launching team, numbering thirty men, took up the stations assigned to them, each man watching Martin Laycock, directing proceedings from the boat's bows.

Now William Nancarrow, with conscious dignity, went to a small wooden table, set conveniently by, on which stood a bottle of French red wine and a glass. He filled the glass with wine and gave it to Maggie and she, somewhat flushed in the cheeks at being the centre of attention, turned and walked towards the boat. The whole crowd was utterly silent, watching her and listening, and for a brief interval the only sound heard on the slipway was the lapping and slapping of the water, a few yards from the lugger's stern.

Maggie raised her glass aloft, took a deep breath to steady herself, and spoke in a loud, ringing voice that carried clearly all round the harbour.

'I wish prosperity to this boat and name her the *Gus Tallack*, and I ask God's blessing on her and her crew.'

She drank some of the wine from the glass, then dashed the rest against the boat, and such was the splendid timing achieved by the launching team in removing chocks and struts that as the wine splashed against her bows the *Gus*

Tallack began to move, slowly at first, with scarcely a sound, but very soon, as the rollers turned, picking up speed in a way that was almost frightening to behold.

A burst of clapping broke out among some of the onlookers but most were watching, hearts in mouths, for now the lugger was beginning to run, rolling and rumbling down the slipway with a noise like thunder. There were shouted instructions from Martin Laycock, a scraping of boots on the granite setts as men lay back on the check-ropes, and then, with a satisfying splash that brought the spray up over her stern, the *Gus Tallack* was afloat in two or three fathoms of water.

The crew, having cast off the check-ropes, waved their caps and gave a cheer, which was echoed and very quickly drowned by the cheer that went up from the watching crowd. Brice, at the helm, gave a salute, and as the lugger moved out on the ebb, the water deepening under her, he very slowly brought her round until her stem pointed seawards.

By now the crew were at work; there were a few quiet commands, a flapping of canvas, a cheeping of blocks; and Billy Coit, in charge of the tack, looked up at the two brown sails as though willing them to draw. And in another moment or two, as the boat cleared the lee of Scully Point and the hot wind came breathing down on them, bringing a scent of Goonwelter furze, the sails very gently and gracefully filled.

Jim, standing with Brice at the helm, watched as his mother, on the slipway, grew smaller and smaller still. He put up a hand to wave to her; a special wave, for her alone; and saw the flutter of her blue and white sleeve as she waved back to him. Brice also was watching her. He watched until, as the distance lengthened, her figure grew blurred and merged with the crowd. He turned his head and looked at Jim and Jim, as yet too full to speak, looked up at him with a smile of pure joy.

The boat now began picking up speed, making westward across the bay. Martin Laycock came aft to speak to Brice.

'Going handsome so far, edn she?'

'Yes, she's going like a bird.'

Rachel, with Maggie on the wharf, listening to the good wishes, the congratulations, the compliments, had little to say in reply. She did not approve of the new boat. She had wanted Brice to give up the sea. But men, as she well knew, would do whatever they wanted to do, for it was their nature and couldn't be changed.

'That boy of yours will be the same. He will go to sea, sure as fate, and nothing you say will make him see sense. And he will spare no thought for the feelings of those he leaves behind.'

The well-wishers had moved away and Rachel and Maggie, alone together, began walking slowly along the wharf.

'Jim's got the sea in his blood. He's grown up within sight and sound of it. The pull of it is too strong for him. He could never resist it even if he wanted to.'

'It seems you accept it.'

'Yes. I do.'

'You are wise,' Rachel said. 'I suppose it's been bred in you.'

She herself had learnt acceptance rather late in life and only after much inner conflict. She was beginning to feel her age. Becoming resigned. Bowing to fate. But there were some compensations to make up for the sense of defeat. She accepted that Brice and Maggie would marry and even found satisfaction in it, for it meant that Gus Tallack's property would come back into the family even if, one day, Brice's children would have to share it with Maggie's illegitimate son.

All along the wharf, as Maggie and Rachel strolled along, there were little groups of people still watching the new boat performing her trials out in the bay.

'You launched her brave and fitty, midear,' Kate Cox said as Maggie passed, and old Thomas Lean called out: 'Proper job! Proper job! And a more handsome craft never put to sea.'

Maggie smiled; made some reply; and walked on at Rachel's side. The two were silent for a while. Then Rachel came to a halt.

'We're very different, you and me. I've lived in this place more than thirty-five years but I still feel myself a stranger here, and that's how people see me, I'm sure. But you are at home here. You seem to belong. It's as though you had lived here all your life.'

'Yes, that's how I feel,' Maggie said. 'Polsinney is my home in a way Porthgaran never was. I've been happy here. I've put down roots.'

'Yes, and the tree has borne fruit, in more ways than one,' Rachel said, with a touch of her old acerbity. And after a while she said briskly: 'Well, I must be getting home. *You* may stay here if you like, watching that boat go to and fro, but *I've* got things to do on the farm.'

'I would come and help you but I promised Jim I'd stay here and watch them come in,' Maggie said.

'You'll have a long wait, I can tell you that. They'll be sailing about for hours yet, if I know anything about it. Still, waiting is something you'll have to get used to, once you are married to Brice. And I daresay there is justice in that because God knows he has waited for *you* long enough.'

Rachel went off along the wharf, giving a perfunctory nod to the groups of people who made way for her.

Maggie walked on to the quay, to join the watchers still gathered there, and fair-haired little Cissie Birch, leaving her grannie, Betsy Coit, came with a hop-skip-and-a-jump to take hold of Maggie's hand.

Out in the bay, off Volley Head, the *Gus Tallack*, under full sail, sped smartly before the wind, a few gulls flashing behind her, omen of good things to come.

Outstanding women's fiction in Panther Books

Muriel Spark

Territorial Rights	£1.25	☐
Not To Disturb	£1.25	☐
Loitering with Intent	£1.25	☐
The Hothouse by the East River	£1.25	☐
Going up to Sotheby's	£1.25	☐

Toni Morrison

Song of Solomon	£2.50	☐
The Bluest Eye	£1.95	☐
Sula	£1.25	☐
Tar Baby	£1.95	☐

Erica Jong

Fear of Flying	£1.95	☐
How To Save Your Own Life	£1.50	☐
Fanny	£1.95	☐
Selected Poems II	£1.25	☐
At the Edge of the Body	£1.25	☐

Ann Bridge

Peking Picnic	£1.95	☐

Anita Brookner

A Start in Life	£1.50	☐
Providence	£1.50	☐

To order direct from the publisher just tick the titles you want and fill in the order form.

GF1381

Outstanding women's fiction in Panther Books

Mary E Pearce

Apple Tree Lean Down	85p	☐
Jack Mercybright	85p	☐
The Land Endures	£1.50	☐
Apple Tree Saga	£2.50	☐

Kathleen Winsor

Wanderers Eastward, Wanderers West (Volume 2)	95p	☐

Margaret Thomson Davis

The Breadmakers	£1.50	☐
A Baby Might Be Crying	£1.50	☐
A Sort of Peace	£1.50	☐

Helena Leigh

The Vintage Years I: The Grapes of Paradise	£1.95	☐

To order direct from the publisher just tick the titles you want
and fill in the order form. **GF1181**

All these books are available at your local bookshop or newsagent, or can be ordered direct from the publisher.

To order direct from the publisher just tick the titles you want and fill in the form below.

Name _____

Address _____

_____